The Lethal Deception

ALSO BY MARION BLACKWOOD

Marion Blackwood has written lots of books across multiple series, and new books are constantly added to her catalogue. To see the most recently updated list of books, please visit: www.marionblackwood.com

CONTENT WARNINGS

The *Court of Elves* series contains violence, morally questionable actions, and later books in the series also contain some more detailed sexual content. If you have specific triggers, you can find the full list of content warnings at: www.marionblackwood.com/content-warnings

THE LETHAL DECEPTION

COURT OF ELVES: BOOK FIVE

MARION BLACKWOOD

Copyright © 2022 by Marion Blackwood

All rights reserved. No part of this book may be reproduced in any form or by any electronic or mechanical means, including information storage and retrieval systems, without permission in writing from the publisher, except by reviewers, who may quote brief passages in a review. For more information, contact info@marionblackwood.com

ISBN 978-91-987259-7-1 (hardcover)
ISBN 978-91-987258-9-6 (paperback)
ISBN 978-91-987258-8-9 (ebook)

Editing by Julia Gibbs

This is a work of fiction. Names, characters, places, and incidents either are the product of the author's imagination or are used fictitiously. Any resemblance to actual persons, living or dead, events, or locales is entirely coincidental.

www.marionblackwood.com

*For everyone who has ever been one more setback
away from setting it all on fire and watching
everything you have built burn to the ground*

down the red steps. The guards who had been stationed in the throne room gave me a nod as I passed them before moving deeper into the castle. My footsteps echoed through silent halls.

There were much fewer people in the castle now than there had been back when Volkan ran the place. The first thing I had done as the new ruler of this court had been to free all the slaves. Everyone who had wanted to leave had been allowed to do so. And everyone who I needed in order to keep things up and running had been offered their job again, but with a normal wage instead. Most of those had accepted. Thankfully. It cost money, of course, but I still needed people who worked in the kitchen, tended the greenhouse, cleaned, delivered messages, and other odd jobs. The half-naked people who had just been standing around in the throne room all day, however, had all left to do something more fulfilling with their lives.

Warm afternoon winds caressed my body as I stepped through the final door and emerged onto the rooftop patio. A few comfortable couches and divans in white and gold were arranged around a low table made of red stone. Plants in pale pots dotted the area and vines covered in fresh green leaves clung to the delicate structure that had been built to provide shade. I left the cozy space behind and instead moved to the other side of the small building that housed the stairwell.

A wide and flat area stretched out before me. It was completely empty. The afternoon sun painted the red stones in hues of gold.

I strode to the middle of the deserted rooftop.

And then I tipped my head back, threw out my arms, and let it all out.

"Another no, I take it?" Leaning back in my seat again, I cocked my head. "I forget, was there something about the taxes that you were unhappy about?"

"No, Lady Firesoul," he stammered.

"Hm." I shifted my attention to the lady in the green dress next to him and raised my eyebrows expectantly. "Anyone else?"

She quickly dropped her gaze and shook her head. When I swept my eyes over the rest of their little disgruntled group of nobles, they all did the same. The flames flickering in my hair disappeared.

"Good. You may leave." I stared them down for another few seconds before looking up and raising my voice to carry across the whole throne room. "All of you."

Clothes whispered against stone as the people who had lingered in the red stone hall bowed to me and started towards the doors. I watched the firelight from the shallow flame pools gleam off some very particular pieces of jewelry. Every single member of the group of dissatisfied elven nobles was wearing a black bracelet. Another wave of irritation pulsed through me.

It had been months since I took over the Court of Fire, but I still couldn't seem to get through a single week without someone questioning my rule in one way or another. And everyone who opposed me was wearing that black bracelet that marked them as a believer in the divinity of the High Elves. I knew that I had made an enemy of High Commander Anron the day I ruined his plans by ramming a sword through Volkan Flameshield's chest. But his interference in my court still annoyed me.

Once the doors had banged shut behind the last of the courtiers, I pushed myself off the sturdy throne and strode

"And how else do you expect there to be enough money to rebuild the bridge?" I arched an eyebrow at him. "Or perhaps you are not interested in that? Though I doubt that is the case. After all, the bridge is on the way to *your* estate, and without it, you have to take a massive detour to get to the city."

The scowling lord puffed up his chest and harrumphed. "That is not the point."

"Exactly," an elven lady in a green dress filled in. "The point is that you should just get your slaves to do it for free. That way, we don't have to waste money on it."

Staring down at her from atop my red throne, I let the silence stretch on for a deliberate second. The group of elven nobles below the raised dais shifted uncomfortably while the rest of the people in the throne room flicked nervous eyes between me and them.

"You know full well that there are no more slaves in the Court of Fire," I finally said, my voice deceptively smooth.

"Well, there should be," the scowling lord huffed.

Fury flashed through me. As if they could see it in my eyes, the courtiers around the room shrank back slightly and tension crackled through the warm air.

"I know what it is like to be a slave, and I will keep none myself." Fire flickered like highlights through my long red hair. I sat forward on my throne. A lethal smile, cold and sharp like a knife, spread across my lips as I locked eyes with the lord below. "But if you are offering to take up that position yourself, then who am I to refuse?"

His mouth fell open. "Wh-wha..."

"No?" I slid my gaze to the three people standing behind him. "Then perhaps your family?"

He flinched and cast a panicked glance at his wife. "I, uhm..."

CHAPTER 1

I resisted the urge to bang my head against the wall. Or better yet, bang someone else's head against the wall. And also to set the throne room on fire. Not necessarily in that order either.

Ruling a court is easy. There are a bunch of senior attendants who handle everything from tax collection to infrastructure to crop yields. They have decades of experience, they are intelligent and efficient, and they are all experts at what they do. So yes, ruling a court is easy. Taking over someone else's court after you stabbed them in the chest and then were crowned the first female half-elf ruler in living memory, who then decided to change the economic structure of the court by freeing all the slaves while also being targeted by a near mythical race of High Elves setting themselves up as gods, on the other hand, is… not easy.

"You simply cannot raise the taxes in this way," said an elven lord with short brown hair and a constant scowl on his face.

Fire shot out around me. Waves of orange and red washed over the floor and spilled out over the edges while a column of flame shot straight up into the bright blue sky. I knew that it produced enormous heat, but I felt none of it. Fire licked my skin. Played in my hair. Whirled around me like a burning storm. I relished the feeling of just pouring out all of my anger and frustration and watching it physically manifest around me before disappearing into the sky.

"Shouldn't you be saving some of that for our fight?" a voice suddenly cut through the inferno.

Letting the fire die down, I turned towards the small building that I had come from. An elf in tightfitting leather armor was leaning against the red stone wall with her arms crossed. Idra. There was an amused twinkle in her black eyes as she raised her eyebrows at me.

I grinned at her. "Oh there is plenty more where that came from."

"Yes, raw power has never been the problem for you, has it?" She pushed off the wall and started towards me. Her shining white hair brushed the top of her shoulder as she cocked her head slightly and shot me a challenging look. "Control has."

"Which I am working on, thank you very much."

"Uh-huh." Idra jerked her chin towards the open end of the roof to my left. "Then throw a small fireball that way."

Turning in the direction she indicated, I raised my arm and then shoved forward with my hand.

A column of crackling fire shot out.

"I said fire*ball*," Idra pointed out rather superfluously.

I blew out a sigh. After lowering my arm again, I turned back to face her. "Yes, well, I said I'm working on it."

"You need to work faster. When the High Elves come for you, you need to be able to wield fire like Volkan did."

"Volkan had centuries to perfect his fire magic."

"Which he barely used because he focused on honing his ability to cast visions instead. You need the fire magic more than he did." Falling into a battle stance, she twitched her fingers at me. "Now, let's go."

I knew that she was right so I just blew out another sigh, tied up my hair, and then squared up against her. She struck. Ducking under her arm, I jabbed towards her side but she was already moving.

Leather creaked as she raised her hand and twitched her fingers again. "Fire up."

After taking a second to get ready, I called up the flames. Fire whooshed down over my arms. Idra gave me an approving nod. I attacked.

My ability to walk through walls was as natural to me as breathing. I didn't need to think about how or when to do it. It just worked. But when I was crowned Lady of Fire and drank that bowl of flames, I had been given two new magic powers: fire-wielding and worldwalking.

Worldwalking had been a pleasant surprise. When someone else did it to me, I always felt nauseous. But when I was the one directing it, the feeling was completely different. Like actually riding the horse yourself instead of bouncing along behind the saddle when someone else was riding. Getting the landing right had taken a few weeks, to Mordren's endless amusement, but I got the hang of it pretty quickly. Wielding fire, on the other hand, was a much harder skill than I had anticipated.

Flames fluttered in the air as I swung my fist towards Idra again. She blocked the strike with her forearm, her fire-resistant armor soaking up the flames, before throwing a merciless punch towards my stomach. I leaped backwards.

"I still don't understand why they're even here," I said, picking up the thread of conversation, while moving back into position again. "After I told King Aldrich that the supposedly valuable information was a fabrication created by Volkan and Anron, everyone knows that the High Elves are here for more than diplomatic ties."

Idra feigned right and then slammed a boot towards my knee. Fire surged down my leg in response and Idra pulled back her kick just in time. Nodding in acknowledgement of the move, she shifted her weight on the red stone roof again.

"Not to mention that those diplomatic ties have already been established," she answered. "And yet they still keep finding reasons to stay."

"Exactly. I don't like sitting around and just waiting for them to take the first shot."

She zigzagged across the stones and aimed a strike at my ribs. "A war with the High Elves would end badly."

Twisting aside, I rammed my elbow into her back. "I know. But I still don't like it. Being passive like this. It's only a matter of time before–"

The door to the stairwell banged open. I pulled back the punch to Idra's stomach and turned to stare across the red stones as one of the elves working as a messenger in my court skidded to a halt on the warm roof.

"Lady Firesoul," he pressed out, clearly winded from the dash up the stairs. "King Aldrich has called an urgent meeting."

Straightening, I locked eyes with him. "About what?"

Summer winds whirled across the stone roof and sent his

long blond hair fluttering behind him. After gulping down another breath, he swallowed and met my gaze.

Dread filled my stomach. And somehow, I knew what he was going to say before he said it.

"The High Elves are moving on the Court of Trees."

CHAPTER 2

Leaves rustled in the branches above us. Evander took his arm from around my waist right as Idra materialized next to us in the silent glen. Ever since the day I removed the slave collar from around her neck, Idra had never worldwalked anyone else. Anywhere. At any time. I wasn't entirely sure why, but I believed it was a matter of principle. Volkan had made her worldwalk people on different missions all the time, and now that she was free, she probably wanted to feel that she was no longer simply someone else's mode of transportation. Or so I thought, at least. Which was why I was the one who had worldwalked Evander here.

"This way," Evander said.

Moving with confident steps, he led us through a shortcut that would take us to the place that King Aldrich had specified. Afternoon sunlight filtered through the pale green canopy above and cast shifting shadows over his lean muscled body as he expertly weaved through the trees. He looked at home here in the woods.

"It's too quiet to be an invasion," Idra observed as we followed Evander through another glen. "Too peaceful."

"I agree." Sweeping my gaze over the forest around us, I took in the tangle of trees and the odd buildings that were located between them in no discernable pattern. "And if they wanted to invade a court, why even go for this one? The Court of Trees is the worst possible one both to take and hold. There is no capital city to conquer. Everything is just a huge chaotic mess spread out across a gigantic forest."

"Indeed."

Figures became visible between the tree trunks. I flicked my gaze over them. Only the king, along with his guards, and the Court of Shadows had arrived so far. Surprise flitted through me. I had thought for sure that we would be the last to arrive since we'd had to worldwalk to a place farther away. It was only possible to worldwalk to a place that you had already seen, and the closest place I had seen had been that glen back there.

I glanced at Evander. Good thing he knew all the shortcuts.

Noticing my look, he flashed me a smile.

"Kenna," King Aldrich said as we came to a halt next to them.

All three of us bowed.

"My king," I said.

He gave me a distracted nod and then went back to scanning the forest. Presumably for any trace of the other princes. Or possibly invading High Elves. I slid my gaze to the Court of Shadows.

"Mordren," I said, meeting his intense gaze. "Eilan. Hadeon. Ellyda."

"Kenna," Mordren replied smoothly while Eilan gave me a nod.

Ellyda didn't reply. Apparently lost in her own head, she was staring straight ahead at something no one else could see. Hadeon wasn't much better. He was scowling at the silent forest around us with a troubled look in his red eyes.

"It doesn't make any sense," he grumbled. "It can't be an invasion. It's too quiet."

I cast a glance at Idra, who had said the same thing only minutes before, but she was busy studying Hadeon.

"We—" I began but the sound of snapping branches and crunching leaves cut me off.

Turning towards the noise, I found Prince Edric stalking towards us with Ymas and Monette beside him. A moment later, something dark blue became visible through the trees on the other side. Prince Rayan and Princess Lilane glided through the forest and approached us as well.

"Thank you for coming so quickly," King Aldrich said before anyone else could speak up. Raising a hand, he motioned for us to start walking. "A short while ago, word reached me that the High Elves were moving half of their forces into the Court of Trees."

"Are they attacking?" the Prince of Stone asked as we all fell in beside the king.

Aldrich shook his head. "As far as we can tell... no. We are not sure what it is that's going on, but I have a hard time believing that Iwdael just woke up one day and decided to invite them in. Which is why I want you all here too."

"I would feel a lot better if you had let us bring more guards, my king," Edric said. There was genuine concern in his gray eyes as he looked at the King of Elves. "What if it is a trap so that they can attack you?"

"Your reservations are noted, but we can't make it seem like *we* are the ones who are attacking. This might be another kind of trap."

On my right, Mordren turned to look at King Aldrich. "You think they are trying to provoke us into starting a fight?"

The king was silent for a few seconds. "Possibly."

Leaves crunched under our feet as we strode across the moss-covered forest floor at a brisk pace. Wooden buildings of varying sizes watched us as we made our way towards Prince Iwdael's castle. The sounds of people talking and moving started trickling through the branches. When the great defensive walls made of dark wood at last rose before us, the noise of bustling people was so loud it echoed between the trees.

I frowned.

There was a long line of elves standing outside the walls, and they looked to be queueing for something. Bronze breastplates shone in the sunlight before them. A pair of tall elves with long pointed ears that stuck up through their hair were attaching something to the wrists of the people at the front. Alarm bells went off inside me.

"Is that what I think it is?" I said, staring at the scene before us.

"Bracelets," Ellyda's sharp voice replied. "The High Elves are the ones who have been handing out those black bracelets. They haven't just been tolerating the religious zealots who believe that they are gods. They have been encouraging them."

Mordren and I exchanged a troubled glance, but no one said anything. A cloud of worry hung over our group. Several people cast uncertain looks at King Aldrich, but his brown eyes were focused on two people standing on the grass inside the gates. High Commander Anron and Prince Iwdael.

The guards at the gate stood promptly aside when the King of Elves strode towards them. Forming a half-circle behind him, we followed Aldrich through the gates and into the gardens outside the palace.

It was swarming with High Elves. Imposing figures in polished armor were moving across the fresh green grass, carrying packs and other supplies. The whole area pulsed with power, and the urge to kneel increased with every step.

"Iwdael. High Commander Anron," King Aldrich said in a powerful voice as we came to a halt in front of the two of them. "You are looking very busy."

The implied question was loud and clear, but Anron only gave the king a nod and a pleasant smile.

"Yes, my king," Prince Iwdael said. He was standing with his hands clasped behind his back, looking calm and at ease. "I realized that it must be awfully uncomfortable for the High Elves to live on the beach at this time of year. No offense, Rayan, but it's very hot in your court in the middle of summer." He shrugged. "So I invited them to stay here until the worst of it has passed."

"How very generous of you," King Aldrich said.

"Yes, I was very surprised," High Commander Anron began as he smiled again, "and immensely grateful, when Prince Iwdael offered to house some of my people so that they could get out of the blistering sun for a while."

King Aldrich said nothing. His silver-trimmed white robes rippled slightly in the wind while he searched Iwdael's face for traces of distress. Something that would tell him whether Iwdael was saying and doing this under duress.

As if Anron could feel it, he gave us all a nod and then said, "Well, I will leave you to it."

Long brown hair shifted over immaculate armor as he

turned and strode away. As soon as he was out of earshot, everyone shifted their attention back to the Prince of Trees. Iwdael was still standing with his hands clasped behind his back, looking at us with a casual expression on his face.

"Iwdael, what the hell is going on?" Prince Edric demanded.

"What I think Edric is trying to say," Rayan cut in smoothly with a small exasperated glance at the Prince of Stone, "is, have they threatened you into doing this?"

"Oh, not at all." Iwdael's smile sent a wave of calm certainty over us. "As I said, I am doing this completely willingly."

The Prince of Trees was eccentric enough that it might be the truth. But there was still something bothering me. As if he was thinking the same thing, King Aldrich spoke up.

"What about the High Elves distributing bracelets to your people outside the walls?"

"Yes, well, I figured it was better to just let people believe what they want." He shrugged again. "Like you said, forbidding something, especially something religious, only makes people cling to it harder. Better to try it and then discard it than being forced to abandon it before you have come to that conclusion yourself."

His words washed over me. He was making a lot of sense.

Another gust of wind whirled through the woods. Branches swayed around us and the smell of warm grass and roses filled the air. Iwdael's long brown hair, decorated with leaves and twigs, fluttered across his face. Unclasping his hands, he raised them and pushed his hair back behind his pointed ears.

A ripple of shock pulsed through our group.

"Iwdael," King Aldrich said, his voice deceptively calm. "What is that?"

Golden light from the afternoon sun shone down on the black bracelet around Prince Iwdael's wrist.

The Prince of Trees glanced towards his wrist before looking back up at us. A mischievous smile flashed over his lips as he winked at us. "Like I said, better to try it out yourself and then discard it."

The twinkle in his yellow eyes made me want to smile too.

"I really should go and help them get settled in," Iwdael said with a wave towards the High Elves. "But you're of course welcome to stay as long as you like." He gave us all a nod. "Fellow princes." His eyes met mine. "And ladies." Turning to Aldrich, he executed a sweeping bow. "My king."

Before anyone could say anything else, he whirled around and started across the grass. His rich purple and gold shirt shimmered in the sunlight. I stared after him.

"Is he serious?" Prince Edric blurted out into the silence that settled around us.

A thoughtful look passed over Evander's face. "This is eccentric. Even for him."

"Did you notice?" Rayan Floodbender began. His gleaming purple eyes swept over us, meeting each of our gazes in turn. "He was using his powers of mood manipulation on us."

I blinked. I hadn't realized that. Not until now when Rayan pointed it out.

"So, is he lying?" Edric prompted and turned to the king. "Is he doing this willingly or are they somehow forcing him to do it? Maybe through that bracelet?"

Silence fell around us. For a few moments, only the chattering and bustling of the High Elves across the grass broke the stillness as we all waited for the King of Elves to proclaim his judgment.

The king was still staring after the Prince of Trees.

At last, he heaved a deep sigh and turned to face us. "I can't tell."

Worry flitted through my chest. I glanced at Evander, who knew the Prince of Trees better than me. He shrugged as if to say that he couldn't tell if Iwdael was lying either.

"So what do we do?" I asked into the tension that was building around us.

Summer winds brought another breeze smelling of warm soil and blooming flowers to our lungs as we once more waited for King Aldrich to make a decision. The Prince of Stone was scowling while Rayan only looked worried. Mordren met my gaze briefly before shifting it back to the king.

"We send a steady stream of spies here to monitor the situation," King Aldrich began.

He looked at each of us in turn and there was a hardness in his brown eyes. My heart thumped in my chest. At last, the King of Elves spoke up again.

"And we start mustering our armies for war."

CHAPTER 3

Nervous tension rippled through the room. From atop my throne, I watched the gathered nobles below exchange worried glances before they straightened their spines and looked back at me. There was not a black bracelet in sight.

"Understood, Lady Firesoul," said the serious-looking elf at the front. "We will start getting our forces ready straight away."

I gave him a nod in acknowledgement.

"Can I just ask," he continued. "How likely is it that there is going to be a war?"

"For now, this is just a precaution," I said. "It is always better to have an army ready and not need it instead of needing an army and not having it."

That seemed to make the nobles relax slightly. In truth, I considered it very likely that the situation with the High Elves would come to a head sooner rather than later, but I decided to keep that to myself for now. No need to spread unnecessary panic.

"Well said, Lady Firesoul." He inclined his head. "I will coordinate the efforts of the noble houses and keep you updated on the progress."

"Thank you, Osfer." Looking up, I swept my gaze across the rest of the throne room. "Any other questions?" When no one spoke up, I raised a hand and motioned towards the doors. "Okay. Then that's all."

The rustling of clothing as they all bowed to me was drowned out by the boom of the doors as some of my servants once more opened them to let the rest of the people back in. I had only wanted my most trusted senior nobles present when I gave the orders to start mustering forces, because otherwise someone might leak it to the High Elves. They would probably find out anyway, one way or another, but there was no reason to make it easy for them.

Soft murmuring started up as a cluster of the nobles' attendants drifted into the throne room. Pushing myself off the sturdy red throne, I started down the steps. Idra came striding towards me from one of the passageways that led to the guards' wing of the castle. I changed direction and moved towards her.

The nobles and their private guards were only one part of the armed forces that the Court of Fire could muster. The largest section was the soldiers that Prince Volkan had kept on payroll, and that I had wisely decided to keep when I stole his throne. They had been Idra's to command before and I didn't see any need to change that. After all, between the two of us, she was by far the one most suited for the post.

I locked eyes with her from across the room. "How goes the–"

Idra's eyes went wide and she opened her mouth to yell something, but I was already moving. There was so much panic in her dark eyes that I threw myself backwards on instinct.

A whistling sound cut through the murmur of the crowd. It was followed by a sharp thud as a knife buried itself in the wall where I had been only a fraction of a second earlier. Another knife shot towards me. I threw up a shield of fire while diving aside again.

"Assassin!" Idra bellowed into the oblivious crowd.

The knife sped through my insufficient flame shield intact and slammed into the wall above me while I rolled to my feet and whipped my head around for the source of the blades. Snapped out of their conversations, the nobles cried out in alarm right as another voice cut through the room.

"Death to the usurper!" a male voice screamed from somewhere on the other side of the sea of nobles. "Death to the pretender!"

Chaos erupted as half of the crowd ducked and ran for cover while the other half threw up protective spells or charged towards where the voice had come from. All it did was create a stampede that no one could get through efficiently. Since the sea of panicking elves and humans was in the way, I couldn't risk shooting any flames towards my unseen attacker. Instead, I made as if to run towards him.

"Stay here!" Idra snapped at me, shoving me backwards as she sprinted into the screaming crowd.

After shifting my fire shield into position, I put my back against the wall and dropped into a defensive stance while scanning the room with wary eyes.

Idra's lethal body disappeared between two groups of humans right as the guards who had been stationed in the throne room reached me and formed a protective barrier around me.

The panicked screaming died down but people were still stampeding towards the doors. Minutes dragged on. When I was fairly certain that no other attacks were coming, I relaxed my stance and let the fire before me die down.

"Go find out if anyone saw who did it," I told the guards around me.

They exchanged a look, as if reluctant to leave me unprotected, but in the end did as I ordered. Only my most loyal and battle-ready nobles had stayed when all hell broke loose. I marked each of their faces. An assassination attempt was bad for one's health, but it was very good for finding out who would have your back in a crisis.

From across the room, guard after guard met my gaze and shook their head after talking to the people still left inside. I blew out a sigh. No one had seen anything.

Movement from the great stone doors caught my attention.

People were leaping out of the way as an elf with shoulder-length white hair came stalking through. Idra often kept her face a passive mask, but in the months we had known each other, I had learned to read the micro-expressions on her face. There was no need for that now. As she plowed through the crowd, it was impossible to miss her state of mind. She was pissed.

"I lost them," she ground out as she prowled up to me and looked me up and down. "Are you hurt?"

"Did you see who it was?" I asked.

She locked eyes with me. "I said, are you hurt?"

I blew out a half-exasperated huff. "No, I'm not hurt. So, did you see who it was?"

"No." Annoyance flickered in her eyes. "Like I said, I lost them."

"It's fine." I jerked my chin, motioning for her to follow. "I think I know someone who can find them."

Anger still swirled in her eyes but she fell in beside me as I started down a narrow corridor. Morning sunlight filtered through the windows and painted the red stones in pale light. I could feel Idra fuming beside me, and I knew that she was beating herself up for the fact that an assassin had managed to take not one, but two, shots at me and then get away without her stopping them. I also knew that nothing I could say would make it better so I kept quiet.

As we turned down another empty hallway, Idra finally spoke up.

"You didn't make it hot enough."

"I know." Tipping my head back, I let out a small sigh. "But I wanted a shield, not a wave that would turn half of the people in that room into charcoal."

Idra kept her gaze on the path ahead. "A fire shield works well on some types of magic. It doesn't work at all against solid objects, like blades, unless you can make the fire hot enough to melt it."

"I already said I know," I muttered. "But I still can't add more heat without also adding more mass. At least not reliably."

"Shitty reason to get assassinated."

"Yes, but I wasn't. Was I?"

"Barely." As we paused outside a door on the outskirts of the castle, Idra turned to face me. "You need to figure out how to use your powers consistently and reliably. Your enemies aren't going to wait. And as you just saw, I'm apparently not good enough to protect you all the time either."

For a moment, I only looked back at her. Behind the

irritation in her eyes was something else. It looked a lot like worry. And a hint of regret.

"For what it's worth," I began, brushing a hand over her arm before gripping the door handle before me, "you don't have to protect me all the time."

Before she could answer, I pushed down the handle and swung open the door to reveal what looked a lot like a cozy living room.

Comfortable sofas and armchairs were scattered around the room in no particular order, desks and tables and chairs occupied the spaces between, and there was a hearth against the inner wall. Rugs covered the floor, and mismatched candelabras and other decorative pieces dotted some of the furniture. It looked like someone had stolen stuff from a whole bunch of different places with various interior designs and then just put it all in the same room. Which was of course exactly what had happened.

"Kenna!" came a cheerful voice from one of the couches.

Loose brown curls fluttered around Valerie's face as she jumped up from her seat and vaulted over the backrest before landing on the mat-covered floor behind. Theo looked up from where he had been sitting by one of the tables and he pushed to his feet as well.

"Hey, Kenna," he said before turning to the elf next to me and inclining his head. "Idra."

There was a wide grin on Valerie's face as she strode towards us. "What brings you to our lawless corner of the castle?"

One of the first things I had done after I became Lady of Fire was to offer Valerie and Theo a job. I knew just how skilled their gang, the Hands, was at navigating the shadier parts of town, so I had asked if they wanted to put those skills to use by working for me as spies. Far from everything of importance happened inside castles, so I needed someone who could keep an eye on the shady part of the world too. In exchange, I had offered them a home here to do with as they pleased, a steady salary, and I turned a blind eye to whatever extracurricular activities they engaged in. Needless to say, they had been most willing to accept.

"Well," I began as I closed the door behind us and moved farther into the room. "I was almost assassinated fifteen minutes ago."

Valerie snorted. "Right." When I said nothing, she raised her eyebrows. "Wait, are you serious?" Before I could answer she shifted her gaze to Idra while pointing at me. "Is she serious?"

"Yes," Idra confirmed with a dark glare in my direction.

"But we don't know who was behind it," I continued. "So could you see what you can find out?"

"Why are you so calm?" Valerie shook her head at me before looking over her shoulder at Theo. "Why is she so calm? Would you be that calm if you were assassinated?"

"Probably not," he said. "Well, apart from the fact that I'd be dead, of course."

I heaved a sigh that was half exasperation and half amusement. "Almost assassinated. I said that I was *almost* assassinated. Anyway, can we focus, please? Could you try and find out who was behind it?"

"Of course!" Valerie gave me a look as if that should have been obvious. Then a wide grin spread across her face and she put two fingers to her lips and blew a long whistle. "You hear that, gang? We've got work to do."

From all over the room, people whose presence I hadn't even noticed popped up out of seemingly nowhere. Even more strolled in from the corridor that led to all of their bedrooms. I suppressed a laugh. Even though I could literally walk through walls, I knew that I would be hard-pressed to match the stealth of these human thieves.

"Alright, we're moving out," Theo said and waved a hand in the air.

Half of the people in the room started grabbing gear off shelves while the rest only fired off a salute to their gang leaders. Some slunk past us towards the door, flashing me a smile on the way, while others climbed out through the windows. I watched the organized chaos around me until Valerie's voice pulled me back.

"I'll come find you when we know more," she said.

"Thanks," I replied.

After one final grin, she took a running start towards the window and then leaped out. Theo winked at me before following her.

Next to me, Idra let out what I swore was an amused huff. I shook my head at the now empty living room before starting towards the door again.

It was only nine o'clock in the morning and I had already given orders to muster our army *and* almost been assassinated.

Idra was right, I really needed to get better at using my fire magic.

Before another attack happened.

CHAPTER 4

Magic flowed inside me, warm and sparkly, as I stepped out of the luxurious stone bath and dried myself with a large fluffy towel. Idra had been right. With both the High Elves making their moves and some unknown party trying to have me assassinated, I needed to focus more on mastering my fire magic. So I had spent the whole day doing just that. It was slow going, but at least it was going.

Moving into my bedroom, I threw open the doors to one of the closets. I still hadn't heard back from Theo and Valerie, and Idra was busy mustering our troops, so there wasn't anything more I could do about that now. However, there was one thing I needed to do. I had to talk to Mordren.

Clothes rustled as I pushed outfits aside while considering.

We needed to coordinate our efforts in finding out what the High Elves were up to. But that didn't mean I had to play nice. A wicked smile spread across my lips as I selected a strapless black dress that I knew would make Mordren's mind go to all kinds of places.

I had just finished brushing my hands down the silken black skirt when a voice came from outside the door.

"Lady Firesoul," one of my guards called through the thick stone. "Prince Mordren is here."

Surprise, and pleasure, swirled inside me. I guess I wasn't the only one who had been wanting to meet.

"Let him through," I called back.

A moment later, the heavy stone door swung open and a dangerously beautiful elf in a sharp black suit sauntered across the threshold. He had been about to say something, but when his eyes fell on me, he stopped. Mouth still slightly open, he watched me from across the rich red and gold rug that spanned the floor. The door clicked shut behind him.

A sly smile spread over his lips as he raked his eyes up and down my body. "Kenna."

I cocked my head, matching his smirk. "Mordren."

He started towards me. Decorated oil lamps made of metal and glass hung on hooks across the ceiling, and the light from the flames illuminated his sharp cheekbones and painted golden highlights in his night-black hair. Lean muscles shifted underneath dark fabric as he moved. I wondered if he knew just how damn attractive he looked.

Dragging my gaze to his face again, I found a slight smirk playing over his lips.

I stifled an amused huff. Oh, of course he did.

"I heard you were almost assassinated today," Mordren said as he came to a halt two strides away.

Waving a casual hand in front of my face, I scoffed, "Ah, they're exaggerating."

He stared me down. "How close was it?"

"Like I said, they're exaggerating. It's nothing to worry about."

"I said, how close was it?" Mordren took a step forward. Reaching out, he placed a hand under my chin and tipped my head back so that I met his intense gaze again. "Answer."

His touch sent a thrill through my body. I grinned up at him. "Or what?"

A wicked glint sparkled in his eyes and he tightened his grip on my jaw. "Or there are other ways to make people talk."

"Careful now, remember that I was the one who told King Aldrich that the Court of Fire didn't require you to have a chaperone anymore. I could just as easily change my mind."

"Is that a threat?"

"More of an observation."

Lifting my hand, I placed it against the inside of Mordren's forearm and pushed his hand away from my chin. He let me. His arms fell back down by his sides but he didn't step away. I held his gaze.

"So I'd do my best to stay in my good graces, if I were you." With deliberate slowness, I raked my eyes over his lean muscled body before locking eyes with him again. An evil smile spread across my lips. "Now, strip."

Amusement and surprise bloomed in his eyes, and he let out a disbelieving laugh. I only raised my eyebrows expectantly. He shook his head, but then moved his hands towards his belt.

Holding my gaze, he unbuckled his black leather belt and slowly slid it out of the belt loops on his pants. I watched him, a smug smirk on my face.

A spark of devilish mischief flashed in his eyes.

And then he struck.

He moved like a viper. Shooting forward, he wrapped his belt around my wrists while his shadows darted out and slithered around my arms and legs to help the process. My stunned surprise gave him a second's advantage.

Fire flared to life along my limbs in order to force the shadows away, but Mordren only sent more black tendrils to ensnare me. While I'd been busy trying to free myself from his shadows, he had finished tying his black leather belt around my wrists, and now he had stepped back. I was vaguely aware of him reaching up and removing something from the ceiling, but I had to focus solely on beating back the shadows.

Suspicion rose inside me.

Even though I couldn't really spare the attention, I whipped my head around to look at what he was doing. My eyes widened. *Oh, no he didn't.*

After he had finished removing one of the oil lamps from its hook in the ceiling, Mordren placed it neatly on a desk and then prowled back towards me. His shadows were effortlessly keeping my flames at bay. I added more heat to them.

Panic rang through me when the carpet under my feet almost caught fire as a result, and the flames along my limbs winked out. Aided by his shadows, Mordren grabbed my bound wrists and walked me two steps backwards until I was standing directly under the now empty hook in the ceiling. Holding my gaze, he forced me up on my toes, guided my tied hands into the hook, and then let go.

Yanking against the restraints, I tried to get out of the exposed position he had put me in, but it was useless.

Wicked satisfaction gleamed in Mordren's eyes as he took a step back and raked his gaze over my body. "Now this brings back memories."

I glared at him. "Seriously. Again?"

"Well, I did not get a chance to enjoy it last time. I had to chase after your thief friend, remember?"

"How is that my fault?" I muttered.

Craning my neck, I looked up at the belt around my wrists and sent a burst of fire magic towards it. Flames spread along my arms. And burned uselessly on top of the belt without affecting it. I blew out a frustrated sigh.

My fire magic treated my clothes as part of my body, which was why I could use it without the risk of it burning through my clothes and leaving me naked. The problem was when I *wanted it* to affect my clothing. Or in this case, the restraints keeping me tied to the ceiling. It was possible to make the flames burn through the belt. I just hadn't quite figured out exactly how to do that yet.

Graceful fingers took my chin in a firm grip and forced my head back down. I stared into a pair of glittering silver eyes from only a breath away. A lethal smile spread across Mordren's mouth.

"You really should know better than to try to threaten me." Keeping his grip on my jaw, he brushed his lips over mine. "My little traitor spy. You know that there is only one way this ends."

"I seem to recall several times when I successfully outmaneuvered you."

"Do you now?" He released me and took a step back. Lifting a hand, he held my gaze while slowly loosening his black silk tie. "Then by all means, give it your best shot."

After tearing my gaze from the way the tie slid over his crisp black shirt as he pulled it off, I turned my attention back to the leather belt. Fire whooshed over my arms again. It crackled faintly but did no damage to the belt.

"What is the problem?" Mordren taunted as he prowled around me until he disappeared behind my back. "Can you not get your fire magic to do what you want yet?"

"Of course I can," I huffed. "It just takes a little time."

"Hmm. Perhaps this will help."

"What are you–" I fell silent as something dark appeared in my vision. "No! Stop that, you insufferable…" A groan escaped my lips as Mordren tied his black silk tie over my eyes. "Bastard."

Deprived of my sight, I couldn't tell where he was anymore, so I started slightly when his dark voice spoke softly right into my ear. "You should be thanking me. I am helping you. You think too much. You need to feel more."

"Feel more?" I grumbled. "Oh, I'm feeling something alright."

Even though I couldn't see the flames along my arms anymore, I redoubled my efforts to make them burn through my restraints. Faint hissing sounded, but the belt stayed firmly in place. I poured more heat into the fire.

Warm fingers brushed over my shoulder blades. A small moan slipped from my lips as Mordren gently brushed my hair aside and draped it down over my shoulder instead. I put more force into the flames around my wrists.

Victory sparkled inside me as a faint smell of burnt leather rose.

I grinned. *Finally.*

A slight burst of pain flickered through my body. My concentration broke in a flash and the fire along my arms spluttered out.

Mordren let out a dark laugh and drew his fingers from my neck and down between my shoulder blades.

Biting back a curse, I brought the flames to life again.

The tight bodice of my dress loosened slightly as Mordren's clever fingers started undoing the fastenings down my back. My body squirmed underneath the brush of his fingers. I sent a burst of power to the flames.

Burnt leather filled the air again. I added more power and—

Another flicker of pain pulsed through my body, shattering my concentration.

"Would you stop that?" I yanked in frustration against the leather belt but it still refused to break.

Mordren had finished undoing the fastenings and started, with torturously slow movements, to strip me of my dress. His fingers brushed over my now exposed back before reaching around and pushing the tight black fabric down over my breasts. Leaning forward, he kissed that sensitive spot at the crook of my neck. My treacherous body shuddered with pleasure.

"What is the matter?" He smiled against my skin. "Am I distracting you?"

I arched my back as he slid the dress down my stomach while he continued to leave a trail of kisses from my neck and over my shoulder. My breathing was growing labored. Dark desire coursed through me as Mordren's hands dipped lower, sliding the black fabric of my dress further down my body. I pulled futilely against my restraints again.

The dress came free, fluttering down around my legs and leaving me standing in only my underwear. My skin prickled at the sudden exposure, even though the air in the room was warm. Mordren had pulled back. Since I was still blindfolded, I couldn't tell where he was but my heart was pounding. I knew he was raking his gaze over my body.

In an effort of pure will, I sent flames whooshing over my arms again. The smell of burnt leather appeared in the air once more.

And then another pulse of pain shattered my concentration like a broken mirror.

"No!" I moaned. It came out sounding much more pitiful than I would have liked. I yanked against the sturdy leather belt in frustration. "Stop doing that."

Mordren's fingers brushed over my ribs. I shivered with pleasure.

"Beg me," he breathed against my mouth.

Refusing to let him win, I brought the fire back to life. A flash of pain broke it instantaneously.

Another frustrated moan slipped my lips. Mordren's hands trailed down my body. Still standing on my toes, I arched into his touch as he made his way down my hips and then up along the inside of my thigh.

A wave of desire coursed through my body, making me tremble.

He withdrew.

The sudden loss of his touch was almost jarring. Still blindfolded, I turned my head from side to side, trying to figure out where he was by sound alone. His fingers threaded through my hair at the back of my neck and he trapped the long red curls in his fist.

Then he tightened his grip and tugged hard, forcing my head back. "Beg." His commanding voice vibrated through my bones from only a breath away.

Burning desire pulsed through my whole body like waves.

"Please," I gasped, breathless. "You win. Please. I'm begging you."

A midnight laugh danced over my skin. Mordren stole a kiss from my lips before releasing me and stepping back.

I sucked in a shuddering breath and it took me another few seconds before I could clear my head enough to summon the fire again. This time, Mordren let me do it without breaking my concentration.

One final time, the smell of burnt leather spread through the air.

The belt snapped.

With the sudden loss of resistance, I crashed down to my knees on the floor. Reaching up, I yanked the silk tie from my eyes only to find a pair of black shoes and pant legs in front of me.

Mordren leaned down and ran a hand over my throat before tilting my chin up so that I met his gaze. A villainous smile of pure victory and satisfaction graced his lips. "My beautiful little liar, on your knees before me once again."

Smacking his hand aside, I shot to my feet and stabbed a finger at him. "You are going to pay for this."

He let out a dark laugh and cocked his head. "So you keep saying."

When his intense eyes raked over my curves, I became acutely aware that I was only wearing my black lace underwear while he was still fully dressed. A sly smile spread over his lips, as if he was thinking the same thing.

With a smug look in his eyes, he advanced on me. I let him back me across the floor.

The back of my legs met the cold stone of my bedframe.

Mordren kept coming.

"How much do you want to bet," he began as he came to a halt before me. After tracing gentle fingers over my cheekbone, he took my jaw in a firm grip. "That I can make you beg at least once more before the night is over?"

Grabbing the front of his shirt, I pulled his face closer to mine. "Come try it."

He pushed me backwards. I landed on the soft mattress

and tried to maneuver myself into a better position while Mordren stripped off his shirt and then straddled me.

I flashed him a wicked smile before throwing myself into the mission of getting sweet revenge on the Prince of Shadows.

CHAPTER 5

Mordren's chest rose and fell in a steady rhythm. Lying on my side, I watched the light play over the sharp ridges of his abs while sleep slowly pulled its heavy blanket from my exhausted body.

"You know, I could come back if you want."

I flew out of bed. Fire flared to life along my arms as I landed in a battle stance on the floor while panic bounced around inside me. On the other side of the bed, Mordren had done the same. Dark shadows shot towards the sound of the voice.

"Wow," the voice continued. "Touchy."

I blinked at the skinny human who was standing on the carpet, inspecting the black tendrils that now encircled her arms.

"I mean, it's a bit superfluous," she commented. "If I'd wanted to slit your throats while you slept, I wouldn't have offered to come back."

"Valerie," I groaned.

With shadows still wrapped around her wrists, Valerie lifted one hand in a cheerful salute. "Morning."

Rolling my eyes, I let the fire along my arms die out while yanking up a silk robe and draping it around my naked body. "Yes, it certainly is."

Mordren arched an eyebrow at her but withdrew his shadows as well. "You were planning on slitting our throats while we slept?"

"No." She gave us a small shake of her head as if that was the silliest thing she'd ever heard. "I simply pointed out that if I had been planning on doing that, I wouldn't have told you that I could come back later. I mean, what kind of assassin would do that?"

Mordren muttered something under his breath while his shadows disappeared completely.

"Seriously, you..." Valerie trailed off. Her brown eyes dipped below Mordren's waist. Moving slowly, she met my gaze again while her eyebrows climbed towards her hairline. Then a wicked grin spread across her mouth.

I threw a pillow at her.

"What?" she said innocently while ducking the fluffy projectile.

Across the bed, Mordren shook his head and turned around while retrieving his pants from the floor. With his back to Valerie, he cast me a look. Satisfaction gleamed in his eyes and a smug smirk played over his lips.

I threw a pillow at him too.

He let out a dark chuckle while a wall of shadows sprang up, both to catch the pillow and to allow him to get changed in peace. Blowing out another exasperated groan, I turned back to Valerie.

"How did you even get in here?" I waved a hand towards the door. "There are supposed to be guards out there."

She grinned like a fiend. "A thief never reveals her tricks."

"Uh-huh." Rubbing my forehead, I made a mental note to go over castle security again. After dragging a hand through my messy hair, I retied the sash around my robe and then met her gaze again. "So, did you find anything?"

"Yeah." All traces of mischief disappeared from her face and a serious expression settled across her features instead. "What do you know about *the Ghosts*?"

"Who?"

"Figured as much. They're hitmen. Not exactly top-tier assassins, but they're not amateurs either. Theo and I ran into them once back in the Court of Stone."

"Seriously?" I stared at her. "They came after you?"

"No. We were robbing a house when they showed up too. Said they were there to kill the guy who lived there and told us to take a hike." She shrugged. "We did."

"Huh. And now they're after me?"

"Yeah."

The shadows on the other side of the bed rippled and then Mordren stepped out, dressed in his sharp black suit once more. While the shifting dark wall disappeared, he turned towards me and narrowed his eyes. "I thought you said that it was not serious."

"Didn't you hear what she said?" I shot him an exasperated look while waving a hand in Valerie's direction. "They're not top-tier."

Mordren leveled a commanding stare on me. "She also said that they are not amateurs."

"Exactly. So I have a bunch of mediocre assassins after me." I shook my head. "Who cares? We have bigger problems. Like the fact that Anron has moved into the Court of Trees and that Iwdael is wearing one of those black bracelets."

"I mean," Valerie interrupted, "it's technically possible to worry about more than one thing. Like, you could worry about both the assassins and the High Elves at the same time."

I shot her a dark glare.

She raised her hands. "Just saying."

"We're going to sneak into the Court of Trees today and see if we can find out what they're up to," I said to her instead, changing the topic. "Wanna come?"

"Would it not be better if Valerie and her colleagues focused on this group of assassins instead?" Mordren cut in smoothly before she could reply.

Raising a hand, Valerie pointed towards him while a grin flashed across her lips. "You know, for once I actually agree with the well-equipped prince over there. We'll see what else we can dig up about the Ghosts while you go play in the forest."

"Are you–" I began but she kept talking.

"Besides, I'm more of a city girl anyway. Don't really like the woods. They're just so... woodsy."

I threw my hands up in an exasperated gesture. "Fine. Just... You said it yourself. They're assassins. So please don't do anything stupid. Or dangerous."

Valerie snorted. "When have I ever done anything stupid or dangerous?"

Before I could remind her of any of the numerous times she had done things that fit either or both of those categories, she flashed us another grin and winked.

"Have fun in the forest!" she called.

And with that, she fired off a playful salute, whirled around, and then disappeared out the door. The guards outside cast startled looks between her and us. I waved them off.

Once the door had clicked shut again, I turned back to Mordren and arched an eyebrow at him. "Seriously?"

He smoothened an invisible crease in his suit. "I am not quite sure what you are referring to."

"Right," I huffed.

Rounding the bed, Mordren advanced on me. I stood my ground. He stopped a single stride in front of me and then reached out to place a hand on my cheek. A hint of worry swirled in his eyes.

"You are not nearly concerned enough about this attempt on your life," he stated.

"Of course I'm concerned," I admitted. "It's more like... I'm not surprised. At my coronation, Anron practically told me that he would be coming for me. It was only a matter of time. Which is why we need to figure out what they're up to."

"Indeed." Drawing his hand along my jaw, he tipped my head back and brushed a soft kiss against my lips. "I have to head back to my court, but I will see you in the Court of Trees at noon."

"Good."

Very slowly, he withdrew. For a moment, we only stared at each other. Close enough to touch. Close enough to pull him back to me and rumple that immaculate black suit of his. But we would have time for things like that later. When the High Elves had been dealt with. When no one was trying to assassinate me any longer. When the Court of Fire was firmly under my control. Until then, these stolen moments in between schemes would have to suffice.

"I'll see you soon," I said.

The serious moment evaporated and he gave me a smug smile. "Yes, you will."

Shining black hair fluttered behind him as he strode towards the door. I watched his lean muscles shift underneath dark fabric until he disappeared out of sight. The guards gave him a respectful nod as he passed. I shook off the memories of last night and made my way towards my closet.

There were still a few more hours until we were meeting up again to spy on the High Elves, which meant that I had some more time to practice my fire magic.

And besides, if we were sneaking into the Court of Trees, there was one more person I had to find.

CHAPTER 6

A gentle breeze carried the scent of warm grass and summer flowers through the forest. I took a deep breath. Sunlight fell in through the bright green canopy above and warmed my skin while the leaves rustled around us. The Court of Trees really was nice in the summer.

Something dark moved in the corner of my eye.

Evander's step faltered a little as he whipped his head towards the approaching figure.

"Hello, Mordren," I said without looking.

"Kenna," came the smooth reply from between the trees.

A moment later, Mordren Darkbringer strode out in front of us. I came to a halt. Evander did the same, except he crossed his arms and raised his chin as well.

"Why is he here?" Evander challenged in a tone that few would dare to use when addressing the Prince of Shadows. Not to mention that he hadn't even actually addressed him, but instead had spoken as if he wasn't there.

"Why are you here?" Mordren looked down at Evander with an indifferent expression on his face. "I do not recall you having any abilities suited for this kind of mission. Or any abilities at all, in fact."

An indignant flush painted red splotches on Evander's cheeks, but before he could say something that would escalate the argument, I cut him off and turned to Mordren.

"He's here because he knows the Court of Trees better than any of us." I started walking again. "Now enough bickering. Let's go."

For a moment, the forest was silent. Then the soft crunching of leaves behind me informed me that Mordren and Evander had followed me. Birds chirped in the branches above us as we walked in silence towards the high defensive walls that protected Prince Iwdael's castle.

The murmur of people grew louder the closer we got, but we were approaching from the back so we still hadn't run into anyone who would recognize us from afar.

"I could just walk through it," I said when we finally reached the tall wooden barrier, "but I assume you have some kind of plan for how you are going to get inside."

"Of course," Evander replied. With a contemptuous glance towards the silent Prince of Shadows, he turned right and made his way along the wall. "Follow me."

A wolfish smile spread across Mordren's lips, but since Evander was now walking ahead of us, he thankfully didn't see it. I suppressed a sigh.

I knew that Mordren disliked Evander because he had betrayed me and Eilan last year and locked us in that mausoleum basement. Considering everything Mordren and I had done to each other, I found it a tad hypocritical, but I still understood the feeling. What Evander's problem with Mordren was, however, was something I still hadn't been able to figure out. He had thought that Mordren was as bad as

Volkan and that he was going to leave us hanging when we were slaves. Since that hadn't happened at all, I didn't really understand what it was about the Prince of Shadows that made Evander so incredibly confrontational all the time.

"This is it," Evander said and pointed to a section of the wall that looked exactly like every other section. "There's a back entrance here but it's locked from the inside."

I studied the slab of wood. "Do I need a key?"

"No, just lift off the bar and pull it open."

"Any guards?"

"Nope. It's used by people who engage in... discreet encounters."

"Ah." I gave him a nod. "Alright, I'll see you in a minute then."

Silk brushed against my skin as I stepped through the wall and into the castle grounds.

Whipping my head from side to side, I made sure that no one was close enough to spot me. Sounds of activity came from the other side of the wooden palace, but this section was hidden by a mass of hedges and the occasional tree. I turned back to the wall.

The inside of it looked just as unassuming as the outside. Frowning, I ran my hands over it.

There was a branch running horizontally across it, but it looked to be a part of the wall. Another small branch bulged outwards underneath it.

Placing my hands under the horizontal branch, I pushed upwards. It dislodged easily. I raised my eyebrows but placed the branch on the ground. After casting another quick look over my shoulder, I grabbed the bulge and pulled.

Cracks appeared in the smooth wood.

And then a door swung open to reveal Mordren and

Evander. I flashed them a grin.

"So, apparently you are not completely useless after all," Mordren commented with a smug glance in Evander's direction.

Evander shot him a vicious look. "As opposed to you."

With his chin raised, Evander stalked through the doorway. He only made it one step before he flinched as if in sudden pain. Whirling around, he glared at Mordren, but the Prince of Shadows only looked back at him with a neutral expression on his face.

Murder shone in Evander's dark green eyes but he continued walking. Mordren sauntered through the doorway as well before turning and helping me put the bar back on the door.

"Seriously?" I said under my breath while we lifted the bar off the grass.

A soft click sounded as the branch slid back into place. Mordren glanced at me. There was a sly smile playing at the corner of his lips.

"I have no idea what you are talking about," he replied smoothly.

And in that moment, I recanted my previous statement. I knew exactly what Evander's problem with Mordren was. Though, as much as I hated to admit it, I did find Mordren's constant power plays kind of hot.

A warm summer breeze rustled the fresh green leaves around us as we snuck through the rows of hedges and approached the front of the castle. With each step, the sounds of people grew louder. Stopping just out of sight, we peered around the corner.

Colorful tents had been erected in a haphazard fashion across the lawn in front of us. High Elves, elves, and humans were mixed together, talking and drinking from wooden cups. It looked like some kind of event.

"What are they doing?" I asked.

Evander kept his eyes on the scene before him, but shook his head. "I don't know."

Though, that didn't really surprise me. Prince Iwdael threw parties whenever and however he wanted, so it could just be a spontaneous celebration of something.

Shielding my eyes from the sun, I scanned the open stretch of grass ahead.

No sign of the Prince of Trees.

"Anron is here," Mordren said.

I shifted my gaze to a cluster of humans who were standing around a very tall elf in bronze armor. A pleasant smile graced High Commander Anron's lips, but his blue eyes shone with intelligence. I couldn't make out what they were saying, but the humans were nodding enthusiastically. They also looked a bit angry. Shaking my head, I swept my gaze over the rest of the gathering.

Captain Vendir disappeared into a yellow and brown striped tent a short distance from his High Commander, while another soldier in armor fastened a black bracelet around someone's wrist.

We needed to split up.

"We should split up," Mordren said.

Amusement rippled through me. I knew that he couldn't actually read minds, but sometimes I still believed the lie he perpetuated.

"I agree," I said.

"I will keep an eye on Anron."

Nodding, I slid my gaze to the yellow and brown striped tent. "I'll take Captain Vendir."

"Okay," Evander said on my other side. "I'll see if I can figure out where Prince Iwdael is, then."

I gave them both a nod. "Good luck."

They nodded back and then split off from our little group. Mordren summoned a haze of shadows and kept to the shade as he made his way closer to the High Commander, while Evander disappeared back the way we had come.

After drawing in a bracing breath, I set my sights on the tent across the grass and snuck away as well.

The chaos that seemed a part of everything in the Court of Trees helped hide me as I moved closer to my target. Between the random bushes, tents, and oblivious groups of people, it was easy to move without having to walk for too long in the open. Keeping my back straight and my strides confident, I closed in on the tent.

Whatever this gathering was, it had a pleasant atmosphere. As if people were discussing interesting things, making friends, and generally having a good time. I wasn't sure if it was due to Iwdael's mood manipulation or if people genuinely were enjoying themselves, but it was making me nervous. People should feel wary around the High Elves. Not comfortable.

Yellow and brown fabric fluttered before me as a sweet-smelling summer wind whirled through the castle gardens. I strolled around the back of the large tent.

As soon as I was out of sight, I dropped down. Lying on my stomach in the warm grass, I carefully lifted the tent wall and peered inside.

Captain Vendir was sitting with his back to me.

I jumped to my feet and phased through the cloth wall before he had a chance to turn around.

The inside of the tent was much darker than the bright

lawn outside, so I had to blink repeatedly while moving into position behind a stack of crates. Once my eyes had adjusted to the gloomier conditions, I peered out from my hiding place.

Vendir was still sitting with his back to me. He was bent across a desk and looked to be writing something. Shifting my position slightly, I tried to see what it was.

Though I was too far away to make out any details, I got a glimpse of what looked like a letter. Staying silent, I continued studying him.

Another couple of minutes ticked by uneventfully. Then he straightened and folded up the document right as the tent flap was pushed open. Vendir shot to his feet.

"–and then I told him that..." The elf who had been talking to her friend as they moved into the tent trailed off once she noticed Vendir. Coming to a halt in the middle of the tent, she blinked at him. "Oh."

Her blue dress rustled as she knelt down, placed a hand over her heart, and bowed her head. Next to her, the other elf did the same. From my position behind the crate, I frowned at them. I vaguely recognized them as minor nobles from the Court of Trees, but I couldn't remember their names. What I could see, however, was the awe and reverence that filled their faces as they bowed before Captain Vendir.

The captain seemed to see it too.

Embarrassment flashed over Vendir's handsome features and he drew a hand through his long blond hair while he shifted uncomfortably.

I stared at him in surprise. That was not what I had been expecting. High Commander Anron seemed to relish the feeling of people treating him as if he were a god. Captain Vendir did apparently not share that sentiment.

"Please, stand up," he said. His voice was much gentler than I had expected it to be. "Was there something I could help you with?"

The two females rose to their feet again, but the admiration stayed on their faces.

"We apologize for the interruption," the one in the blue dress said. "We didn't know you were in here."

"It's quite alright," Vendir said.

Another few seconds passed but the two elves said nothing. Uncertainty flickered in Captain Vendir's brown eyes as he glanced between the two of them.

"Was there something I could help you with?" he repeated, his voice still gentle.

"What's Valdanar like?" the second elf blurted out.

She was wearing a rather spectacular yellow dress that made her look like a cross between a daffodil and the sun. Her pale blue eyes glittered as she looked at Captain Vendir. He blinked in surprise.

"Oh." He cleared his throat. "It's… uhm… big."

She opened her mouth, but could apparently not think of anything to say. Fortunately for them all, the awkward situation was interrupted a moment later when High Commander Anron strode into the tent. He had been about to say something, but stopped when he noticed the two female elves.

Their eyes widened.

With hurried movements, they dropped down on their knees again.

"High Commander Anron," the one in the blue dress said, her voice serious.

Anron watched them for a few seconds. Satisfaction gleamed in his eyes as he took in their kneeling forms. From behind the stack of crates, I barely dared breathe.

"Ladies," he said at last. "Would you mind giving us a few minutes?"

They scrambled up and hurried towards the exit instantaneously.

Once the tent flap had swung shut behind them again, Anron turned to Captain Vendir. Cocking my head, I studied the captain.

All traces of uncertainty and discomfort were gone. He stood with his spine straight and his hands behind his back, his face wiped of all emotion. A soldier waiting for orders from his superior.

"Is it done?" Anron asked.

"Yes, High Commander," Captain Vendir replied.

"Good. Give it to Fendar. He's waiting outside."

Vendir nodded in acknowledgement before turning and picking up the letter from the desk. After placing it in an envelope, he inclined his head to Anron and then moved towards the exit again.

"And Vendir," Anron said right before he could disappear through the tent flap. His blue eyes were hard as they locked on his captain. "We are gods. Remember that."

Something swirled in Vendir's brown eyes, but he quickly dipped his chin in deference. "Yes, High Commander."

As soon as I realized that Anron was going to follow Vendir outside, I threw myself through the tent wall and hurried towards the nearest corner.

A High Elf with dark red hair waited just outside the entrance to the tent. He nodded when Captain Vendir handed him the envelope.

Indecision flitted through me. *Should I follow him, or stay with Vendir?*

The redhead made the decision for me when he took off straight through the crowd and towards the main gate. There was no way for me to follow him without being detected.

Something cool and silken brushed my arm. I turned to find Mordren approaching me from the other side. He pulled back his shadows as he came to a halt next to me.

"Anron has been spending a lot of time with the humans," he said by way of greeting. "I am not sure why, though."

"Huh." I ran a hand over my jaw. "Captain Vendir wrote some kind of letter and gave it to that redhead over there."

"What was it about?"

"No idea. But he seems uncomfortable with people treating him as if he's a god."

Mordren's eyes tracked Vendir from across the grass. "That is interesting."

"Yes, but I'm not sure how we can use that. He also follows Anron's orders without question."

"I see."

Movement by the castle wall drew my attention. An elf with short brown hair met my gaze and then shook his head. So, Evander hadn't been able to find Prince Iwdael.

Worry seeped into my bones.

Something was definitely wrong. The problem was that we didn't have enough information to act on. There were too many odd things happening and I couldn't fit them all into a cohesive plot yet.

Drumming my fingers against my thigh, I watched Anron as he joined another group of humans.

I didn't like waiting around for someone else to make the first move.

But right now, we didn't have a choice.

CHAPTER 7

Swords clanged between the stone walls. For a moment, I just remained standing there, watching the soldiers as they sparred on the dusty stones. Elves, male and female, dressed in the red and gold armor of the Court of Fire. Fighting with blades or magic. Determined and serious. And loyal. To me. They were my army. It was still such a surreal feeling.

"We're still waiting for most of the nobles' soldiers," Idra said as she came striding between the rows of sparring elves. "But it'll be fairly easy to incorporate them once they get here."

"Good." I turned to face her as she came to a halt next to me. "Any issues?"

"No. The ones Volkan kept on payroll will follow you because you proved yourself by killing him." She tipped her head from side to side. "And besides, you're still paying them." Twisting slightly, she met my gaze head on. "And the slaves you freed and offered actual jobs... they'll be loyal to you forever."

I glanced towards the group of elves on the far left. A muscular elf with short brown hair slammed his sword into his shield before advancing on his opponent. Kael Sandscorcher. He had challenged Volkan in the tournament's first match, and lost. When I had taken the slave collar off his throat and offered him a paid job in the army, he had actually teared up.

"But the nobles with those black bracelets are still trying to turn people against you," Idra finished. "So I'll keep an eye out for traitors."

"Thank you."

She nodded. After sweeping one last look across my army, I turned and moved away from the training fields. Idra fell in beside me.

The bright sun beat down mercilessly on us as we made our way back towards the red stone palace. Since it was the middle of summer, temperatures were about as high as they got. And in the Court of Fire, that was a lot. At least it was dry heat. Glancing up, I studied the burnt blue sky above us. Not a cloud to be seen. It must be awfully hot for the soldiers to be training in this kind of weather.

Since I received my fire magic, my sense of heat had changed. I could still feel when things were warm or cold, of course, but the feelings were more muted. Scorching days like these didn't really affect me all that much. It was a rather interesting side effect. One I appreciated a lot at times like these.

The chattering of people and bustling of a city surrounded us as we left the barracks and training fields behind. Elves and humans dressed in loose clothes that provided respite from the heat moved up and down the street. Some bowed their heads as I passed, others only continued on their way. I watched a group of children play in a fountain while their parents inspected a horse near the stables.

"Do you really think it will come to it?"

"A war?" Idra followed my gaze and watched the kids for a while too before shifting her attention back to the street ahead. "I don't know. The High Elves are clearly here for more than diplomatic ties, which means that they will reveal their hand at some point. As for how far they will go to get whatever it is that they want?" She shrugged. "Who knows?"

Tearing my gaze from the playing children, I focused on the road before us as well. "I don't like just waiting for them to make the next move."

"I know."

We'd had this conversation several times already, but Idra knew how on edge I was so she only answered in the same calm way that she always did.

"What would you do?" I glanced at her from the corner of my eye. "If you were the ruler?"

Idra was silent for a few seconds. "I wouldn't send our people into battle unless I had to. Especially since we don't even know our enemy's strengths and weaknesses."

She was right. I had felt enormous power around Anron when he got into an argument with Volkan, but I still didn't understand what it was. Reaching up, I raked my fingers through my hair and blew out a deep sigh.

"You're right. As usual."

"As always," she corrected.

I turned to look at her. There was a slight smirk playing over her lips. The sight of it warmed my heart. It had taken a while for Idra to start showing emotions. She still didn't do it all that often, but compared to when she had been Volkan's slave, it was a remarkable change.

"Bah," I huffed in mock affront. "And here I was–"

The street exploded.

My body flew sideways as Idra shoved me out of the way right before what looked like a lightning strike hit the street in the spot I had been occupying. I slammed into the red stone wall while the blinding white light from the concentrated explosion died down. Pain spiked through my shoulder, but I hadn't wanted to phase through the wall since I didn't know what was on the other side.

"Go!" Idra bellowed as dark shapes landed on the street.

The air crackled.

I leaped backwards through the wall behind me just as another white bolt zapped the stones where my feet had been. The flash of brilliant light illuminated the living room I had ended up in. Stumbling over a side table, I tried to find my way back to Idra.

The door crashed open.

An elf with long white hair pulled back in a braid darted into the living room. I yanked out my sword and knife. Sounds of battle came from outside and I barely had time to see Idra fighting half a dozen people on the street before the elf in front of me drew a pale sword and charged me.

Throwing up my own sword, I blocked hers while swiping towards her stomach with my knife. She twisted aside just in time and then attacked from the side. With a quick strike, I parried her thrust and countered. Once more, she danced aside and then swung at me from the side.

Wood clattered as I leaped away, crashing into a small table as I did so. She didn't press the advantage. Instead, she only kept backing me across the floor. I frowned. What was she doing?

Clanging steel came from outside. It was followed by a dull

thud. I cast a quick look over my shoulder. The open front door was directly behind me now. Fighting in a cramped living room was not ideal. And besides, I needed to get outside to help Idra. Making a split-second decision, I broke and ran for the closest wall.

She didn't try to stop me.

Dread welled up inside me, but before I could realize my mistake, I was already outside.

The white-haired elf darted after me.

As soon as she was outside, a blinding bolt of white light zapped towards me. I threw myself aside a fraction of a second before it hit me. The air smelled of ozone. Rolling to my feet, I shoved a hand towards her.

Fire roared to life.

Her eyes widened and she leaped back and slammed the stone door shut right before a column of flame smacked into it. Fire licked the red stones and heat washed over the alley, but the wall remained intact.

A sound came from behind me.

On instinct, I whirled around and yanked up my sword. Metal clanked as the sword meant for my chest slammed into my own blade instead. Another attacker, this one human, flicked his wrist to disengage our blades before swinging at me again. I rammed my knife into his arm.

A cry echoed between the buildings. It was almost loud enough to drown out the sound of a door crashing open. I yanked out my knife from his arm and threw myself sideways as the white-haired elf sent another bolt of lightning from above.

My mind was screaming at me. She needed to be outside for the white lightning to work, that was why she had backed me around the room until I made a break for the wall. I had to get back inside.

Clashing steel rang out behind the white-haired elf and the human with the sword. Idra was fighting four people at once. Two more lay dead at her feet. I couldn't leave her.

Silver glinted in the bright sunlight. I leaped back as the human man swung his sword at me once more.

As soon as my feet touched the ground, I jumped again.

A sizzling beam of white light hit the stones I should have been standing on.

Pain shot through my ribs as the sword-wielding human landed a glancing blow to my side while I was busy trying to get away from another bolt of lightning. Sucking in a sharp breath between my teeth, I swung at him. The air crackled. Before the blow could land, I was forced to abort the attack and throw myself sideways to avoid another lightning strike.

I couldn't stay in the same place for more than a second, or I would be hit by that lightning, but I also couldn't just keep jumping around when there was a man trying to shove a sword through my heart. Fighting like this was impossible.

Another burst of pain pulsed through me as the man's sword split the skin on my arm while I tried to get away from the white-haired elf's attack.

Irritation burned through me like wildfire.

Behind their backs, Idra was still fighting four people at once.

"Idra!" I screamed as I jumped out of reach once more while drawing my arms back. "Under!"

She didn't take her eyes off the fight but she jerked her chin down in acknowledgement.

"Now!"

As soon as the word was out of my mouth, two things

happened. I slammed my arms forward and Idra threw herself flat on the ground.

A wall of fire roared down the street. Panicked screams filled the air as the attackers tried to get away. The man with the sword had been far too close to escape and disappeared in a dark red inferno. Behind him, the others scrambled to get out of the way.

The elf with the white lightning dove through the nearest window. Glass shattered around her and rained down the street right before the wave of flames washed past. The four people who had been attacking Idra had panicked at the sight of the wall of death and ran in the other direction. One of them was smart enough to leap through an open doorway but the others kept running.

Idra, pressed flat against the bloodstained ground, was left untouched as the flames raced past above her. As soon as she was in the clear, she leaped to her feet.

"Run," she said.

I didn't even stay to see what happened to the other three assassins. The wall of flames would burn out before it reached the end of the empty street, so it wouldn't harm anyone else, and we needed these precious few moments I had bought us.

Ramming my blades back into their sheaths, I sprinted up the street in the other direction with Idra next to me. The assassins didn't seem all that interested in pursuing us now that more than half of them were dead, but I still didn't feel safe until we had passed through the wrought metal gates and were back inside the castle walls.

Adrenaline still pulsed through me from the fight and the sprint.

"You okay?" Idra asked as we made our way inside.

"Yeah." My chest heaved so I took another breath before continuing. "You?"

She nodded. "The one with the white lightning... I've heard of her. She's a mercenary."

My hands were starting to shake so I drew my fingers through my hair and then shook out the muscles of my arms to stop that from happening. Dried blood was still crusted on my skin.

"She's not with the Ghosts?" I asked.

"No." Idra came to a halt once we reached the empty throne room. Placing a hand on my uninjured arm, she pulled me to a stop as well. Only when I had turned to face her did she continue. "As far as I know, the Ghosts sometimes hire her for jobs as an independent contractor."

I frowned at her. "A group of assassins hire a mercenary?"

"Yes. If they really want to make sure their target ends up in the ground. And she's not cheap."

A frustrated groan ripped from my throat. It echoed through the high-ceilinged hall and sent one of my messengers running towards us.

"How are the High Elves even paying them?" I dragged my hands through my hair again and shook my head. "It's not like they earn money."

Idra looked back at me with steady eyes. "I don't know."

"Lady Firesoul," the messenger said as he skidded to a halt next to me. "You're hurt."

"I'm fine, Nicholas," I replied.

Nicholas glanced from the blood running down the side of my ribs to the cut on my arm and then back to my face. I heaved a deep sigh.

"Alright," I said in defeat. "Send word to Imelda in the Court of Shadows. She'll be able to heal me."

"Yes, Lady Firesoul," Nicholas said. "Right away."

I watched his blond head disappear out the door before I turned back to Idra. "We need to figure out who is funding the Ghosts and cut off their source of money. They're hired killers. They're not trying to assassinate me because they hate me. They're doing it because someone is paying them to. So, we cut off their funding and they'll stop trying to kill me."

"And how do we do that?"

"I haven't figured that part out yet."

"Sounds like we need to talk to those weirdos again."

Despite the aftereffects of the assassination attempt still racking my body, I laughed. "Yeah, we do."

So, while we waited for Nicholas to come back with Imelda, Idra and I went to find a couple of thieves.

CHAPTER 8

Night had drawn its blanket over the city. The dark heavens were dusted with silver glitter and a bright moon shone down on us where we waited in a shadowed alley.

"Several of our people saw a man with fresh burns on his arm return to this house." Theo nodded towards the building across the street. "He also fits the description of the guy you saw dive into the doorway when you sent that wall of fire."

I nodded. "Alright."

"How do you want to play this?"

"I'm going to sneak inside and see if it's him. And if it is, I'm going to make him tell me how they're getting paid." Tearing my gaze from the house across the street, I turned and looked at Theo and Valerie. "You might want to wait outside for this part."

They exchanged a glance.

"You're thieves," I said. "Not killers."

Valerie arched an eyebrow at me. "You do remember the

time when we hired you to set fire to Collum Skullcrusher's headquarters, right?"

"Yeah." A small chuckle escaped my lips. "Yeah, I do. But this is different."

"Seems pretty straightforward to me."

Theo nodded as well. "If someone tries to kill us or our people, as far as we're concerned, they deserve what's coming to them."

Silence fell over the alley as I studied their determined faces. Not for the first time, I was struck by the amount of love, and loyalty, in their eyes when they looked at me. We hadn't even known each other for an entire year yet, but they had already made me a part of their family.

A soft smile blew across my lips. "Okay. How are you getting inside?"

"The roof." Valerie grinned. "And then the window."

"Of course it is." I shook my head in mock exasperation and then waved a hand towards the front door. "Well, I'll be taking the stairs."

She snorted. "Amateur."

"Kenna."

All three of us turned around to find the source of the voice striding out of the shadows behind us. Moonlight made Idra's white hair shimmer like a river of silver. I had just opened my mouth to reply when a second figure became visible in the gloom. Surprise flitted through me. I frowned, but before I could comment, Idra spoke up again.

"The other safe house was a bust." Idra crossed her arms as she came to a halt in front of me. "If the lightning mercenary was staying there, she's long gone now."

"I suspected as much. She seemed like a professional." I

shifted my gaze to the elf who had stopped next to her. "Evander. What are you doing here?"

"I'm helping you, of course." Emotions flickered in his dark green eyes. "Information about the Court of Trees isn't the only thing I can contribute with, you know."

Ah. I barely prevented myself from blowing out an exasperated sigh. So, Mordren's comment about his uselessness when we were sneaking into Iwdael's castle had really struck a nerve.

"I tried to make him stay behind, but unless you wanted me to actually kill him…" Idra met my gaze and shrugged before shooting Evander a pointed look.

He flinched when her black eyes fell on him, but then he raised his chin. "We're all here now, so let's just do this. How are we getting inside?"

"First we climb up onto the roof, and then through the window," Valerie said cheerfully.

Idra appeared entirely unfazed but Evander's eyes widened. When a grin spread across Valerie's face, I had a sudden feeling that she had done it on purpose.

"They're using the roof," I clarified. "We're taking the stairs. Follow me."

"Race you inside," Valerie said before she and Theo leaped onto the nearest wall.

While they scrambled upwards and disappeared into the darkness, I started towards the front door. All the windows were dark, meaning that the assassin inside was probably trying to sleep off his wounds from the fight earlier today. I still kept my footsteps soft as I made my way to the door and slipped through it.

With the building now blocking the bright moonlight, the hall inside the door was even darker than the night outside. I ran my hands over the door until I found the locking mechanism. Very carefully, I turned it.

There was a faint click as it unlocked.

For a moment, I remained standing there motionless. Listening for any sound of an assassin stirring. When nothing happened, I slowly pushed down the handle and swung open the door. Idra and Evander snuck through while I started towards the stairs.

Since the staircase was made of stone, there was thankfully no risk of creaking floorboards. I wasn't sure how proficient Evander was at breaking into people's homes, so anything that made it less likely that he would mess up was a blessing.

After peeking into the other empty rooms, I moved towards the only one with a closed door. Presumably the bedroom. Once I reached it, I waited for Idra and Evander to catch up before I edged open the door.

"You took your time."

I nearly jumped out of my skin.

Valerie's brown eyes glittered with mischief where she was standing right inside the door. Next to her, Theo slapped his forehead.

My eyes darted towards the sleeping figure on the bed before meeting Valerie's gaze again.

"He's been self-medicating," she answered in response to my silent question, and nodded towards the pile of empty liquor bottles next to the bed.

Giving her a nod, I moved into the darkened bedroom. The man sleeping on the bed had bandages all over his arm and he appeared to be completely knocked out. Not a great state to be in if you worked as an assassin. Though to be fair, if I had burns that severe, I would probably have self-medicated quite heavily too.

I drew the knife from my thigh holster while moving towards the bed.

"Get the chair," I said to the room in general.

Idra lifted out the chair from by the desk and placed it closer to the bed, while Theo and Valerie pulled out a couple of belts from one of the drawers. Evander remained hovering awkwardly by the door.

Stopping next to the bed, I stared down at the man lying there on his back. He was definitely one of the people who had attacked us in that street, and the one who had dived into the doorway to escape my flames. I studied his features for another few seconds before lifting my knife and placing it against his throat.

"Wake up," I said.

Nothing happened.

I glanced at the empty bottles of alcohol again. He really was completely out of it. Moving the knife a little farther away, I drew back my other hand and slapped him across the face.

He jerked upwards but I slammed my free hand down on his chest and forced him back while repositioning the knife against his throat. Once he felt the cold kiss of steel, he stopped struggling. Blinking furiously, he tried to take everything in.

"Remember me?" I said.

His eyes darted down to his burned arm before focusing on my face again.

"Good." I jerked my chin towards the chair. "We're going to have a little chat."

A scarred hand wrapped around his uninjured arm.

"I assume you're also familiar with Idra Souldrinker," I continued.

All color drained from his face as he looked from the hand around his arm to the elf attached to it. With one pulse of her magic, he would be dead.

"Good," I said again. "Please have a seat."

With Idra's lethal touch on his skin, he could do nothing except let her walk him to the chair and push him into it. Valerie and Theo tied his arms to the chair with the belts. The assassin winced when the leather bit into the bandages, but he remained silent.

Theo and Valerie withdrew to the wall, but Idra remained standing behind the assassin's back. Spinning the knife in my hand, I advanced on him.

"Who is paying you?" I asked.

Only the softly blowing wind outside answered me.

Fire flickered in my hair. Placing my hands on his arms, I leaned down closer to him. Idra placed her hand on his shoulder from behind to make sure that he didn't try anything.

"It really would be in your best interest to answer my questions promptly and efficiently," I said, my voice laced with threats.

He remained silent.

"That looks like some really nasty burns." I cast a pointed look at his bandaged forearm before flames whooshed to life on my shoulder. They slowly spread down my arm and towards the hand I still held pressed against his forearm. "I bet it would be really painful if someone decided to burn those bandages off."

Dread surged in the assassin's pale eyes, but he clamped his jaws together. The fire continued down towards my hand. I held his gaze.

The flames reached my palm.

He jerked against the restraints.

Idra tightened her grip on his shoulder.

The smell of burnt cloth filled the room as his bandages caught fire.

A whimper slipped his lips.

And still, he said nothing.

Irritation crackled through me.

Extinguishing the flames, I straightened and rammed my knife back in its holster. "I really don't have all night, and you're clearly not fazed by a little torture, so how about we skip the warmup."

Steel rang into the dead silent room as I drew the sword from my back and moved so that I stood to his side instead of in front of him. Suspicion and worry swirled in his eyes as he watched me.

Gripping the sword two-handed, I touched the edge to his right wrist as if taking aim, and then I lifted the sword high. "It's going to be really difficult for you to make a living without your hands."

Pure terror flooded his eyes.

"You have three seconds."

He thrashed against his restraints, but Idra kept him mercilessly pinned to the chair.

"One."

A sob ripped from his throat.

"Two."

"Stop!" he screamed. Primal fear pulsed in his eyes as he stared up at me while trying to yank his hands away. "I'll do whatever you want. Just, please... don't cut my hands off."

I let the silence stretch long enough for him to truly understand that I could change my mind if he stopped cooperating. He swallowed.

"Who is paying you to kill me?" I asked at last.

"We don't know."

Rolling my eyes, I raised the sword again.

"No!" he shrieked and pulled against the restraints. "I swear, I'm telling the truth. Someone is transferring money into our account anonymously. We even tried asking the bank, because it's not every day someone hires you to kill a prince. I mean, a lady. Ruler. It's a high-profile job. But the bank just says the client wishes to remain anonymous. And you know what they're like. The banks never betray their clients' privacy."

As much as I hated to admit it, he was making perfect sense. If I was trying to have a prince assassinated, I wouldn't exactly want my name connected to the payouts either. And the banks acted like independents states so they didn't pick sides.

"What's your account number? The account that these payments are transferred to?"

Paper rustled by the wall as Theo pulled out a small notebook. I watched the assassin's face for traces of lies while he spoke a series of numbers.

"How many of you are there?" I asked once Theo had finished writing down the account number.

"About twenty."

Twenty? By all the gods and spirits. I stifled a groan and instead narrowed my eyes at the assassin once more. "Where are they?"

"I don't know. We move safe houses all the time." He glanced at the sword in my hands. "For this exact reason."

Raising my gaze, I met Idra's eyes from across his shoulder. Her nod confirmed that she didn't think he was lying either.

"Anything else?" I asked, even though I already knew that there was nothing more of value he could tell me.

He shook his head.

I slit his throat.

A gasp rang out from the doorway. It was quickly drowned out by the wet gurgling sound that the assassin made as he died.

Turning around, I found Evander staring at me from beside the door. Shock, and something else, swirled in his eyes. He opened his mouth. Whatever he had been about to say, I didn't want to hear it.

So I flicked the blood off my sword and strode past him.

Back out into the night.

CHAPTER 9

*D*espite the cozy space we were in, the mood in the room was sour. Candles burned brightly throughout a room filled with plush couches and armchairs while rows of bookshelves and a few soft carpets provided the study with an even more comfortable feeling. Valerie and Theo had taken a detour to the kitchen, so there were currently only three people in the room. Idra was seated on a red couch, her face devoid of all expression. From an armchair on the other side of the table, dark green eyes glared at me.

"You tortured him," Evander said, breaking the tense silence at last.

"Yes." I met his gaze. "What did you think I was going to do? Ask nicely?"

"You set his already burned arm on fire. And then threatened to cut his hands off. There are more stops between that and asking nicely."

"He's an assassin. He wasn't going to tell me anything unless I made him."

"Was. Not is. He *was* an assassin. He's dead now."

Raising my eyebrows, I spread my hands. "Are you going somewhere with this?"

"You didn't have to kill him!" Evander's words ripped from his throat with much more force than I had expected.

I frowned at him. "Of course I did. He was being paid to assassinate me. Their whole group is *still* being paid to assassinate me. If I had let him live, he would've just tried to kill me again as soon as my back was turned. It was him or me, and in a situation like that, I'm going to choose myself every day of the week."

"But why did you have to do it in such a… brutal way? You could've just had Idra kill him with a painless touch. But no, instead you had to slit his throat and watch him drown in his own blood."

Ringing silence filled the room once he had finished. For a few seconds, I only stared back at him without saying anything. Leather creaked faintly as Idra at last shifted in her seat. Her black eyes slid to me.

The reason why I had killed him myself instead of asking Idra to do it was very simple, but I was still reluctant to explain it to Evander. Idra was magically gifted at killing and she had more experience with taking someone's life than anyone I had ever met. I knew that she could handle it. Knew that she wouldn't have lost any sleep over it if I had asked her to use her magic on the assassin. After all, he had tried to kill her too. But Idra had spent her whole life killing people on someone else's command. And enough was enough. If I wanted someone dead, their blood should be on my hands. Not hers.

"He was mine to kill," was all I said.

Evander made a frustrated noise and threw his hands up.

From her place on the red couch, Idra held my gaze for another few seconds. Then she gave me a slow nod, and I think she understood.

"I don't understand why you are complaining about this," I continued. "You weren't even supposed to be there. I didn't ask you to come specifically because I didn't want you to see all that. *You* are the one who forced Idra to bring you along."

"It doesn't matter if I'm there to see it or not!" Evander sat forward in his armchair. There was a storm of worry and desperation in his eyes as he looked at me. "What matters is what you do, regardless of who sees it. If you torture and kill someone when no one is looking, you're still a person who tortures and kills people. Is that really the person you want to become?"

"Then what was I supposed to have done?" My voice rose in exasperation too. "Should I have just let him keep coming at me until he finally succeeded in killing me?"

"That's not what I'm saying!"

"Then what are you saying? If he hadn't dived out of the way when I sent that wall of fire, he would also have been dead. How is that any different from this?"

Evander let out a frustrated groan and shot to his feet. Irritation danced over his handsome features as he stalked towards the door and threw it open. "I need some air."

Letting my head fall back against the backrest, I closed my eyes and heaved a deep sigh. Evander's stomping footsteps echoed from the hallway outside, but they were growing fainter with each step. I focused on how soft the cushion behind me was in order to try to calm my own flickering anger.

"What's his problem?" came a voice from the doorway.

Opening one eye, I found Valerie and Theo strolling across

the threshold. Their hands were full of plates containing everything from fruit to bread to cheese to what looked like pastries. Valerie had jerked her chin in Evander's direction as she walked inside but was now completely focused on maneuvering the plates onto the table without dropping anything.

"I don't know," I said since I didn't want to rehash the argument we'd had. Sitting up, I scanned the low table before me. "Please tell me you brought cake."

Metal clinked as Theo dumped his plates on the table too. Valerie moved aside a mountain of grapes to reveal a big chocolate cake that she then proceeded to push towards me.

"Of course I did." A wide grin spread across her mouth. "What kind of amateur midnight snacker do you take me for?"

I laughed, feeling the heaviness of Evander's words disappear. Valerie was good like that. Leaning forward, I reached for the chocolate cake and cut myself a large piece.

"So, we now know that someone anonymous is paying the Ghosts to kill you," Theo said as he settled onto the couch next to Idra.

There were two plates piled high with cheese and fruit in his hands. He handed one of them to Idra. Genuine surprise flickered in her eyes. Then she reached out and took the offered plate.

"What are we going to do about that?" Theo finished as he placed his own plate on top of his knees.

"We need to shut down the payments," I said. "I kind of just want to stalk into the bank and order them to stop the transfers. I'm the ruler of a court now, so I should be able to do that."

"Won't work," Valerie said around a mouthful of bread and garlic butter. "Got no authority there."

Shoving a big piece of cake into my mouth, I grumbled, "I know. But still, it would be nice."

The dancing candlelight cast the room in a warm glow. Turning slightly, I watched the dark night outside the window. Glittering silver stars still covered the heavens, and the moon bathed the courtyard outside in pale light. I ate some more of the delicious chocolate cake while mulling over my options.

"Oh!" Valerie suddenly exclaimed.

Jumping to her feet, she accidentally slammed her knee into one of the fruit trays, which sent it skidding over the edge. Idra's hand shot out and caught it before it went over. Something between amusement and exasperation tugged at the corner of her lips as she pushed it back in place while she cast a glance at the excited thief.

"What if we plot a burglary?" Anticipation bounced around in Valerie's brown eyes as she pointed straight at me before moving her finger from person to person. "Huh?"

"What?" A frown passed over Theo's face as he looked back at her. "Robbing a bank is suicide, Val. You know that. Everyone knows that." Holding her gaze, he hiked a thumb in my direction. "In fact, weren't you the one who told her that?"

"No, no, don't shoot me down yet." She jumped from foot to foot and then jerked her arms down in a victorious gesture. "Oh, this is brilliant. Okay, hear me out."

Three frowning faces looked back at Valerie as she launched into an explanation of how her plan was supposed to work. By the time she was finished, the furrowed brows had climbed higher up on everyone's forehead.

"That's actually... a pretty smart plan," Idra said into the silence.

"Aha!" Valerie grinned. Then she let a mock scowl settle on

her face as she slapped Idra's arm with the back of her hand. "Though no need to sound surprised. I am rather brilliant, you know."

Idra started slightly and stared at the spot on her arm where the thief had so casually touched her, but before she could say anything, Theo cut in.

"Yes, once you peel back like fifty layers of crazy."

"Oh shut it." Valerie threw a grape at him. "You're just as crazy as I am. You just hide it better."

Theo tipped his head from side to side and then shrugged. "Well, can't argue with that."

I laughed and shook my head. "I agree with all of you. Yes, you are definitely crazy. And yes, this plan of yours is pretty brilliant and might actually work."

"Ha!" Valerie winked at me. "Told you so."

"But we're going to need some stuff to pull this off."

"Yep. Are you thinking what I'm thinking?"

"I am indeed." I matched Valerie's smile and gave her a quick rise and fall of my eyebrows. "Who wants to go visit the Court of Shadows in the morning?"

CHAPTER 10

"So that's what we're planning," I finished. "Do you have anything that will work?"

Ellyda stared at the wall above my shoulder. Light from the tall windows fell across her face and made her violet eyes glitter. Though, they were still very blank and out of focus. On my other side, Theo glanced between the two of us. The silence stretched on.

"Yes," she said once a good minute had passed.

Dragging her gaze from the wall, she blinked a few times before her eyes focused on my face. For a while, she only stared at me. Then she abruptly turned around and walked out the door. Her brown hair, tied back in its usual messy bun, bounced slightly with each step. And then she was gone.

"Uhm..." Theo watched her disappear, an uncertain look on his face. "Is she...?"

"She does that," a voice said from the other side of the door.

I turned to see Eilan and Mordren striding through the doorway, and my breath hitched slightly. He really was beautiful. They both were. But there was something about the way that Mordren carried himself, with a sense of absolute power and control, that made my heart start pounding faster in my chest. I knew that it was ridiculous. The High Elves had infiltrated the Court of Trees and were probably planning how to take over all of our courts, and I also had a group of assassins trying to kill me. It was the worst possible time to be distracted by things like this, but at that moment, all I could think about was how much I wished that Mordren and I had more time.

"She'll be back with what you asked for soon," Eilan finished. He nodded at Theo and then turned to the final person in the room. Pale green eyes shimmered in the bright sunlight as he smiled and nodded at Valerie as well. "Nice to see you both again."

"Oh." The sound was like a mix between a small exclamation and a whimper. Clearing her throat, Valerie shook her head. "I mean, hello."

Mordren rolled his eyes. Biting my lip, I suppressed a chuckle, but Valerie was thankfully not looking in either of our directions.

While the two thieves went to greet Eilan, Mordren approached me. Placing a hand on my arm, he steered me towards the side of the room. His eyes looked far too serious for my liking.

"What's wrong?" I asked once we were out of earshot.

Mordren shifted his position so that he was standing with his back to the others, and he also kept his voice low. "Eilan just came back from the Court of Trees."

"He was there as…?"

I left the sentence unfinished, but we both knew what I was referring to. Eilan had gone to the Court of Trees as one of his shapeshifter aliases. And more precisely, as that blond elf with a bland face who had worked as one of Prince Iwdael's spies for years. Very few people knew that Eilan was a shapeshifter. Valerie and Theo were currently not among those select few, which was no doubt why Mordren didn't want them to overhear.

"Yes," he confirmed.

"And?" I prompted.

"Iwdael refuses to reveal anything. Every time Eilan has tried to breach the topic of what the High Elves are doing there, he gives him some excuse or other and brushes him off."

"Wait, so he's not even talking to his spies about it?"

"Exactly." A worried frown creased Mordren's dark brows. "Whatever it is that the High Elves have on Iwdael, it must be something very important to him."

Blowing out a sigh, I massaged my forehead. "Great."

On the other side of the room, Valerie was explaining something to Eilan. Waving her arms around, she mimicked what looked like an explosion before throwing her head back and laughing. Eilan smiled too. While she was still busy sucking air back into her lungs, Theo slapped the side of her ribs and then picked up the threads of the story.

"How are things on your end?" Mordren asked. "No more attacks, I hope."

"Oh, well, uhm." I cleared my throat before shifting my gaze back to him. "I was kind of almost assassinated again yesterday."

"Kenna." There was a dangerous note to his voice.

"What?" I threw my hands up. "It's not like I ask them to try and kill me."

"What happened?"

"They attacked me and Idra when we were walking back from the barracks. We fought, I sent a wall of flame at them, and then we escaped."

"Did you managed to track any of them down afterwards?"

"Yes, one of them."

"And?"

"I tortured him and threatened to cut off his hands until he told me what I wanted to know. And then I killed him."

"Good," Mordren said, entirely unfazed by the gruesome deeds I had just admitted to. "Did you learn anything useful?"

"Not really. Well, partly. But to do something about it, we need her help."

Right as I nodded towards the other doorway, Ellyda reappeared. There was a pile of what look like assorted junk in her arms. Taking a step forward, I made as if to join her and the others by the table, but a hand shot out before I could.

Strong fingers gripped my chin and turned my head until I faced Mordren again. He stared me down until I stopped trying to move.

"If there is anything I can do to help you deal with these assassins," Mordren began, "anything at all, just say the word."

My heart stuttered slightly at the intensity of his gaze. "Yeah. I will. Thanks."

"Good."

Clearing my throat, I gave the hand still holding my jaw a soft swat. He flashed me a smirk but released me.

"Though, I'm pretty sure you'd still make me beg for it," I said under my breath as we started towards the table.

Mordren let out a dark laugh. Draping a possessive arm over my shoulders, he cocked his head and glanced down at me. That wicked smirk of his still played over his lips. "Well, I do like it when you beg."

"Bastard." I jabbed an elbow in his ribs that he pretended not to feel. "I will get my revenge on you, you know."

"So you keep saying."

The whole right side of the dining room table was now packed with items of all shapes and sizes. Ellyda was standing next to a pile of metal balls, sifting through them and inspecting several seemingly at random. Eilan, Theo, and Valerie were arranged in a semi-circle and they all appeared to be waiting for something.

Eilan raised his head and threw us a half smirk as we came to a halt next to him as well. "Finished flirting slash threatening each other?"

A sharp smile spread across Mordren's lips. "Oh you wish, brother."

"Where is *your* brother?" Valerie blurted out, her eyes on Ellyda, before Eilan could retort.

Ellyda only continued squinting at the metal ball in her hands. Her eyes were sharp, but they were only focused on that strange object as she fiddled with some kind of gears on the side of it. For all I knew, she wasn't even aware that we were in the room anymore.

"Hadeon is overseeing the mustering of our army," Mordren replied smoothly when the silence stretched on.

"Just like Idra," Valerie said. Concern blew across her face for a second. "Do you really think there will be a war?"

It was the same question I had asked Idra only yesterday. Mordren and I exchanged a glance, but it was Eilan who answered.

"I don't know," he said, his gorgeous face betraying a hint of worry as well. "But it's always better to be prepared."

"I just have a bad feeling that–"

"Here," Ellyda interrupted, making everyone start in

surprise. She shoved the small metal ball into Theo's hands. "See if you can get it into your pocket."

Blinking at her, Theo hesitated for a second. When she only continued staring at him, he at last cleared his throat and lurched into motion. It took some maneuvering, but he managed to squeeze the ball into his pocket.

"Good," Ellyda said and nodded to herself. "Then it's stable."

"What does it do?"

She looked back at him for a good ten seconds, as if she needed time to process what he had said, before finally replying. "It explodes."

Panic surged in Theo's gray eyes. With frantic movements, he yanked out the ball again and put it back on the table. "By all the gods." He sucked in a shuddering breath while his eyes darted between the exploding ball and the elf who had handed it to him. "Maybe tell me that before I shove it into my pants."

Ellyda frowned at him in silence for another few seconds. Then she gave him a single nod. "That's a valid point. I suppose it would have been rather inconvenient for you if it had blown your junk off."

Next to me, Eilan pressed a desperate hand against his mouth but still failed to completely stop the chuckle that slipped his lips. Theo shot him a disgruntled look, which only made Valerie laugh as well. I smiled and shook my head at them.

"This one here will create a cloud of smoke if you smash it," Ellyda continued as if nothing had happened, and pointed at a small glass vial filled with a black swirling substance. Shifting it aside, she motioned towards a cluster of tiny glass balls. "And these will set off a series of popping sparkles. While these ones…"

I made mental notes about all the inventions she showed us. The banks might be completely protected against magic, but they weren't as concerned with regular burglary stuff.

Mostly because no one would be insane enough to actually try to rob a bank with only smoke and mirrors as their tools.

Or would they?

CHAPTER 11

The urge to kneel pulsed through the grand hall. From atop my sturdy red throne, I watched as High Commander Anron and Captain Vendir strode through the throne room. Courtiers parted like the sea before a warship.

"High Commander Anron," I said as they came to a halt below the red stone steps. "Captain Vendir."

A sharp smile spread over Anron's lips. "Kenna."

Irritation flashed through me at the deliberate use of only my first name but I shoved it aside. Ignoring his obvious attempt to bait me, I instead gave him a pleasant smile that was laced with just a bit of poison.

"What brings you to my court?" I asked.

"Just a social visit." He matched my venomous smile. "I trust that the start of your rule is going well?"

"Of course," I replied, as if I hadn't almost been assassinated, *again*, just two days ago. "And what about you? I saw that you moved into the Court of Trees."

"Only half of us. The others are still enjoying the beach."

"And are you? Enjoying yourself?"

There was a satisfied glint in his blue eyes. "Iwdael is such a gracious host."

"Hmm."

"Well, I won't take up any more of your time." Anron glanced towards a group of elven nobles who had appeared behind him. They all wore black bracelets. "There seem to be other people who wish to speak with you. Good luck, Kenna."

Without waiting for a reply, he moved aside, but still stayed in the throne room. Captain Vendir followed.

From the group who had waited behind them, a male elf with short blond hair stepped up. Fire glinted off the black bracelet around his wrist. I raised my eyebrows in a show of indifference, but my heart was pattering in my chest. Whatever was about to happen had been orchestrated by Anron, which meant that it couldn't be good. Why did it have to be today of all days?

"Lady Firesoul." The words rang out across the throne room. "I challenge you to a duel for the throne."

A stunned laugh ripped from my throat. "Excuse me?"

"I challenge you to a duel for the throne," he repeated.

"Edus Quickfeet," I said, looking down at the elf below the red stone steps. "If you wanted a shot at the throne, you should have entered the tournament. Like I did."

Edus jutted out his chin. "You didn't beat Prince Volkan in a fair fight. You tricked him. That was the only reason you won."

Fire flickered through my red curls and a wolfish smile spread across my lips. "Ah, but no one ever said that you had to fight fair."

"It's not right. Which is why I now challenge you to a duel."

"But you have no right to demand a duel. That is not how succession works in the Court of Fire."

For a fraction of a second, his eyes darted towards High Commander Anron. Displeasure flashed across Anron's face.

"You're just scared to fight me," Edus Quickfeet blurted out.

The courtiers in the throne room sucked in a collective gasp. No one would have dared say something like that to Volkan Flameshield. Well, except for me, that is. Right before I killed him.

"Fine." I flicked a lazy hand and pushed to my feet. "If it's a fight you want, it's a fight you'll get."

Drawing my blades from their place behind the throne, I started down the steps. The other people in the throne room scrambled out of the way and didn't stop until they were standing a safe distance away.

Eyes darting from side to side, Edus retreated a step as well. "Right now?"

"Yes." I cocked my head. "Or have you suddenly lost your nerve?"

He cast another treacherous look towards High Commander Anron. "No, of course not."

Steel rang through the high-ceilinged hall as Edus drew his rapier. I had reached the bottom of the steps and advanced on him without stopping. After rolling his shoulders, he dropped into an attack position.

And then he flew across the floor.

Literally.

A burst of fire appeared under his boots and he shot towards me with impossible speed. I threw up my sword to block his thrust. Metallic dinging echoed between the stone walls.

Shoving his blade downwards, I rammed my knife towards his ribs. But he was already gone.

A blur of brown and green flashed in the corner of my eye, and I barely had time to leap aside before a rapier cut the air where I should have been standing. The crowd gasped. Whirling around, I drew my sword in a wide arc to force him backwards. He evaded it effortlessly.

Sparks gleamed along the floor as Edus Quickfeet darted towards me again. I jabbed at him, but he was already changing direction.

Pain vibrated through my leg as he kicked my knees out from underneath me. Hitting the floor less gracefully than I would've preferred, I dove forwards and rolled to my feet while spinning around.

The surprise twist almost caught Edus in the chest and he had to abort his attack at the last second. I jumped to my feet and went on the offensive.

His brown pants and green shirt blurred at the edges as he zigzagged across the floor, ducking my strikes while trying to score one of his own.

It took all my concentration just to survive the next few seconds. He was moving far too fast to hit, and almost too fast for me to block as well. I couldn't keep fighting like this.

My control on my fire magic still wasn't as good as I would have liked, especially not for a battle in such close quarters and among so many innocent spectators. But I would have to risk it.

Fire roared through the throne room as the flames in every pool along the floor and every fire pit flared upwards. The courtiers screamed in panic, but it was only meant as a diversion so the fire had just shot towards the ceiling without getting near anyone.

However, the move made Edus' step falter and he whipped his head around while ducking.

That gave me the second I needed to pin down his location.

With a twist of my hand, I summoned a ring of fire that surrounded the distracted Edus before he could figure out what was happening.

My heart slammed in my chest. This move took a lot of control on my part, and I had to keep the flames in check every second to prevent the ring from breaking. With nervous energy still bouncing around inside me, I squeezed the handle of my knife. The circle of fire tightened around Edus.

"It doesn't matter how fast you can run," I said from outside the flames, "when you can't walk through fire."

The fiery barrier tightened further. With his rapier still raised, Edus turned around and around, looking for a way out. There was none.

"Do you know how long it takes for someone's skin to start melting?" That cold ruthless smile was back on my lips. "Want to find out?"

"No," Edus pressed out.

"No? You really should have thought about that before you came into my halls, demanding a duel for *my* throne."

"Please." His chest was rising and falling rapidly now and his sword hand was shaking. "Please don't."

"You want me to spare your life?"

"Y-yes."

I closed the final distance to the now very tight circle of flames. As I passed through the wall of fire, I banked the flames enough for everyone to be able to see us clearly, but not enough to let Edus escape. Dark red fire clung to me as I stepped out of the flames and into the ring. It licked my skin and the black fabric of my clothes, and lifted my long hair so that it billowed behind me.

Edus flinched, his eyes wide, but there was no more space to back away. I advanced on him until I was standing a single step in front of him. Staring him down, I spoke loudly enough for the whole throne room to hear.

"Then beg for my mercy."

Metallic clattering joined the crackling of the flames as Edus threw his sword away. It skidded through the circle of flames before slamming to a halt against a metal fire pit. With fear in his eyes, the blond elf dropped to his knees and pressed his forehead to the cold stones before my feet.

"Please, Lady Firesoul," he said. "I'm begging you to spare my life."

I locked eyes with High Commander Anron from across the flames and the crowded throne room. He stared back at me. No one dared move. I wasn't even sure Edus was breathing anymore.

"Please," he whispered below me.

I let the silence stretch for another few seconds.

When I finally spoke up again, I kept my eyes on the High Commander across the room.

"If you ever come after me again, I will end your entire bloodline. Am I making myself clear?"

"Yes," Edus whimpered.

A small opening appeared in the flames behind him. I kept my eyes locked on Anron. "Get out before I change my mind."

Edus scrambled to his feet and all but ran through the opening I had created for him. Not even stopping to pick up his rapier, he darted out of the throne room in a rather undignified way.

Dark red flames continued licking my skin and playing in my hair as I kept my eyes on Anron.

At last, a cold smile spread across his lips and he inclined his head slightly. Then he broke eye contact and strode towards the exit. Captain Vendir, his face still carefully blank, followed him without question.

Only when they had disappeared out the great stone doors did I let the flames die down. The rest of the courtiers were still standing frozen on the red stone floor, glancing between me and where Edus had disappeared.

I waved a hand in the air. "No more petitioners today."

Without waiting to see what they would do, I spun on my heel and stalked towards a doorway leading deeper into the castle. The soft rustle of clothing and clinking of jewelry informed me that the courtiers had probably bowed before leaving the throne room.

After sheathing my blades, I smoothened down my black clothes while stalking through the palace. I was angry. And tired. And I wanted to talk to someone. But at the same time, I didn't want to talk to anyone.

Why did I always have to fight for every single thing all the time?

Shaking my head, I set course for the stairwell that would take me up to the rooftop terrace.

I needed to blow off some steam.

CHAPTER 12

Waves of fire roared into the golden sky. Spinning around, I drew my arms in a wide circle and then shoved my hands forward. Another crackling column of flames shot across the low stone railing and cut through the warm afternoon air. It felt like taking all my anger and just throwing it out. Very therapeutic.

Twisting my hand, I made the river of fire turn and soar upwards instead. I technically didn't need to use my hands for my fire magic to work, but until I had mastered how to use it as effortlessly as my ability to walk through walls, it was easier to have a visual representation of what I was trying to do.

A warm breeze rolled over the rooftop terrace. My hair fluttered behind me as it played in my loose curls. Letting the fire die out, I blew out a long sigh.

High Commander Anron was already trying to kill me covertly with that group of assassins. Did he really need to challenge me so publicly too? I had banked on the fact that I would have fifteen years to master my fire magic before someone would try to challenge me for the throne. I had gotten lucky with Edus Quickfeet, and he hadn't even been much of a threat. If someone who was actually skilled with battle magic decided to force me into a duel for the throne, my reign would be a very short one. I needed to become more dangerous. And fast.

Footsteps sounded behind me.

I turned around to see who it was and a flicker of irritation pulsed through me. It immediately made me feel like a horrible person, but I was in no mood for a lecture right now.

"Hey," Evander said as he moved closer.

Bracing my forearms against the warm stone railing, I shifted my gaze back to the pink and golden sky beyond the roof. "Hey."

Silence fell for a few seconds while Evander closed the distance between us and then took up position next to me. He leaned his arms against the railing as well, and for a few moments, we only watched the sun set over the sandstone city.

"How are you feeling?" he asked at last.

"I'm pretty fed up with people trying to kill me all the time. But other than that, I'm fine."

He nodded. Another few seconds of silence fell across the roof. I listened to the bustle of the city below and savored the feeling of warm summer winds on my face.

"I'm sorry for going off on you like that the other day," he said after a while.

When I didn't immediately reply, Evander placed a hand on my arm until I turned my head towards him. His dark green eyes were full of sincerity.

"I care about you," he said, holding my gaze. "You know that, right?"

"Yeah." I gave him a small smile. "I know."

"And I'm just trying to look out for you. I just want to make sure that you don't start doing things that you'll regret later."

"You know... whenever I'm confronted with a problem, my first reaction actually *isn't* to kill it."

"I know. Of course, I know that." Taking his hand off my arm, he gestured vaguely towards the castle around us. "But you're surrounded by people like that. Mordren and Idra... as soon as something happens that they don't like, *their* first reaction is to kill it."

Surprise flitted through me. Was that really how other people saw them? I knew that neither Mordren nor Idra had a kneejerk reaction that involved killing people. Threatening them, sure. But kill first, ask questions later? Never. But apparently, other people thought they operated like that. I wondered how Idra and Mordren felt about that. If they wanted to have that kind of reputation or if it bothered them.

"And I don't want them to turn you into someone you're not," Evander continued. "So I just... I want to be there to remind you of who you really are."

"But what if I am a person who kills people?"

"You're not."

"That dead assassin would disagree."

"Edus Quickfeet wouldn't." He picked at the stone railing and cast a glance at me from the corner of his eye. "You could have killed him. But you didn't."

A long sigh escaped my lips, and for a moment, I said nothing. "No, I didn't."

"And that's what I'm trying to tell you," Evander said while bumping my shoulder with his. "You're not a bad person."

"What a ringing endorsement."

He laughed and shook his head. "You know what I mean."

I only gave him a smile in reply because I wasn't actually sure if I did understand what he meant. Pushing a loose curl back behind my ear, I turned to face him.

"So, have you figured out what *you* want to do yet?" I asked, changing the topic.

Surprise flashed across his face. Then he reached up and scratched the back of his neck while a sheepish smile spread over his lips. "No, not yet."

Evander didn't technically have a job. Ever since I had freed him from the slave collar, he had stayed in the Court of Fire. I didn't pay him for anything, but I also didn't charge him for living in the castle. When he had worked for Prince Volkan, all he had done was stand around in the throne room and occasionally consult on something connected to the Court of Trees. I had asked him what he wanted to do with his time now, but he still hadn't figured it out.

Dragging his fingers through his short brown hair, he tilted his head back and stared up into the sky for a few seconds. "It's just... back when I lived in the forest, we worked all the time. Tending our garden, hunting, doing whatever that we needed to survive from day to day. So I have a whole bunch of skills that I'm fairly good at, but nothing that I excel at."

"That makes sense. But skills aren't set in stone. If you practice something, you get better at it." I let out a short chuckle. "I mean, look at me. I had no idea how to wield fire magic, but I'm learning. So forget what you can and can't do. If you *could* do anything, what would it be?"

"I don't know."

"But if–"

"If I could do anything," he finished for me. Turning to face me, he threw his arms out in a helpless gesture. "I still don't know."

My brows creased slightly in genuine surprise. "You don't have any goals? Any dreams at all?"

"Well, I…"

"What?"

"Okay, I know this sounds silly." Evander grimaced and cleared his throat before continuing. "But all I really want is just a comfortable life where I don't have to worry about anything."

Before I could reply, another set of footsteps sounded against the roof. My fingers brushed my sheathed blades, but when I saw who it was, I let my hands drop again. Idra was standing on the red stones halfway between us and the stairwell.

Evander grabbed the railing when her black eyes slid over him, but she had clearly come here for me because she met my gaze.

"Kenna," she said. "Mordren sent word. He needs you in the Court of Shadows."

Worry pulsed through my body. Before she had even finished her sentence, I was striding towards her. "Has Anron made a move?"

Idra shot me an exasperated stare. "Don't you think I would have told you if something like that happened?"

"Good point." Shaking my head, I let out an embarrassed laugh. "Sorry. Today is… I'm just a bit on edge today. What does Mordren want?"

"He didn't say. But it sounded important."

Evander had followed me from the railing and shifted his gaze between me and Idra when I stopped in front of her. "Should I...?"

"He only asked for Kenna," Idra replied, her voice impassive.

"Well, then." Evander straightened his spine while a smile that didn't touch his eyes appeared on his mouth. "I guess that's my cue to leave." Meeting my gaze, he gave me a serious look. "Remember what I said."

Without waiting for a reply, he strode towards the stairwell, giving Idra a wide berth as he passed her. I watched his dark green shirt shift across his back until he had disappeared out of sight.

Idra studied me with perceptive eyes, but didn't ask. That was another thing I really liked about her. She never pushed. Never tried to force others to share. She knew that if I wanted to talk, then I would tell her.

I wasn't even sure what to say, so I just pushed aside the tangles that Evander's words had created in my chest.

The sun was sinking lower over the city. Red and purple streaks painted the horizon in darker colors and cast long shadows over the heavens. I drew a deep breath of warm evening air and shook out my muscles. Meeting Idra's gaze, I flashed her a smile.

"Well, let's go see what Mordren wants then."

CHAPTER 13

The Court of Shadows lay empty and silent around us. I watched the candlelight cast gleaming reflections in the smooth black walls as Idra and I made our way deeper into Mordren's castle. My heart pattered nervously in my chest.

"I have a bad feeling about this," I muttered to Idra.

Every day since the High Elves had moved into the Court of Trees, I had just been waiting for the other shoe to drop. Today was already bad enough in itself. And now, something else had apparently happened too.

Up ahead, the cozy dining room that Mordren and the others ate all their meals in was dark. I frowned. Where was he?

Worry bloomed in my chest, but Idra was striding towards it with confident steps so I continued forwards as well. When we finally crossed the threshold, my heart was slamming against my ribs. If something had happened to Mordren–

"Surprise!"

I yanked out my sword and knife while fire whooshed to

life around my body. The candles around the room flared up as I lit them with my magic so that I could see who was attacking me. Dropping into a defensive position, I raised my weapons and faced the ambushers.

Someone chuckled. Loudly. I blinked at the scene before me.

Hadeon was grinning at me from next to the table. His muscled arm was slung over Ellyda's shoulders, and she was studying me with a smug expression on her face. Next to them were Eilan and Mordren, wearing matching smirks, while Theo and Valerie looked like they had just popped up from behind one of the couches. The shield of fire around me sputtered out.

"What the actual fuck?" I blurted out.

"Uhm," Theo began before being cut off by Valerie.

Lifting the chocolate cake in her hands, she flashed me a beaming smile and shouted, "Happy birthday!"

"I..." Looking between the six of them, I trailed off. Adrenaline was still pumping through my body, ready to deal with another ambush, and my heart was thumping in my chest. I lowered my weapons and forced out a long breath. "By all the gods and spirits. You do know that people are actively trying to assassinate me at the moment, right?" Shaking my head, I rammed my blades back in their sheaths. "Maybe don't surprise me in the dark."

"Told you she would think it was an ambush," Ellyda said, that smug look still on her face, as she turned and looked up at Hadeon. "Pay up, brother."

Twisting my head, I met Idra's gaze. She was standing next to me, completely relaxed, and hadn't even reacted when they had surprised us. I narrowed my eyes at her.

"You knew about this?"

Barely hidden amusement drifted over her face as she lifted one shoulder in a nonchalant shrug.

"Of course you did," I huffed.

"I said," Valerie began in an even louder voice than before, "happy birthday!"

Staring at me pointedly, she waved the chocolate cake around so much that the top layers almost slid off. A laugh ripped from my throat. Holding her gaze, I shook my head in disbelief and laughed again, feeling the last of the tension drain from my body.

"Thank you," I said and gave her a warm smile.

"Happy birthday," Idra whispered softly before moving farther into the room.

With a wide grin on her face, Valerie made her way to the table and pushed the now slightly crooked cake onto the smooth wooden tabletop. Eilan winked at me before helping her get it into position next to the stack of plates and silverware. Theo headed for the decanters while Hadeon fished out a small purse that he then grudgingly handed to his satisfied-looking sister.

"How did you even know that it was my birthday?" I asked.

Mordren sauntered towards me. The candles I had lit all around the room made his eyes sparkle. Or perhaps it was the smugness on his face.

Stopping a single stride in front of me, he drew his fingers up my throat and over my jaw before tipping my head back so that I met his gaze. "I could make princes grovel at my feet with the secrets I know. Do you really think I cannot find out when your birthday is?"

"Besides," Hadeon called from across the room. "Back when you stayed here with us, you said you've never celebrated your birthday."

"And that's just sad," Valerie filled in. "Like, really sad."

Growing up, I had never liked my birthday. I could tell that my mother and adoptive father hated that day, and even though I hadn't understood the true scope of it back then, their emotions had rubbed off on me. So I disliked my birthday as well, and had never had either opportunity or cause to celebrate it.

"Exactly," Hadeon finished. "So then we knew we just had to celebrate your next one."

Warmth sparkled through my whole soul as I looked at the seven people gathered in the room.

"Thank you," I said and truly meant it.

Mordren brushed his lips over mine and then stepped back. With a smile drifting over his mouth, he placed a hand on my back and guided me towards the table. "Theo informed us that chocolate cake is your favorite."

I looked at the blond thief across the table. "It is."

"See!" He grinned and tapped his temple. "I'm not just good-looking. I'm observant too."

"Says the guy who can't for the life of him seem to notice when girls, and guys, are flirting with him," Valerie chimed in from across the table.

"I notice it," Theo huffed with a mock scowl in her direction. "I'm just not interested in the whole love and sex thing. Like, what's the big deal?"

She pressed a hand to her chest in a show of shock. "What's the big deal?"

"Exactly." A sly smile spread across his lips as he flicked a glance between her and Eilan. "And besides, you're interested in it enough for the both of us."

Valerie choked on her wine. A furious blush crept into her

cheeks, but if Eilan noticed it, he didn't show it. I laughed and shook my head at the two of them.

Silverware clinked as the gorgeous shapeshifter cut several pieces of cake and placed them on the plates that were arranged around it. After coughing to get the wine out of her windpipe, Valerie grabbed a plate and started stuffing her face with it. As if that would make the red on her cheeks disappear. Theo smirked at her but grabbed a plate for himself too.

The slices were disappearing with alarming speed, but Eilan kept cutting up new ones. I watched as Mordren grabbed two for us while Hadeon dove onto the remaining couple.

"What's with the lurking?" he boomed across the room even though the person he was speaking to was only a short distance away.

Idra leveled a flat look in his direction. "I'm not lurking."

"Standing by a wall and brooding is like the definition of lurking." Hadeon closed the distance between them and shoved a plate into her hands before clapping her on the shoulder. "Have some cake."

She snapped her gaze between the place on her shoulder where he had touched her and the plate he had so casually shoved into her hands, and for a moment, I wasn't sure if she was about to say thank you or break his jaw.

"So, what's–" Hadeon began but his sister abruptly cut him off before he could finish.

"Kenna."

Ellyda was the only one who had actually taken a seat at the table. With her legs curled up under her, she had been staring at the open book before her while everyone grabbed their plates. There was an untouched slice of cake and a tea cup next to her elbow. Steam rose into the air in lazy circles.

"Yes?" I replied hesitantly. She looked very serious.

Her violet eyes were clear and sharp as she held my gaze. "It's your birthday today."

"I know."

"Yes, but you hadn't planned on telling us that." She narrowed her eyes at me. "Failing to inform us about things that matter to you has consequences."

Idra frowned at her. "Is that a threat?"

Ellyda was silent for a few seconds. When she shifted her gaze to Idra, it took a while for her eyes to come into focus again. A slight tension fell over the room. Right when several people were about to interrupt, Ellyda finally spoke up again.

"Yes," she said matter-of-factly.

Then she picked up her tea cup and returned to her book.

The room held its breath. Idra's dark eyes were locked on Ellyda, but it was clear that the strange elf was no longer listening.

"I like her," Idra announced, the ghost of a smile playing over her lips.

Hadeon drained his entire wine glass and mumbled something under his breath. I chuckled and dug into my cake.

It was heavenly. Not only did it taste like melting dark chocolate, there was also a hint of orange in there that paired perfectly with the richness of the chocolate.

While the others spread out across the dining room, I gingerly placed the small plate back on the table and snuck out of the room before anyone could notice. I needed a minute to get my head on straight.

When I had come here, I had believed it was because something bad had happened. And that feeling was still bouncing around inside me. I didn't want the festive mood to be spoiled by my worries so I just needed a little time to breathe and remind myself that no one was trying to assassinate me right now and that the High Elves had not launched an attack right now.

The black glass-like walls watched me impassively as I made my way down the corridor and approached the nearest window.

Warm night air smelling of jasmine filled the hall as I threw open the tall window. Drawing myself up on the windowsill, I swung my legs over it and leaned against the frame. And then I breathed.

Nothing bad would happen tonight.

"Kenna."

I didn't even need to turn around to know who it was. Cloth whispered into the silence. And then Mordren gracefully seated himself next to me on the windowsill.

"Are you okay?" he asked.

"Yeah, sorry. I just needed a moment to gather my thoughts."

"Tell me what is bothering you."

"I just… I just can't shake the feeling that something bad is about to happen." Not looking at him, I braced myself for a reply dismissing my worries.

Mordren paused for a second before saying, "I share that sentiment."

Whipping my head around, I looked at him in surprise. He was staring into the starlit night outside and there was a distinct trace of worry on his beautiful features. I wasn't sure if I was relieved or sad that it wasn't just me.

"I do not know if I agree with King Aldrich's decision to do nothing while the High Elves move into the Court of

Trees," Mordren continued. "But those are the orders we have been given, and we have to respect them."

"So, what do we do?"

"Tomorrow? Whatever the king decrees." He turned to meet my gaze and a smile spread across his lips. "Tonight? We enjoy the moment of joy and peace we have together."

Another warm night breeze blew in through the window and made his dark hair ripple over his black suit. I smiled at him. "Well said."

Reaching into the inside pocket of his suit jacket, he pulled out a slim case covered in black satin. I raised my eyebrows in surprise. Mordren took my hand and gently placed the case in it.

Still holding on to my wrist, he leaned forward and brushed a kiss on my cheek. "Happy birthday."

His breath against my skin sent waves of heat through my body, but Mordren drew back before I could do anything about it. Sitting there on the windowsill next to me, he watched me with those intense silver eyes of his. I swallowed and looked down at the black satin case in my hand.

With my heart suddenly pattering in my chest, I pried open the case.

I sucked in a gasp.

A stunning necklace stared back at me. A thin gold chain lay against the small black pillow, and attached to the delicate chain was a large red gemstone shaped like a teardrop.

"It is a blood ruby," Mordren explained. "It is a gemstone that has been imbued with magic that will temporarily keep all the blood in a person's body." A wicked glint crept into his glittering eyes as he looked me up and down. "So the next time you decide to drive a sword through your own chest, you will be able to stay alive until a healer arrives."

A surprised laugh erupted from my throat. I gave his shoulder a shove. "Bastard."

He smirked at me, apparently very satisfied with himself.

Holding his gaze, I fondly drew my fingers over the necklace while a serious expression settled on my face. "I love it. Thank you."

"May I?" He motioned towards my neck.

I nodded. We climbed off the windowsill and returned to the black corridor inside. Still holding on to the open case, I straightened just inside the window while Mordren took a step closer to me. He kept his eyes on me as he reached out and lifted the necklace from the satin pillow.

A soft snap echoed into the silent hall as I closed the case and placed it on the windowsill. My heart pounded in my chest. Raising my hand, I swept my long red hair over my shoulder and then turned around.

The brush of Mordren's fingers against my heated skin sent a shudder of pleasure through my body. After tracing a hand over my bare shoulder, he draped the necklace around my throat and then clasped it behind me.

Leaning forward, he kissed that sensitive spot below my ear.

Another shudder coursed through my body.

With my heart still slamming against my ribs, I turned around to face him. The look in his eyes made me almost forget how to breathe.

He reached out and traced gentle fingers over my cheek. Closing my eyes, I sucked in a shuddering breath.

"Kenna." His voice was so full of emotion that I barely dared open my eyes.

When I finally did, I found serious eyes holding my gaze. Moonlight fell in through the window and painted silver highlights in Mordren's night-black hair. His eyes glittered like liquid starlight.

"I love you."

My breath hitched and my heart skipped a beat. Mordren Darkbringer, the Prince of Shadows, the most feared elven prince in all the courts. A powerful ruthless schemer who had been through so much, who had brought princes to their knees, who could have his pick of anyone in the lands. He had said that he loved me. Me. Logic would dictate that I shouldn't believe it. That it was too outlandish to be true.

But after everything we had done for each other, I didn't doubt it for a second. So instead, I reached out and placed my hand on his cheek. And then told him what my wicked little heart had known for months now.

"I love you too."

He drew in a shuddering breath that was so full of emotion that it made my chest tighten.

I slid my hand to the back of his neck and pulled him towards me.

His lips crashed against mine. Passion and relief and love, blazing love that could set the world aflame, pulsed through me as Mordren wrapped me in his arms and held me close.

And in that moment, I knew one thing for certain.

No matter what dangers tomorrow held, Mordren and I would face them together.

CHAPTER 14

"Hey, who ate all the cake?" Valerie called as she stared down at the now messy table full of empty plates.

From my spot on the couch, I grinned at her. "I'm pretty sure it was a group effort."

Evening had turned into night, but my birthday party was still in full swing. It was as if everyone knew that this might be our last chance to just relax and enjoy ourselves for quite a while. Shoving the thoughts of tomorrow aside, I poured Mordren another glass of wine.

"If I did not know better, I might think that you were deliberately trying to get me drunk," Mordren said as he took the offered glass.

"Well, it would only be fair," I said while picking up my own glass. "Since you've seen *me* wasted, but I still haven't had the same pleasure."

A smirk slid home on his lips. "That is because, as opposed to you, I am not a lightweight."

I snorted. "Uh-huh."

Metallic clattering filled the room. We all turned to find Theo scrambling to return an empty decanter to the tabletop after having demonstrated some kind of acrobatic move involving the table. Or at least that was what it looked like based on the way he and Hadeon were standing. From her chair by the table, Idra rolled her eyes.

"Eilan," Mordren suddenly called. "Did Herman send a different kind of wine this time?"

Eilan's pale green eyes glided over my face before settling on Mordren. "No, but he did say that the vineyard was trying something different with this batch."

"Hmm. I will go and see if we have some other vintages left. This one tastes more bitter than it should."

Of course it did. I had been spiking Mordren's wine with high-percentage alcohol for the past hour. I wanted revenge for that time he had bossed me around while I was really drunk, and when I had also accidentally told him that he was hot after he forced a mugger to beg my forgiveness.

Eilan, who had picked up on what I was doing very quickly, winked at me as Mordren pushed himself up from the couch and started towards the kitchen. His stride was a little more unsteady than it normally was.

A wicked grin spread across my face. He really should have learned by now not to let me anywhere near his wine bottles.

The dark purple cushion shifted as Valerie threw herself down next to me on the couch. Leaning closer, she wiggled her eyebrows at me.

"So…" she began, drawing out the word. Her brown eyes sparkled mischievously. "What's it like? Sharing a bed with an elven royal?"

I choked on my wine. Slapping a hand in front of my

mouth, I narrowly prevented myself from spitting it all over her face.

"What?" She shrugged innocently. "I've been meaning to ask you for months."

After forcing the wine down, I cast a glance over my shoulder to check if someone else might have overheard her question.

"You're stalling," she announced. Running her tongue over her teeth, she gave me a quick rise and fall of her eyebrows. "What does a lethal body like that feel like against your own?" Her eyes darted briefly towards Eilan. "How is it having someone like that pin you to the mattress and–"

"By all the gods and spirits," I groaned.

"Well?"

"It's... nice."

She leveled an unimpressed stare at me. "Nice?"

"Okay." I cleared my throat a bit self-consciously. "It's hot. It's really fucking hot, okay?"

"Hmm." Her eyes once more drifted to the gorgeous elf across the room.

Eilan was standing across the table from where Theo was still showing Hadeon some kind of move. His long black hair shifted over his lean muscled body as he continued to absentmindedly spin a knife in his left hand.

"I'll be right back," Valerie declared and jumped to her feet.

It took great effort to hide the smile on my face as she strode straight towards Eilan and unceremoniously slid onto the tabletop right in front of him. Eilan started slightly in surprise. I couldn't hear what Valerie said, but she pointed towards the knife in his hand and then magicked something made of silver from her own sleeve. She twitched her fingers and it was gone again. Eilan raised his eyebrows, while Valerie wiggled hers.

"I saw you speaking to Valerie," Mordren said as he slid down next to me on the couch again. Uncorking the new wine bottle, he arched an eyebrow in my direction. "What did I miss?"

The memory of what she had been asking about made my cheeks flush. I cleared my throat. "Nothing at all."

Strong fingers wrapped around my jaw. I tried to force the red color from my cheeks while Mordren turned my face towards him. It apparently didn't work all that well.

"Nothing, huh?" he said, his eyes searching my face.

"Nope."

Leaning forward, he placed his lips next to my ear. "Why do I find that hard to believe?"

A shiver of pleasure coursed through me when his breath danced over my skin.

While his attention was focused elsewhere, I withdrew the small bottle of liquor that I had been hiding. His new vintage was waiting unattended on the table.

"Because you know what a good liar I am," I whispered into his ear while promptly spiking his new bottle of wine as well.

Mordren's dark laugh caressed my skin as he kissed my jaw before drawing back. I gave him a sly smile. The bottle of liquor was once more nowhere to be seen.

"What's with the eye rolling?" a loud voice suddenly boomed across the room.

Hadeon was standing with his arms spread wide. And he was staring at Idra.

Still seated in her chair, Idra looked back at him with a neutral expression on her face. "I just don't understand why you are still trying. Look at him." She nodded towards Theo. "He has like a third of your body mass. How can you possibly think that you will be able to pull off the same moves as him when you're all muscle and he's all flexibility?"

"It's not about that. It's about technique."

"Really?" Idra raised her eyebrows and waved a hand towards the table. "Then I shouldn't be able to pull it off on my first try either."

Hadeon crossed his arms. "Exactly."

A sharp smile spread over Idra's lips. "How about a bet, then?"

"Bring it on."

"If I can pull off that move on my first try, you have to go swim naked in that pond I saw out in the gardens."

Surprised laughter erupted from Hadeon's throat. Then he raised a large hand and pointed straight at Idra. "You're on. But if you can't, you have to do the same."

"Deal."

"Oh I can't wait to see this."

Wood scraped against the floor as Idra rose from the chair. The rest of the room stopped to watch. Even Ellyda, who had disappeared into a remarkably thick book, lowered the leather-bound tome enough to peer over the top of the page. Beside me, Mordren drained his glass. I hid my smug smile and instead watched the scene about to unfold.

With a slight smirk playing over her lips, Idra prowled up to Hadeon. Arching a pale eyebrow, she waited for him to back away so that she could take his place between the wall and the table. He flashed her a challenging grin before stepping aside.

Only the soft creaking of furniture broke the silence as the rest of us sat forward in anticipation while Idra moved into position, estimating the distance between the two surfaces.

She jumped.

Kicking off against the wall, she vaulted backwards and placed her palms on the tabletop before pushing off that as well and landing on the other side of the table in a crouch.

Deafening silence pulsed through the room.

Then Valerie let out a long whoop.

"That was freaking awesome!" she called while pumping her fist in the air.

Hadeon was staring at her with his mouth open. "No way."

"Told you." Idra flashed him a smug smirk. "Now, get ready to swim."

That snapped Hadeon out of his shock. Waving his hands in front of his face, he stalked around the table towards her. "No, no, no. There's no way that was your first time doing that."

"Are you calling me a liar?"

"I'm calling you a cheater."

Idra raised her chin in a cocky gesture, even as Hadeon towered over her when he came to a halt right in front of her. "If I were you, I would choose my next words very carefully."

"Oh please." He snorted and flicked a dismissive hand. "I could easily take you in a fight."

Idra snickered and flicked her eyes up and down his body. "Keep telling yourself that if it helps you sleep at night." That sharp smile slid back onto her lips. "But what this all sounds like to me... is you trying to weasel out of losing a wager."

I swore I could hear an evil chuckle from behind the thick book that Ellyda had once more disappeared into.

Red flashed over Hadeon's already alcohol-flushed face.

Uncrossing his arms, he stabbed a hand at her. "I *never* welch on my bets."

"Well." She lifted one shoulder in a casual shrug. "Then I guess you have some midnight swimming to do."

Grumbling curses under his breath, Hadeon stalked towards the hallway that would take him to the front door. With that smirk tugging at her lips, Idra followed.

Next to me, Mordren let out an exasperated groan. "Oh, by the spirits." Pushing to his feet, he drained his glass. "I'd better go make sure they don't drown each other."

Wicked satisfaction swirled inside me. Mordren usually spoke properly. Formally. But not right now. The alcohol must be starting to really get to his head.

"Yeah, that's probably best," I replied.

He eyed the table for another second. And then shrugged and snatched up the spiked wine bottle before hurrying after Hadeon and Idra. He zigzagged a lot more than he should have.

Sipping at my own wine, I just sat there with a smile on my face and watched for some time while the others continued to laugh and joke.

Just as I reached for the decanter to refill my glass, Eilan collapsed onto the couch. There was a mischievous smile playing over his lips as he scooted closer to me while holding my gaze. "So, what did you spike it with?"

I lifted the bottle I had been hiding all night.

He chuckled. "Nice."

"Thanks for backing up my lie."

"Oh, I would never turn down a chance to drink my little brother under the table."

Comfortable silence fell over the couch for a few moments. On the other side of the room, Valerie and Theo were engaged in a dramatic discussion about something that we were too far away to hear clearly. Paper rustled as Ellyda turned the page where she sat in her armchair. I slid my gaze back to Valerie. Candlelight cast dancing shadows over her smiling face and her brown eyes sparkled with life.

"Don't take this the wrong way," I began as I tore my gaze from Valerie and turned to face Eilan instead. "But you're gorgeous."

A surprised laugh slipped his lips and he shook his head. "How could I possibly take that the wrong way?"

"What I mean is, you're gorgeous."

"You already said that."

"And," I continued as if he hadn't interrupted, "you're a really nice person too. You must have people throwing themselves at you. I mean, I've seen how they look at you and act around you. But I've never seen you engage with anyone. Why is that?"

"Oh. Uhm…"

I looked at him curiously. "Are you just not interested in that sort of thing?"

"No, it's not that." Eilan was silent for a while before continuing. "Being in a relationship is… very complicated for someone like me."

"What do you mean?"

He fell silent again. A whole swarm of emotions whirled in his light green eyes as he stared at the starlit night outside the window. Picking up a discarded dinner knife from the table, he started to absentmindedly twirl it in his hand.

"It's not that I don't want to be in a relationship." He blew out a small sigh. "It's that I don't want to be in a relationship with someone if I have to lie to them all the time." Tearing his gaze from the window, he met my eyes and drew in a deep breath. "I can't just go around telling people that I'm a shapeshifter, which means that I need to keep the core part of my identity secret from any potential partner. And if they don't know that I'm a shapeshifter, they don't really know me at all, so what's the point?"

"You've never told anyone?"

"Oh, I have. Over the years, I have told a few people. The ones I truly thought might be the one for me." He shrugged. It was a casual gesture but he couldn't quite hide the pain in his eyes. "It's never worked out."

"Why not?"

"The problem is that I'm not just one person. I'm several people." Lifting a hand, he motioned towards me. "You say that I'm a nice person. And I am." He flicked his hand to indicate his own body. "This version of me, at least. But I'm also the Void. And a whole bunch of other people, and not all of them are nice. Some of them are arrogant. Domineering. Cruel. And they're not just different skins. They're different versions of me. They have to be."

Realization dawned. "Otherwise, the ruse would never work. Of course. People would see through the lie unless the shapeshifter form was real enough to be an actual person."

"Exactly. They're all real. And they're all me." He shrugged again. "Which means that in order for someone to actually love me, the real me, they also have to love every version of me. Even the bad ones. That's why it's so complicated. Why relationships never work out for me."

I couldn't even imagine what that must be like. To almost never be able to tell anyone who you really are. And the few times when you actually do, realize that the other person doesn't accept you for everything that you are. It must be awful.

Reaching out, I took his hand. There were no words to express what I wanted to say, so instead, I just held his gaze and gave his hand a squeeze. He seemed to understand because he nodded and gave me a small smile.

Boisterous laughter echoed from down the hall.

All of us turned to look as three people strode across the threshold. Hadeon, his clothes dry but his hair wet, grinned widely as he sauntered inside while Idra, who was fully dry, followed with a smirk on her face. After them came Mordren.

Water fell in muted drops from his whole body as he stalked into the dining room. His black suit was plastered to his skin, his shoes squeaked as he walked, and every part of him was soaking wet.

"What did you do?" Eilan asked. Amusement shone on his face as he frowned at his brother. "Fall into the pond?"

"I didn't fall into the pond," Mordren declared and stabbed a hand towards Hadeon. "He pushed me in."

The red-eyed warrior let out another rumbling laugh, not even bothering to deny it.

"And my shadows aren't working properly." Shaking his head, he waved a hand in my direction while offhandedly tossing out, "What did you do, spike my wine?"

An evil smile spread across my lips.

Stopping dead on the floor, Mordren stared at me in utter disbelief. "You *spiked my wine?*"

"I don't know why you're so surprised." I grinned at him and lifted my shoulders in a nonchalant shrug. "It's not as if it's the first time I've messed with your wine bottles."

Black shadows flickered chaotically around Mordren. Then he took a step forward.

"Ohh, you're in trouble now," Theo called from across the room.

Placing a hand on the dark purple cushion, I jumped over the couch's backrest. A small pulse of pain shot through me right as I landed, and I stumbled a step before getting back to my feet. Mordren kept coming.

Shadows shot towards me.

I leaped backwards on instinct, but the dark tendrils wavered and slithered off course. It didn't matter, the move had still distracted me long enough for Mordren to close the distance between us. I reached the wall at the same time as Mordren reached me.

This close, his shadows had managed to curl around my ankles, preventing me from phasing through the wall.

Mordren placed his hand against my collarbones and pushed me back against the black glass-like material. Tilting my head back, I looked up into a pair of silver eyes from only a breath away. Candlelight glinted in the water that clung to his dark hair.

"You spiked my wine?" he repeated, his voice low enough that only I could hear.

Behind his back, the others had returned to their previous conversations. As if the Prince of Shadows pushing me up against a wall and threatening me after I had tampered with his wine was an everyday occurrence. Though, to be fair, it wasn't as uncommon as it probably should have been.

"Yep," I replied, a victorious grin on my mouth.

While still keeping me trapped against the wall with one hand, he leaned closer. "You will pay for this."

His words were a dark promise that sent a pulse of heat through my body.

"Is that so?" I drew my fingers along his jaw. "Then by all means, come try it." A wicked smirk drifted over my lips as I brushed them against his mouth. "My prince."

"Ah, my little traitor spy. The things I will do to you." Taking a step back, he released me and cocked his head. "Well, shall we?"

Running a hand over his chest, I moved past him and started towards the hallway that would take me to Mordren's bedroom. The Prince of Shadows followed.

He threaded his fingers through mine as we weaved deeper into the black castle.

One last night.

One last breath.

Before the storm broke.

CHAPTER 15

Worry pulsed through me. Ordinary citizens were strolling up and down the sandstone street, smiling and chatting. I glanced towards the rooftops. A burnt blue sky was visible between the houses and the bright summer sun beat down on the city. Dark shadows should be easy to spot. So far, there were none. But that didn't mean anything.

It had been two days since my birthday, and nothing bad had happened yet. The High Elves hadn't made any more moves, and no one had tried to assassinate me or challenge me for the throne again. I knew that it was illogical, but the fact that nothing had happened only made me more worried. Which was why I had once more gone to check on the army.

They were ready.

The only question was when, and for what, they would be used.

Casting a glance over my shoulder, I turned down another street that would take me back to the palace. Idra had stayed behind at the training field, albeit reluctantly. But after I had rather forcefully pointed out that I was perfectly capable of walking through my own city by myself, she had relented.

What I hadn't wanted to admit, however, was that if there was another assassination attempt about to happen, I would be in a much worse position to survive it now that I was alone.

Shaking my head, I stalked towards the next cross street. I truly hated feeling unsafe in my own court.

Feet thudded against stone.

I yanked out my blades and called up a shield of fire around me while giving myself a mental slap. Why did I have to jinx it?

A male elf with short blond hair skidded around the corner and almost slammed straight into me. He let out a yelp and leaped out of the way of the flames licking my skin.

I blinked at him in surprise and extinguished the fire. It was one of the elves possessing the worldwalking ability who worked for me as a messenger. "Nicholas."

"Lady Firesoul," Nicholas blurted out. "I went to the training field but Idra said that you had already left so then I went back but you weren't there either and I..." He trailed off and shook his head. "I'm rambling. What I'm trying to say is that King Aldrich sent an emergency message. You need to get to the Court of Water. Right now."

Panic shot up my spine. "Where?"

"The clock tower overlooking the courtyard outside the castle gates. Do you know it? Otherwise I can worldwalk you there right now."

"I know it." While sheathing my blades again, I gave him a nod. "Thanks, Nicholas."

And then I worldwalked away.

Warm winds that tasted like the sea washed over me as I

materialized at the top of the clock tower that he had specified. My heart slammed against my ribs as I turned around until I found three other people already standing by the railing farther away. While trying to smother my panic, I strode towards them.

"What's going on?" I asked without preamble as I closed the distance to the two princes and the king.

"They're waiting," Aldrich Spiritsinger said.

"For what?"

Coming to a halt between Mordren and Edric, I leaned over the railing and looked down at the open space before the gates. A small group of High Elves were standing there on the white stones, and a mass of elves and humans from the Court of Water had gathered on all sides as well. Water rushed down over the high defensive walls, but other than that, there was no movement.

"For Rayan," the king replied. There was such sadness in his voice that I momentarily didn't know what to do.

"Rayan sent word to King Aldrich half an hour ago," Mordren explained. His eyes were still locked on the closed gates below. "The High Elves gave him an ultimatum. Accept them into his court, and accept them as gods, or they will release a fast-acting poison into the water streams."

Shock clanged through my head. Everything in Rayan's court was connected by water. From the great waterfalls crashing over the castle walls, to the canals, to the taps and the wells and the water trickling down the side of buildings. A water-based toxin could poison the whole Court of Water in a matter of minutes. And Rayan would never be able to heal them all in time.

"We have to do something," I snapped. "We have to help him!"

I whirled around, but before I could take so much as a step, a strong hand wrapped around my arm. Edric Mountaincleaver kept his grip on my arm and met my gaze. It was the look on his face, that forced stoic look, more than anything that made me pause. He shook his head.

"There is nothing we can do," King Aldrich said into the oppressive silence. "I have already spoken with Rayan. He will have to do this. High Commander Anron can release that poison long before any of us can get our armies here. So to save his court, he will have to give in."

"Can't he just tell all his people not to drink the water?" I blurted out. But even as I said it, I knew that it would be pointless.

As soon as the toxin was in the water, it would be over. Everyone would have to leave the city, and the Court of Water would become a ruin.

"I know, I know," I interrupted before anyone could say what I had just been thinking as well. "It wouldn't work." Raking my fingers through my hair, I shook my head. "How did the High Elves even know that threatening to poison the water was the way to break Rayan?" A sudden unwelcome thought sprang to mind. "Do you think Iwdael told them?"

"Iwdael is many things," the king began. "But a mass murderer is not one of them. He would never tell the High Elves that they could poison an entire city."

Guilt wormed its way through my chest. "No, of course not."

"That High Commander is a very perceptive one," Prince Edric said into the silence that fell. "And they've been living close to the city. He could've put two and two together on his own."

"Yeah, but..." I trailed off as the gates to the castle swung open.

A ripple went through the citizens gathered below. I watched with a growing sense of alarm as an elf with long black hair and purple eyes strode towards the cluster of High Elves outside the gates. Rayan Floodbender kept his head held high and his spine straight as he stopped a few strides away from High Commander Anron.

"My beloved citizens," Prince Rayan called across the white city. "The spirits of our ancestors will always be with us and watch over us, just as we remember them. But I have also come to realize that our gods of old are back." A slight sharpness crept into his voice. "And who am I to deny the gods?"

The elves and humans crowding the streets stirred restlessly and looked between their prince and the High Elves.

"But please remember that this is only my opinion," Rayan continued. "You, my beloved people, are under no obligations to change your faith to match mine."

Displeasure flashed over Anron's face, but it was gone so fast that I had almost missed it. Prince Rayan might be forced to tell lies, but he was trying his best to make sure that his people didn't follow him into it.

Rayan took a step forward.

His face was an unreadable mask as he slowly closed the final distance to the High Elves. Once he was standing only two steps in front of Anron, he stopped. His violet eyes were hard as he held Anron's gaze.

Then he lowered himself to his knees before the High Elf Commander.

Shock and uncertainty pulsed through the audience.

With his gaze still locked on Anron, Prince Rayan raised

his left hand and offered him his wrist. High Commander Anron produced one of those black bracelets that the other believers wore. Smug satisfaction drifted over his face as he reached down and snapped the bracelet shut around Rayan's wrist. Then he waited.

For a few moments, the two of them only stared at each other.

At last, the Prince of Water forced a breath into his lungs. And then he dropped his gaze and pressed his forehead to the white stones before Anron's feet.

Dread crawled up my throat like bile.

Below us on the streets, large portions of the elven audience bowed down as well.

"They have gone too far." King Aldrich's voice was as hard and merciless as the mountains themselves. "This time, they have gone too far."

I opened my mouth to say something, but then thought better of it, and closed it again.

"What is it?" the king prompted.

"Nothing, my king."

Turning to face me, he locked those observant brown eyes on me. "Speak."

"We shouldn't have let it get this far." It felt wrong to speak to the King of Elves in this way, but if he hadn't wanted me to tell him how I felt, he wouldn't have ordered me to do so. "We should have acted as soon as they moved on the Court of Trees. Now we've lost Rayan and his entire army too. We had five courts and five armies, against their one. Now we're down to three."

"Kenna, that's not–" Prince Edric began before the king cut him off.

"No, she's right. With hindsight, Kenna is right. We

shouldn't have hesitated." King Aldrich let out a weary sigh. "But I didn't know that at the time. The High Elves had made no military moves against the Court of Trees and Iwdael insisted that he had invited them willingly. Not to mention that we still don't know the extent of the High Elves' power. Engaging them in open conflict is extremely risky, which is why I wanted to avoid it if I could. Based on the information I had, I made the decision I thought was right. Apparently, it was not."

Another wave of guilt washed over me. "I'm sorry."

"Don't be." Aldrich placed a hand on my shoulder and gave it a quick squeeze. "Making mistakes is part of being a leader. There is no such thing as perfect, because everyone makes mistakes from time to time. But what separates a good leader from a bad one is how you come back from it. How you learn from it. How you handle the consequences and fix the mess you've made." He gave me a small smile. "Remember that and you will make a fine ruler, Kenna."

Swallowing the emotions that were rising in my throat, I nodded.

Down below, Prince Rayan had straightened and was striding back into his castle. The crowd was split into people awkwardly drifting off and people who approached the High Elves to receive bracelets for themselves.

"What would you like us to do, my king?" Mordren asked.

Aldrich watched the people kneeling before the High Elves for another few seconds before releasing a long breath.

When he turned to face us, his eyes were hard and there was a determined set to his features.

"Tell your people that it is time. Tomorrow, we force the High Elves out of our lands."

CHAPTER 16

The sound of thumping boots echoed across the plains. Standing at the front of our joint army, I watched as High Commander Anron's legion of High Elves marched towards us. The midday sun glinted off their bronze armor.

"That was the last of it," a familiar voice said from behind. "Everyone is here now."

Casting a glance over my shoulder, I found Felix, a half-elf with copper-colored hair, standing behind Prince Edric's shoulder. We had been friends back when I had worked as a spy in the Court of Stone, but he had ultimately taken Monette's side, so I wasn't sure where we stood at the moment. Not that it mattered right now. Right now, we had more important things to worry about.

"From every court?" Prince Edric asked without taking his eyes off the approaching High Elves.

"Yes," Felix replied.

"Good. Get to the back."

We had used every worldwalker from all three of our

courts to transport our army to this wide grassland. It was located halfway between the Court of Trees and the Court of Water, as well as halfway between the coast and King Aldrich's mountain that was at the center of the continent. Our plan had been a surprise attack while the High Elves' forces were split between two courts.

Unfortunately, our plans had not been as secret as we had hoped.

Once roughly half of our army had been worldwalked to this location, the two halves of Anron's forces had become visible in the distance. By then it was too late to back out, so we had scrambled to worldwalk everyone here while the High Elves met up and formed a cohesive legion.

Now, our army was all here.

But so were they.

A cloud of cold dread spread through my chest when I noticed the two shorter figures at the edge of the High Elves' ranks. Rayan and Iwdael. They looked between the tall elves around them and our army on the other side. Worry was clear on their faces.

At least they hadn't brought their courts' armies too.

"High Commander Anron," the King of Elves called as they came to a halt a short distance in front of us. Warm summer winds carried his voice across the plains.

"King Aldrich," Anron replied.

"You have gone too far." Aldrich's long white hair fluttered behind him on the breeze as he faced down the High Elves with a regal expression on his face. "These are our lands. Take those bracelets off our people and leave this continent. Before we make you."

A boom echoed across the grasslands. Armor clanked as

soldiers whirled in the direction that the noise had come from.

"Did that come from your mountain?" Prince Edric murmured softly, still not taking his eyes off the threat before us.

"It doesn't matter," King Aldrich replied. "There is no one left there anyway. I brought everyone here."

Leather creaked and armor clanked once more as our army shifted their attention back to the High Elves again. Whatever had happened at the king's mountain, it didn't present an immediate threat so it would have to wait.

"High Commander Anron," Aldrich Spiritsinger repeated. His strong voice pulsed through the warm air and sent a flock of birds flapping away to safety farther away. "This is your last chance. Leave our continent now, or face our wrath."

On this battlefield, we outnumbered them. By a lot. Even if they were able to use magic as well as we were, they couldn't possibly win. If they had brought Rayan and Iwdael's armies too, then we would've been in trouble. But as things stood now, the most logical thing for the High Elves to do was to retreat.

Anron raised his eyebrows in a show of surprise, but his blue eyes glinted. "Are you threatening armed conflict if we don't depart?"

"Yes."

"Satisfied?" Anron stabbed a hand in our direction. "There's your insurance policy. In case we ever have to explain, we can now claim that they attacked first."

"What are you—"

A gasp rippled through our ranks.

Long shadows streaked across the pale heavens as two winged serpents shot towards us. They were followed by even more beasts. And soldiers. Pure panic blared through my skull as I watched two more legions of High Elves speed towards us. Some from inland, and some from the coast.

The ground shuddered as the air serpents slammed down one after another. Soldiers in bronze armor were marching into position on either side of Anron's legion almost before their mounts' feet had touched the grass. With every High Elf that arrived, the urge to kneel intensified until I could almost feel it physically pressing against my body.

Magic flared to life among our soldiers as they shifted nervously.

"Hold!" King Aldrich called.

"My king?" I asked. My voice was thick with dread.

His brown eyes flicked from Anron to the two other legion commanders who were approaching him. "We need to play this smart. *We* are outnumbered now."

The two newly arrived commanders, one blond and one with black hair, came to a halt on either side of Anron. They were as tall as him. With sculpted bodies and perfectly carved features. Just like him. Just like all the other High Elves. And they radiated power.

"Danser," Anron said as he looked at the dark-haired commander. "Have I satisfied your need for caution?"

High Commander Danser nodded. "Yes."

"Lester, what about you?" Anron asked as his gaze slid to the blond one on his other side.

"I don't care about back-up plans." High Commander Lester flicked a dismissive hand in front of his face. "I'm more interested in knowing where these Low Elves found the audacity to challenge our race like this."

"Yes, it does seem like you have found a particularly troublesome island," the black-haired one added. "And it looks like their magic has evolved quite a lot compared to the other Low Elves."

The blond commander looked down his nose at us. "They don't look very strong to me." He shrugged and waved a lazy hand. "But I agree. If this temper tantrum is any indication, they need to be taught a lesson."

My heart slammed against my ribs. Behind the three commanders, more winged serpents were touching down with squads of soldiers on their backs. Captain Vendir pushed his way to the front and spoke quickly into Anron's ear while handing him something that glinted in the sun. At the edge of their ranks, Rayan and Iwdael were being herded farther and farther to the side until they were standing almost halfway between our army and theirs. They were trying their best to hide it, but fear, as well as regret, blew across their faces.

A sense of panic was spreading through our forces.

"My king," Mordren said in a low voice. "Do we attack?"

"No." Aldrich's face was a carefully constructed mask, but I swore that I could see a wisp of dread swirling in his eyes. "We might be able to talk our way out of this. There might be a way out that doesn't involve most of our people dying or being forced to worship these beings as gods."

Danser motioned between us and Anron. "Well, this is your operation. You have tactical command. What do you want to do?"

"High Commander Anron," King Aldrich called before he could reply.

A smirk drifted over Anron's lips and he arched an eyebrow at us. "Let me guess, you now want to resolve this peacefully instead."

"That would be preferable."

"Then bow down before us, put on those bracelets, and recognize us as gods."

"I do not know exactly what those bracelets do," King Aldrich said. "But I do know that the wearer cannot take them off once they are on. We will not be your slaves."

Anron's blue eyes were like chips of ice in the warm summer day as he stared us down. "You still act as if you have a choice."

Raising a hand, he snapped his fingers.

Armor clanked as our soldiers dropped into a battle stance and magic once more flared to life among our troops. But the High Elves didn't attack.

Anron, Captain Vendir, and the two other commanders, as well as every squad leader, moved until they were standing in one long row in front of the rest of the soldiers.

There was a hum of magic in the air. My instincts screamed at me. Screamed at me to duck. To surrender. To beg their forgiveness. It was the same emotions that I had felt when Prince Volkan and Anron had fought those few times in the Court of Fire. And it was a truly terrifying feeling.

Apparently, I wasn't the only one who felt it.

Our ranks buckled slightly as parts of our army shrank back.

"Compared to us, you are children," High Commander Anron said. A wide smile slid home on his lips as he spread his arms wide. "Let me show you who you are really playing against."

I threw up my fire shield. Next to me, Mordren's shadows flickered around him as well, while Edric raised a short wall from the stone below the grass. Defensive magic surged up from our troops as well.

The ground cracked.

Rushing winds tore across the landscape.

Water gathered into waves.

Crackling fire roared to life.

All the blood drained from my face as I watched Anron, Vendir, and everyone else on the front line rise up into the air as if on invisible wings. Earth and stone joined fire and water, and spun around the rising High Elves like twisting rings.

The power that pulsed through the air grew more oppressive with each second. But it didn't stop.

Levitating high above us, each of them summoned more power. More flames, more water, more earth and stone and rushing winds swirled around each and every one of them where they hovered in the air.

Lightning split the sky.

Our army scrambled backwards, but the flashing bolts of lightning only joined the twisting rings around Anron and the others.

Fear and hopelessness crashed over me like a tidal wave. They could fly. And they could wield every element. *Every* element. The sheer power that they radiated made me want to curl up in a ball.

"Tremble before the power of gods," High Commander Anron bellowed across the plains.

Noise clanged behind me. I whipped my head around to find that sections of our army had abandoned their weapons and magic and dropped to their knees. Cold realization spread through my veins like poison.

This was the day we all became slaves to the High Elves.

This was the day I became a slave.

Again.

King Aldrich Spiritsinger took a step forward. "You are no god of mine."

The ground exploded.

A huge block of stone shot up from the earth and flashed through the air. Deafening booms echoed across the grasslands as stone and lightning slammed into Aldrich's gigantic boulder before it could wipe the High Elves from the sky like a great hand.

Cracked stone rained down over the field as the attacks crashed into each other.

"Come down and fight me if you dare!" King Aldrich bellowed as he stalked towards the High Commanders.

Mordren, Edric, and I exchanged a glance.

And then we attacked.

Flames tore through the air as I sent a fireball straight at Captain Vendir. He threw up a shield of water that cancelled it out, while at the same time raising a wall of stone across the ground.

Idra and Hadeon, who had sprinted past us towards the ranks of waiting High Elves, screeched to a halt as their headlong rush was abruptly cut off. Lightning crackled through the air. Panic pulsed through me and I sent a wave of flame to intercept it, but the lightning bolts passed straight through it and sped towards Idra and Hadeon where they were trapped between the stone walls.

With incredible speed, Hadeon slammed his hand into Idra and shoved her aside right as the lightning struck. My heart almost stopped.

But the blinding light exploded against an invisible shield before him. I whirled around.

Prince Edric was standing with his arms raised, one towards our army and the other towards Idra and Hadeon, and he was using his power of shielding to keep them safe.

With a twitch of his fingers, the stone walls around the two warriors disappeared.

Hadeon stared at Edric in shock, while Idra was doing the same to Hadeon, but as soon as the wall before them lowered, they darted forward.

Another stone wall shot up and blocked their way.

I hurled a column of fire at Captain Vendir but High Commander Lester intercepted it with a blast of water.

A series of cries rang out.

Several of the flying High Elves plummeted towards the ground before finally stabilizing themselves. Mordren sent another wave of his pain magic towards them.

"Coward!" King Aldrich bellowed. "Come down and fight me."

The black-haired commander waved his hand.

Bright orange flames washed over Aldrich, but it didn't even slow him down. The magic passed over his impenetrable stone skin without harming him.

That rallied our soldiers and several of them started throwing their own magical attacks at the High Elves above.

A block of stone shot towards me.

I dove to the side, but Mordren's shadows shoved it off course before it could get near me. Rolling to my feet, I sent a wave of flames towards the High Elf who had sent it.

Water and lightning and fire washed over the King of Elves. But he continued stalking across the battlefield. Walls of stone rose and fell in his wake. Anron looked down at him and I swore I could see a smirk on his lips. Then he started lowering himself towards the ground.

Another pulse of pain magic sent several of the others dropping with him, but they stabilized themselves and replied with a storm of magic of their own.

"Mordren!" Eilan shouted. "Left!"

I blindly threw up a shield of fire to our left right before a water whip cracked into it. Steam hissed as it evaporated. Mordren snarled and sent another burst of pain magic.

Across the grass, Idra and Hadeon were dodging the stone walls that sprang up around them every time they moved.

Steel rang out between the roaring of fire and wind.

Anron had reached the ground and drawn his sword. King Aldrich unsheathed his as well.

I hurled a firebolt at Captain Vendir, who had tried to blow Idra and Hadeon back with a blast of wind, while the king and the High Commander watched each other.

Aldrich attacked.

Swinging his sword with terrible strength, he aimed for Anron's head. The High Commander yanked up his own to block it. Steel crashed against steel. With a flick of his wrist, Anron disengaged their blades and then aimed for Aldrich's side.

The king didn't even try to block it.

He just swung his sword at Anron's other side.

Anron's blade struck Aldrich's stone skin and bounced back without causing any harm, while the king's sword sped towards the High Commander's exposed side. A gust of wind knocked the blade off course right before it could hit. Anron leaped back.

Surprise was evident on his face as he looked from the sword in his hand to Aldrich's uninjured side. A wicked grin spread across my mouth while I sent another spear of flame towards the blond commander above me. Challenging someone who had impenetrable stone skin to a sword fight really was a terrible, terrible move on Anron's part.

King Aldrich darted forward again.

Throwing a wave of fire at him, Anron temporarily blocked his view while he slid aside. Steel glinted in the light as he slammed his sword towards Aldrich's head from the other side.

Lightning exploded above my head. I flinched, but the attack hadn't been aimed at me. It had been aimed at our army. Gritting his teeth, Prince Edric continued holding up the shield that protected our soldiers from the worst of it.

Mordren sent another pulse of pain towards the High Elves, and this time, a few of them dropped all the way to the ground. I shot a wide column of dark red flames at them, but the ones still in the air protected their comrades with shields of stone and water.

Metallic ringing washed over the grasslands as Anron and Aldrich's blades crashed into each other. With a mighty shove, Anron forced Aldrich's sword away. He yanked a dagger from a sheath at his side and rammed it towards the king's throat. Letting the strike go through, Aldrich instead brought his own sword up for a killing strike.

Then he stopped.

Stunned shock, and a hint of fear, flashed over King Aldrich's wise face.

High Commander Anron had a dagger resting against the side of Aldrich's neck.

It was an old-looking wavy dagger.

My blood froze as I stared at the way the markings etched into it seemed to glow from within. I knew that weapon.

The Dagger of Orias.

CHAPTER 17

"Enough!" High Commander Anron bellowed across the sounds of battle. "Or your beloved king dies."

The fire around me sputtered out.

Attacks staggered to a halt all across the grass as everyone turned to stare at the impossible scene before them. The High Elf Commander was pressing the Dagger of Orias against the side of King Aldrich's neck. How in the world had they managed to get their hands on that weapon?

"Drop the sword," Anron commanded as he stared down at the King of Elves.

Aldrich glared up at him for another few seconds before letting the blade slip from his fingers. It hit the grass with a soft thud.

Before us, the levitating High Elves were returning to the ground.

Idra and Hadeon, who were still trapped halfway between our forces and theirs, flicked their gazes between us and Anron. Both Mordren and I carefully shook our heads. They exchanged a glance but didn't try to attack.

"Now," Anron said. His voice carried across the plains and split the tense silence that had settled. "Surrender, put on the bracelet, and bow before your gods. Or your king dies."

Gasps rippled through our soldiers. The creaking of leather and groaning of armor that followed informed me that multiple sections of our army once more got down on their knees. I swallowed. My throat was suddenly parched.

This couldn't be happening.

I had already been a slave. Twice. And I had finally schemed and fought my way to freedom and power. Only for it to be ripped away before I'd even had a chance to enjoy it. Fiery rage burned through the fear. No. This was not happening.

"I will not be a slave again," I said in a soft voice so that only Mordren and Eilan could hear.

Mordren cast me a glance from the corner of his eye. "No, you will not."

With those four words, he had confirmed that we were of the same mind. We would fight our way through this. And if that didn't work, we would run before we ever let the High Elves force us to our knees.

"Alright," a desperate voice rang out from our other side.

My heart sank.

We might be prepared to fight or flee despite the threat to Aldrich's life, but Prince Edric... He loved the king in a different way than the others. King Aldrich had been the Prince of Stone before Edric, and Edric had always looked up to him. As a mentor. A friend. A father. To save Aldrich's life, there was nothing Prince Edric wouldn't do.

"Alright," Edric repeated. He had his chin raised, but I could see the worry in his gray eyes. "I surrender, and you let King Aldrich live?"

High Commander Anron smiled like a predator and motioned for Edric to approach.

The Prince of Stone swallowed.

After a quick glance at us, he started across the grass.

A summer wind danced across the silent plains and caressed my cheeks. We had to somehow figure out a way to get our army out of here before the High Elves could force us into a battle we couldn't win. I flicked my gaze around the area.

Half of the soldiers behind us were on their knees. The other half watched the king and the prince while fear and uncertainty swirled in their eyes. A group of High Elves had skirted around the battlefield and were snapping black bracelets shut around the wrists of the kneeling soldiers. Idra and Hadeon were still surrounded by a forest of stone walls that would make it difficult for them to get back to us quickly. At the edge of the battlefield, Rayan and Iwdael were watching the unfolding events with mixed expressions on their faces. The Prince of Water looked anxious, while Iwdael Vineweaver looked genuinely horrified. Neither of them would be much help. In fact, almost nothing on the battlefield was of much help to us.

No one dared to move as Prince Edric finally came to a halt in front of Anron and Aldrich. The other two commanders had joined them and were now flanking the pair.

Anron flexed his fingers on the dagger and looked expectantly at Edric. "Well?"

With jerky movements, the Prince of Stone dropped to his knees and held out his wrist. High Commander Danser bent down and snapped a bracelet shut around it. That ominous click seemed to vibrate through the air. Anron arched an eyebrow.

Stone rumbled underneath our feet, but Prince Edric tore his gaze from the High Commanders and pressed his forehead to the ground before their feet.

Pain and sorrow flooded King Aldrich's brown eyes.

"Get up," Anron said. "And tell your court to do the same."

After climbing to his feet, Prince Edric moved several steps to the side and then turned to face our army. "The Court of Stone recognizes the High Elves as gods."

A malicious smile stretched High Commander Anron's lips. "As you should."

And then he shoved the Dagger of Orias into King Aldrich's throat.

I staggered backwards.

My heart plummeted into my stomach and poison spread through my veins at the surprised gasp that slipped King Aldrich's lips when the blade punctured his windpipe and tore apart his artery. The shock of someone who had never felt physical pain bounced across the king's face. Then, Anron ripped out the dagger again.

"NO!" A scream of pure animalistic rage and pain tore from Prince Edric's chest as Aldrich crumpled to the ground.

Blood leaked from the wound and painted the fresh green grass red.

Prince Edric threw himself towards the king, but High Commander Lester intercepted him.

Stones rose from the ground.

The black bracelet around Edric's wrist started glowing.

And the stones disappeared.

While Edric was still waiting for the stone wall that was no longer coming to smack the commander away, he took a crushing punch to the gut and collapsed to the ground.

A few strides away, King Aldrich's body spasmed as he choked on his own blood.

I whipped my head towards Rayan. The Prince of Water was on his knees on the other side of the battlefield. Tears ran down his face. His bracelet also glowed.

Wise brown eyes, eyes that had seen so much of the world and looked at it all with kindness, stared up into the burnt blue sky. And then they started glassing over.

Prince Edric, pain clouding his eyes, crawled towards the dying king but the blond commander stomped his boot down on Edric's back and stopped his movements. A strangled cry ripped from Edric's lips.

Only a stride away, kind brown eyes went blank.

I choked back a sob.

King Aldrich Spiritsinger, the King of Elves, was dead.

The silence that fell across the sunny grasslands was so loud it was deafening. For a few moments, I could only stare at the scene before me in utter disbelief.

Behind the three commanders, the ranks of soldiers in bronze armor shifted to let a slim figure through but I was only vaguely aware of it. My eyes were still locked on the body of King Aldrich.

"The king is dead," a clear voice cut through the oppressive silence. "Long live the queen."

I whipped towards the sound.

Princess Syrene swept her long brown hair back over her shoulder and smiled at the stunned army before her. Her violet eyes glinted in the sun.

"You?" Prince Iwdael blurted out as he stared at his wife. "*You* were behind this?"

She lifted her shoulders in a casual shrug.

"I let them into my court!" Iwdael raised his hand and shook it. "I put on this bracelet. For you. So that they would save *you* from execution. And you do... this."

"Oh, don't act so high and mighty. As soon as they had broken me out, you were going to turn on them. Am I right?"

Iwdael flicked a panicked look towards High Commander Anron that all but confirmed her accusation.

Princess Syrene clicked her tongue. "You might love me enough to let them into your court in exchange for my life. But you would never help them take over the other courts and kill the king." She shot him a disgusted look. "You don't have enough ambition for things like that." Flicking a dismissive hand, she shrugged again. "Well, no matter. Because unfortunately for you, when you made that oh-so-selfless deal with High Commander Anron... I had already made one with him too."

Eilan brushed a hand down my arm.

"We need to leave," he breathed.

"If we leave our armies behind, we won't be able to get them back," I whispered back to him. My eyes darted to our two friends across the grass. "And besides, Hadeon can't worldwalk. Idra can, but she doesn't worldwalk other people."

"How could you do this?" Prince Iwdael screamed at Syrene while stalking towards her. There was open fury on his face, something I had never seen before. "You told them where to find the Dagger of Orias. You helped them kill King Aldrich!"

Princess Syrene rolled her eyes and turned towards Anron. "High Commander, would you mind providing some wind?"

He inclined his head. In one smooth motion, Syrene put her hand into a small bag that she had tied to her waist, and then withdrew her fist before throwing a shimmering powder into the air. The gust of wind that Anron shoved at it sent it shooting straight at Iwdael before I could burn the powder out of the air.

The glittering dust slammed right into the Prince of Trees. Trailing to a halt on the grass halfway to Syrene, he coughed in surprise. Then panic flooded his yellow eyes.

Pressing his hands to the sides of his head, he collapsed to his knees and rocked back and forth as if that powder had made his senses, or perhaps his magic senses, go haywire. "Make it stop. Make it stop."

Dread drew its icy fingers down my spine as I watched Prince Iwdael plead desperately on the ground.

Our army stirred in fear. I whirled around just in time to see several of our worldwalkers grab the nearest person and disappear into thin air.

"Oh, no," High Commander Anron said. "No leaving."

Every single bracelet suddenly started glowing with black light.

Felix, who had grabbed Monette's shoulder, blinked in shock and whipped his gaze from his own body to the High Commander and then to the bracelet around his wrist.

Alarm flashed over all our faces as Eilan, Mordren, and I exchanged a panicked look. I turned towards Idra. She and Hadeon were staring at us from across the battlefield.

Hoping that everyone understood what was about to happen, I drew in a shuddering breath and then shouted, "The Hands!"

Idra's hand shot out and wrapped around Hadeon's arm.

And then they were gone.

High Commander Anron snapped his gaze towards the empty spot where they had been standing before whipping back towards us. Water and air and lightning sped across the grass.

But when it reached the area of burnt grass we had been occupying, Eilan, Mordren, and I had already disappeared into thin air.

CHAPTER 18

An empty room with walls made of wood appeared around me. I whipped my head from side to side. No one else was there. Leaping straight through the wall, I left the room that had been mine for a while and darted into the corridor outside. Two elves with long black hair jerked back when I materialized next to them. A few seconds later, two more elves came running in through the front door.

"Are you okay?" all six of us blurted out at the same time.

A laugh that was laced with tension escaped from several throats. Mordren drew me into a tight embrace, and for one second, I allowed myself to breathe. Then I pulled back.

The tall building we were standing in had served as the Hands' headquarters before I had recruited them and offered Valerie, Theo, and their gang a home in my castle. Since we couldn't risk Anron following us, we couldn't go somewhere that he would know about. When I had shouted 'the Hands', I had just hoped that everyone would understand what I meant. Thankfully, they had.

"We can't go back to our courts now," I said as I stepped

out of Mordren's embrace. "Too many people answer to Anron."

"I agree," Eilan said. "And besides, they have Syrene on their side now. She knows far too much about how our courts work."

Sudden dread clanged through me as I remembered our conversation in the dungeons. "She was planning on killing King Aldrich and then all the princes as well. She had a plan." I met each of their gazes in turn. "She knows how to break all the princes."

"Which means that everyone we care about is in danger," Mordren finished.

"So what do we do?" Idra asked. "Hide?"

For a few seconds, we all only looked at each other. Then, as one, we nodded.

"We hide."

Mordren met Hadeon's eyes. "I will get Ellyda."

"I'll get Valerie," Eilan added.

Idra blew out a soft breath. "I'll take Theo."

Normally, Idra didn't worldwalk anyone anywhere. I wasn't entirely sure what it meant that she had both worldwalked Hadeon here from the battlefield and that she was now also offering to get Theo, but I didn't have time to think about that, so all I said was, "Alright, I'll find Evander. Meet back here as soon as you have them."

Hadeon, who was the only one out of the five of us not able to worldwalk, motioned towards the corridor around us. "I'll do a sweep of the building."

I gave him another nod before worldwalking away.

Golden light from the sun fell across huge red walls and painted them with gilded streaks. I barely spared them a glance before taking off at a run straight towards them. I couldn't risk getting spotted by any of the guards in case the High Elves had already been here to relay the new orders.

Silk brushed against my skin as I phased through the red stone walls while sneaking into my own castle like a spy.

When the door to Evander's room appeared, I walked right through it too without knocking. An empty bedroom stared back at me. I cursed. Where was he?

Taking off at a run, I sprinted towards my own rooms. He might be waiting for me to get back.

Since taking over the Court of Fire, I had made sure that there was a route to and from my own bedroom that I could use without being spotted. I had been a spy most of my life, and old habits die hard. As I slipped into my room through a series of empty passageways and unguarded walls, I was incredibly grateful for the sneaky side of my personality.

Another empty room met me as I cleared the final wall.

"Gods and spirits damn it," I swore.

Well, as long as I was here, I might as well pick up a few necessary items. Moving with whirlwind speed, I grabbed a few sets of clothes, my magic-imbued jacket, a few more weapons and tools, and shoved it all into a bag. After slinging it over my shoulder, I strode over to the door and cracked it open.

The guard outside jumped in surprise. "Lady Firesoul. When did you...? How...?"

"Kenna," another voice cut in.

I threw the door open. Evander had been pacing up and down the corridor and was now hurrying towards me.

"What's going on?" he asked.

Grabbing him by the arm, I dragged him down the corridor. "We need to leave. *Now*. Head to the city. I'll meet you in the alley to the left of the gates."

"W-what...?" he began, but I cut him off.

"No time. Go."

Without waiting for him to reply, I ran past the stunned guard and back into my room before phasing through the wall once more. My heart slammed against my ribs as I snuck out of the castle again.

I barely felt it when the warm sun finally fell across my face and caressed my skin. With one eye on the people around me, I made my way to the alley I had told Evander to meet me in. Unsurprisingly, it was empty when I arrived. I crossed my arms and leaned against the rough sandstone wall in order to stop myself from pacing.

This was taking too long. Anron and the High Elves could be here any minute.

My gaze darted towards the red castle towering before me. Fury burned through my soul. This was mine. My castle. My throne. My court. Narrowing my eyes, I seared the image of it into my mind. I would get it back.

An elf with short brown hair skidded into the alley. I was halfway to my weapons before realizing that it was Evander. Striding towards him, I threw my arm around his back instead.

"Where are we going?" he asked.

"I'll explain when we get there."

I worldwalked us out.

Walls made of dark wood replaced the sandstone ones. With my heart still thumping in my chest, I let go of Evander and dropped the bag on the floor before striding into the hallway outside my room.

A deep sigh of relief escaped me when I found Valerie and Theo standing next to Eilan and Idra.

"Mordren and Ellyda?" I asked.

Heavy footsteps came thumping down the stairs behind me.

"Not back yet," Hadeon answered as he joined us in the cramped hallway.

Idra met my gaze. "Did you see it?"

"See what?" I asked.

Lifting a scarred hand, she motioned in the general direction of Prince Edric's white stone castle. "The High Elves are moving all the courts into King Aldrich's castle atop the mountain."

"What?" I frowned at her. "Why?"

Eilan's pale green eyes slid to me. "Hostages."

"Damn." I raked a hand through my hair. "Gods and spirits damn it all."

Next to me, Evander flicked his gaze from face to face. I knew that I should be explaining things properly to him. He needed to know who was behind this lethal deception and exactly what it had cost us. But I just couldn't muster enough energy to relive what had happened on those sunlit plains today. At least not yet.

"So..." Evander began. "What do we do now?"

"We need to free the other princes," I said. "As long as Anron has them hostage, he controls the courts."

"And how do we do that?"

I was all out of bright ideas so I just lifted my shoulders in a helpless shrug and swept my gaze over the rest of them.

"We need to figure out what we're dealing with," Eilan said at last. "If we could–"

Mordren blinked into existence on the wooden floor a few strides away. I opened my mouth to say something, but the look on his face stopped me. Leather creaked as Hadeon shifted his position to see better.

"Where's El?" he asked. There was a hint of panic in his voice.

"Hadeon…" Mordren began.

"Mordren." His voice came out in a growl. "Where is El?"

"She… We were too late." Pain swirled in Mordren's eyes. "She was already gone."

It was as if all the air had been sucked from the room. For a few seconds, no one seemed to be breathing.

Hadeon stared uncomprehendingly at the Prince of Shadows. "What are you saying?"

Mordren sucked in a shuddering breath.

"They took her."

CHAPTER 19

The tension in the hallway was so thick I could have cut it with my knife. Theo placed a sympathetic hand on Hadeon's arm, but the muscular warrior didn't seem to feel it. He was still staring straight at Mordren.

"We will get her back," the Prince of Shadows said.

"How?" Hadeon demanded.

Pain swirled in Mordren's eyes again. "I do not know yet. But I promise you, we will free her."

"You don't have a plan yet, do you?"

"No, but–"

"Then I'm not waiting." He stalked closer to Mordren. "Take me there right now."

"To do what, Hadeon?" Eilan cut in. His pale green eyes were brimming with concern as he gestured helplessly around him. "We don't know how to get her out yet."

Hadeon snapped his gaze between the two dark-haired brothers. "Then I'm not getting her out. I'm joining her."

"You will also become a hostage," Mordren said, his voice soft.

"I don't care."

"It would–"

"No!"

Something snapped inside Hadeon. Taking two quick strides, he shoved Mordren back against the wall and grabbed a fistful of his black leather armor. The thud as Mordren hit the dark wood echoed through the building, but he didn't even raise his hands to protect himself as Hadeon jerked him forwards and then slammed him back against the wall again.

"You worldwalk me to that mountain right now," Hadeon growled in his face. "Or I swear by the spirits of our parents, I will kill you."

Mordren opened his mouth, but before he could reply, Hadeon pressed on.

"It's El." Fear bloomed in his red eyes and the anger bled away as he drew in a shuddering breath. "You know what she's like. How her mind works. Anron and the High Elves... they won't understand. They'll get frustrated and angry because she says and does weird shit." He swallowed to keep his voice from breaking. "They might hurt her for it."

Raising his hand, Mordren placed it on Hadeon's arm. "Okay. I will worldwalk you there. You will look after Ellyda, and we will figure out a way to get you both out."

"Yes. Good." Hadeon let out a long shuddering breath and released his grip on Mordren's armor. Clearing his throat, he smoothened down the crease he had made. "Sorry."

Mordren only gave his shoulder a companionable squeeze as if to say that he understood. While Hadeon stepped back, the Prince of Shadows turned to the rest of us.

"When I returned home to get Ellyda, I saw that the High Elves were using their air serpents to transport key members of our court towards King Aldrich's castle. We need to find out what is happening in there."

"We were just saying the same thing when you arrived," Eilan answered. "If we're to stand any chance of freeing Hadeon and Ellyda, as well as the other princes, we need to know what we're dealing with."

Mordren shifted his gaze to me. "Do you think you could sneak inside?"

"You want her to sneak inside a castle that the High Elves have claimed?" Evander snapped, speaking for the first time since Mordren appeared. "Have you even considered how dangerous that would be for her?"

"Of course I can sneak inside," I interrupted.

"If you want to find out what is happening inside the castle, why don't you do it yourself?" Evander challenged, his eyes still fixed on Mordren. "And besides, what are the High Elves even doing in King Aldrich's castle?"

"Aldrich is dead." Mordren spit out the words as if they were poison, but it still wasn't enough to hide the hurt in his eyes.

Evander rocked back as if someone had slapped him, but before he could respond, Mordren continued.

"And as for sneaking in myself… If I were able to walk through walls, I would do it myself. But I am not. Besides, Kenna is more than capable of speaking for herself." He shot a final withering glare at Evander before his silver eyes slid to me. "You said you were fine with going inside to see what we are dealing with?"

It was halfway between a statement and a question, but I nodded anyway. "Yeah, of course. Just give me a minute to change out of this armor and into something that doesn't make as much noise."

While Evander crossed his arms and glowered at him, Mordren turned back to Hadeon and motioned towards the bag he had dropped on the floor when he arrived. "I brought some clothes for us. You should probably change too before we leave. Unless you are comfortable with the High Elves getting their hands on your armor."

"Oh, hell no," Hadeon replied and reached for the bag. "Those bastards ain't getting that. Or my sword."

"I suspected as much."

Theo and Valerie, who had been standing quietly by the other wall, took a step forward.

"We need to make some arrangements and make sure that our gang is safe," Valerie said. Her gaze drifted to Eilan. "So if someone could...?"

"I'll go with you," Eilan filled in.

"Thank you."

Idra's dark eyes had been locked on Hadeon for the past few minutes, but now she finally tore her gaze from the warrior and slid it to the two thieves. After another second of silence, she blew out an exasperated breath and met my gaze.

"I'll make sure they don't die before you get back," she announced and then stalked over to where Eilan, Theo, and Valerie had formed a separate group.

"Alright." I swept my gaze around the hallway and nodded. "Meet back here later tonight then."

Evander just spun on his heel and stalked away, but the others nodded back.

Drawing in a deep breath, I made my way back into my old room. The dark wooden walls and all the furniture looked exactly like it had almost a year ago when the Hands had let me live there. It felt like decades had passed since then.

Back then, I had still been Prince Edric's spy.

Then I had pulled off an incredibly complicated scheme and blackmailed Mordren Darkbringer into buying me my freedom. And then I had helped him plot against Prince Volkan, which had left me a slave in the Court of Fire. Then I had become the Lady of Fire. And fought the High Elves. And watched the King of Elves be murdered right before my eyes.

And now I was going to have to watch Hadeon surrender himself to keep Ellyda safe while I tried to sneak into the king's former castle in order to figure out a way to free them and all the other princes. And also to get my throne back.

This was going to require one hell of a scheme.

CHAPTER 20

Cold winds blew across the mountainside, bringing with it a taste of snow in the air. Standing pressed against Mordren's chest, I watched from behind a boulder as Hadeon approached the High Elves who had taken up position outside the great doors to King Aldrich's castle. The setting sun painted the white stone palace with streaks of red and purple.

"Halt," the High Elves called. "And hands where we can see them. Who are you?"

"I'm Hadeon Battleborn."

Arrows were drawn and pointed at his chest. "Why are you here, Hadeon Battleborn?"

"Because you have my sister, and Prince Mordren doesn't care enough to try and rescue her. And I don't give a fuck about the rest of the world if she's not in it."

Behind my back, I felt Mordren flinch at his words. It wasn't true. We all knew that Hadeon had to say something along those lines so that the High Elves wouldn't try to use Ellyda and Hadeon to force Mordren out of hiding. But apparently, it still hurt to hear the venom in his friend's words.

"So, you have come to surrender," the High Elf guard said.

"Yes."

"I don't know how you people do things, but this is not how someone surrenders where we're from."

For a moment, the mountain was silent. Only the whisper of a cool wind making lazy arcs around the snowcapped peaks broke the stillness as Hadeon stared back at the High Elves. Then he rolled back his shoulders and slowly got down on his knees.

A cold hand squeezed my heart as I watched them snap a black bracelet around his wrist before dragging him to his feet again and marching him up the slope towards the castle.

We would get them out.

"We will get them out," Mordren said, as if he had heard my thoughts.

"Yeah." Turning around, I met his gaze. "I'll meet you back in the cabin."

It was the same small cabin on the side of the mountain that we had used when we were both trying to steal the Dagger of Orias. The ghost of a smirk on Mordren's lips informed me that he remembered how he had gotten me to grovel at his feet there back then. I gave his chest a shove.

"Don't get any ideas," I muttered.

His hand shot out and wrapped around my arm before I could stalk away. I paused and looked up at him in silent question.

He searched my face for another moment before finally saying, "Be careful."

"I'll do my best."

"You'd better."

"Always so bossy." Grabbing the front of his shirt, I yanked him closer and stole a kiss from his lips. "I'll see you soon."

"Yes, you will."

With one final huff of amusement and mock annoyance, I released my grip on his shirt and took off towards the side of the castle.

The High Elves had claimed the white stone palace, but they apparently didn't know it as well as King Aldrich had because they had left several of the access points unguarded. Snow crunched underneath my boots as I slunk towards a section that would take me into the main ballroom. If the inside of the castle was as poorly guarded as the outside, I should be able to get where I wanted to go from there.

Silk brushed against my skin. I flicked wary glances around the high-ceilinged hall before me as I left the cool mountain air behind and phased through one of the side walls that led into the ballroom.

My heart leaped into my throat.

With my pulse suddenly thrumming in my ears, I dove behind a cluster of white couches and pressed myself against a smooth backrest.

The ballroom wasn't empty. A short distance away was an elf dressed in a regal gown made of purple silk. Princess Syrene. Or, according to her, Queen Syrene.

Edging forward, I peered around the white armrest.

Syrene was standing with her spine straight and her arms crossed, and she was tapping her foot against the spotless floor. But thankfully, she wasn't looking in my direction. She was staring out the open doors to the main balcony as if she was waiting for something.

The sound of great wings boomed in through the doors.

Clamping my teeth together, I tried to force my heart to

keep a steady rhythm as High Commander Anron and his winged serpent landed on the balcony. He slid off his mount and strode towards the doors while the beast took off into the red-streaked sky again.

The only way to get to this castle was by worldwalking. Or so we had thought. With those air serpents, the High Elves could come and go as they pleased.

"Queen Syrene," Anron said in a neutral voice as he crossed into the ballroom and found the brown-haired elf waiting for him in there.

"High Commander," she replied. "You said you would be leaving after the battle. And yet, I find your men making themselves at home in my castle."

He came to a halt a couple of strides away, towering over her as if she were a child. "Did I?"

"Yes. You become gods and make people put on those bracelets. Then you use the magic you're siphoning through them to become more powerful so that you can go back and overthrow your emperor. That's your plan, isn't it?"

Anron took a half step back, blinking in surprise.

"Oh, don't look so shocked." Syrene flashed him a cunning smile. "I know one when I see one. I had a similar plan, remember?"

Having recovered from the moment of surprise, Anron inclined his head and matched the sharp smile on her lips. "Well spotted."

"Thank you." She raised her eyebrows expectantly. "So, why are you not getting ready to head back to your homeland and take the throne you really want?"

"Even with all the elves who have already surrendered to us, the bracelets are not sucking enough magic. I need everyone's magic. And most of all, I need all the princes' power. They have unrestricted access to elemental magic, which is very powerful. I need it all."

"Then maybe you shouldn't have let two of them get away."

Anron's blue eyes flashed, but when he spoke, his tone was calm. "If you have any ideas for how to capture them, I'm all ears."

"I have already solved three of your problems for you by telling you to threaten Rayan's water, using that special herb to make Iwdael's mood-sensing magic unbearable, and telling you to threaten the king to get Edric to surrender." Her eyes were as sharp as his. "But sure, if it will get you back to your homeland sooner, then why not." She gave him a calculating smile. "Leveraging Ellyda won't be enough to get Mordren. Apparently, he wasn't desperate enough to try to rescue her, so her brother surrendered instead. But when I was planning to overthrow them all, those two were only part of my back-up plan anyway." Her smile widened as she cocked her head. "The real key is his brother. Get Eilan, and you will have Mordren on his knees in a matter of seconds."

"I see. And what about Kenna?"

"That's where it gets problematic. I don't know. When I made my plan to take the throne, Volkan still ruled the Court of Fire. I thought I had a way to neutralize his fire magic, but apparently, the gemstone I had planned on using turned out to be fake. And I don't know what Kenna's weakness is."

High Commander Anron ran a hand over his jaw. "Volkan did. He figured it out right before she killed him. I wish he had told me."

"I suppose we will have to figure out another way then. So that you can leave. Soon."

"Indeed." Anron started towards the doors leading farther into the castle. "Walk with me."

Irritation flashed across Syrene's face, but in the end she followed him towards the doors. I remained hidden behind the white couch for another few minutes after they had left. Once I was certain that I wouldn't run into them, I snuck towards the opposite wall. If I remembered the map of the castle correctly, I should be able to get to the guest wing fairly easily from this location.

Empty halls made of pale marble watched me impassively as I snuck through the palace while mulling over the conversation I had overheard.

Based on what had happened on the battlefield earlier today, I had guessed that those black bracelets somehow blocked the wearer's magic. But I hadn't expected them to suck the magic from the person in order to give it to someone else. To give it to Anron. As if he wasn't already far too powerful with those godlike abilities he had displayed on the plains.

Turning yet another corner, I slipped through a series of walls behind the ballroom.

The good news was that Anron and his people weren't planning on staying here as gods. The bad news, however, was that they weren't going to leave until they had put one of those magic-draining bracelets on both me and Mordren. And I intended to keep the hard-earned power I had finally schemed my way into, thank you very much. So if they weren't going to leave until they had my power, and I wasn't going to give up my power, then this was going to get complicated and ugly really fast.

"This will be your room," a voice announced from around the next corner. "Don't wander outside this wing until someone gives you permission. Got it?"

"Got it," Hadeon's voice grumbled. "Now, where's my sister?"

Pressing myself against the cold stone wall, I stole a glance around the corner. Halfway down the corridor, Hadeon was scowling up at an annoyed High Elf in bronze armor.

"That's her room." After stabbing a hand towards the room next to Hadeon's, the High Elf spun on his heel and stalked away.

Hadeon didn't even bother opening the door to his own room. He strode straight for Ellyda's.

I listened to the High Elf's footsteps echo between the white walls while Hadeon disappeared into his sister's room. When the sound had at last died out, I approached the same door that Hadeon had gone through a minute before. Hoping that I wasn't about to interrupt a heartfelt sibling hug, I walked straight through the door.

"–doing, you bloody idiot!" Ellyda's voice cut through the air.

Drawing up short right inside the door, I blinked at the scene before me. Hadeon was backing away from a furious-looking Ellyda, whose vicious glares were sharp enough to draw blood.

Well, so much for a heartfelt sibling hug.

"You should be out there, helping Mordren and Eilan figure out a way to fix this mess," she sniped at him. "But now, you're stuck here too."

"I–"

"And for what? I am perfectly capable of taking care of myself."

"But–"

"Did you even think this through?"

"Well–"

"Did you even try to stop him?"

"Wait, what? Stop who?"

"No," I admitted, answering Ellyda's question that had clearly been directed at me.

I wasn't even sure when she had first noticed me. She hadn't even looked in my direction. But the more time I spent with Ellyda, the more I got the feeling that she only had two core settings to choose from. Either, her ability to perceive the world around her was entirely shut down and she was completely oblivious to everything that happened. Or, she saw and heard and felt *everything*.

"But can you really blame him?" I continued. "When you would have done the exact same thing for him if your roles had been reversed?"

At last, her sharp violet eyes slid to me. She was silent for a while. Hadeon, who had whirled around in surprise at the sound of my voice, was now flicking his gaze between the two of us.

"No, I suppose I can't," she finally said. Her furious expression softened as she shifted her attention back to Hadeon. "I still think you're an idiot for giving yourself up, but in spite of that..." She cleared her throat and looked away. "I am actually glad you're with me, brother."

Taking two long strides, Hadeon closed the distance between them and drew his sister into a bear hug. Ellyda shifted awkwardly on her feet but let him hug her.

"*Thank you,*" Hadeon mouthed at me over her shoulder.

I let out a soft chuckle and gave him a nod.

"So, did you find out anything when you snuck inside, Kenna?" Hadeon asked as he released his sister and stepped back.

"Yeah, I managed to eavesdrop on a conversation between

Anron and Syrene." I turned to Ellyda. "Are the other princes close by? It would be..." I trailed off.

Ellyda was already striding past me and out the door, presumably to retrieve said princes.

Shaking his head, Hadeon let out a chuckle and then moved towards the cluster of armchairs and couches in the corner. I had never visited the guest wing here before, but apparently, King Aldrich had been a firm believer in the importance of hospitality. The guest room Ellyda was staying in was huge. In addition to the grand double bed with fluffy white pillows and covers, there was a spacious seating arrangement, several closets, a desk, and what looked like a door to a private bathroom at the back. If the other rooms were similar to this one, at least Hadeon and the princes would be comfortable while in captivity.

Footsteps sounded in the corridor outside. I had just lowered myself into the armchair next to Hadeon's when four people poured across the threshold.

"Damn, they got you too," Prince Edric growled as his gaze fell on the two of us.

His face was a carefully constructed mask, but I could tell from his bloodshot eyes that he had been crying. It didn't surprise me at all but it still made my heart constrict painfully. Edric had always looked up to Aldrich as a father figure. The death of King Aldrich had shocked me, and I did mourn him even though I hadn't known him all that well. I couldn't even begin to understand what it must have been like for Edric to watch someone he loved like family be murdered right before his eyes.

"No," Rayan Floodbender said from behind his shoulder while he followed him towards a couch. "Look at her wrist."

Both Edric and Iwdael glanced down at my bare wrists.

A soft click sounded as Ellyda closed the door behind the three princes while they all took a seat.

"Huh," the Prince of Trees said. "How come you don't have one?"

Crossing one leg over the other, Rayan cocked his head and studied me with those calm purple eyes of his. "And how did you even get in here?"

Wood creaked faintly as Ellyda unceremoniously dropped down on the couch next to the Prince of Water. He gave her a small smile before returning his attention to me. In fact, everyone turned their attention to me.

"Well," I began and cleared my throat. "Seeing as most of you already know this, I might as well share it with everyone. I can walk through walls."

Iwdael and Rayan, who were the only ones here still in the dark about my powers, raised their eyebrows in surprise.

"I see." Prince Rayan gave me a knowing look. "So, that explains how you found your way into my bedroom in the middle of the night."

"Yeah, and that's how I can get in here without the High Elves knowing."

"Good, then–"

"Enough chitchat," Prince Edric snapped. His eyes were hard as granite as he met each of our gazes in turn. "How do we take the bastards out?"

Silence descended on the pale room. Rayan and I exchanged a glance, but the pause had stretched a little too long so the Prince of Stone cut off any reply before it could be voiced.

"I don't want your pity," Edric growled. "I know that you already know how I feel about... felt about King Aldrich. I know that you can see in my face that I'm affected by this. But

I don't want your pity. I want a plan for how to kill Anron. If I'd had my magic, I could've just dropped this entire castle on their heads, but I can't even move so much as a pebble. Can't shield. I can't even worldwalk." Lifting a hand, he shook his wrist. The black bracelet on it still shone with dark light. "This somehow blocks it. Which means that I can't do this on my own." He glared at the rest of us. "So, what have you got?"

I knew just how much Prince Edric hated looking weak, and if it had been me, I would have hated the pity too. So in the end, I just cleared my throat and sat forward in my armchair. "I eavesdropped on Anron and Syrene on the way in here."

Prince Iwdael flinched at the mention of his wife's name, but didn't say anything.

"Those bracelets you're wearing," I nodded towards their wrists, "don't just block your magic. They siphon it."

"The bastard is stealing our magic?"

"Yes." I nodded and then proceeded to tell them about Anron's plans to return to Valdanar and overthrow their emperor as soon as he had everyone's magic.

Edric's scowl deepened with every word. On the couch, both Rayan and Ellyda looked like they were turning over the information in their heads. Once I was finished, Hadeon opened his mouth to respond, but Prince Iwdael beat him to it.

"So what you're saying is, the High Elves are going to put these bracelets on everyone, drain the magic of our entire species, and then leave without giving us a way to take them off." His yellow eyes flashed with rage in a way I had never seen before. "Leaving us powerless and ruled by Syrene, who will be the only elf with magic in our lands."

Letting out a slow breath, I met his furious gaze. "Yeah."

"Shit," Hadeon commented.

Rayan nodded towards the warrior. "What he said."

"As long as they have you," I continued, "they have your courts. So we need to figure out a way to get those bracelets off you."

"I think I might have an idea," Ellyda said. Her eyes had been focused on the white wall above Hadeon's shoulder, but now she dragged her gaze back to us. "But it will take some time."

"We also need to find a way to neutralize the poison that they were going to release into my court," Rayan added. "Because as long as they hold that over my head, I won't be able to leave, even if you can get this bracelet off me."

"Good point," I said. "We sh–"

"No," Ellyda interrupted. "No, we don't." When everyone frowned at her, she shrugged. "They were bluffing."

Realization dawned as I caught up with her thought process. "Oh, of course. You're right."

"What do you mean 'they were bluffing'?" Rayan asked, his dark brows still creased.

"Didn't you hear what Kenna said?" Ellyda nodded towards me. "They need everyone's magic so that they'll have enough power to challenge their emperor."

"Which means that they can't poison half your city," I finished.

The Prince of Water let out a long sigh and pressed a hand to his forehead. "By the spirits." He shook his head. "I shouldn't have fallen for it."

"You were not the only one who fell for something he shouldn't have," Iwdael Vineweaver added quietly. "Don't beat yourself up."

"Yes, speaking of the deal you made with the High Elves,"

Prince Edric cut in. Turning in his armchair, he leveled a hard stare on the Prince of Trees. "If you had known about Syrene's own deal with Anron, then I would have killed you without hesitation. *But...*" he pressed on when several people attempted to speak up, "you didn't. So all you are guilty of is letting the High Elves into your court and putting on the bracelet. Which is exactly what I have done as well now. However, this plan we're making is most likely going to end with Syrene dead. Are you prepared for that?"

"I sacrificed my court for her," Iwdael said slowly. Deliberately. Each word laced with bitterness. "My court. My *people*. All the elves under my protection are now powerless slaves to the High Elves. Because of her." Tearing his hard stare from Edric, he swept eyes that burned with cold fury around the room. "When the time comes, I will kill her myself."

I couldn't even imagine the guilt he must be carrying because of the deal he had made. Even though it wasn't his fault that Anron had murdered King Aldrich, he had still made a deal with the High Elves to save the person who was directly responsible for Anron murdering the king. He had loved her. A lot. And now he was vowing to kill her himself.

"Good," Prince Edric said.

After nodding to the Prince of Trees, he met each of our gazes in turn.

"Then let's plot murder and destruction."

CHAPTER 21

Moonlight streamed in through the windows and added a touch of silver to the golden light from the candles burning throughout the room. Valerie and Theo were sprawled across one of the couches in what had been some kind of common room for their gang before they moved to the Court of Fire. To their right, Mordren and Eilan sat in separate armchairs but wore matching expressions on their faces. Their dark brows were slightly creased as if calculating the odds of success. Idra had taken up position by the back wall and watched the rest of us silently, while Evander paced in front of the window.

"So..." Valerie began, drawing out the word. "I know that you," she flapped her hand in my direction, "kind of specialize in crazy, but this plan is pretty crazy, right? And we don't even have a whole plan yet. Just a general end goal or two."

"She has a point." Mordren inclined his head towards the brown-haired thief. "If it was only Anron and his soldiers, we might stand a chance of winning a potential battle. But as things stand now... there are six of us against three legions of High Elves and three other courts."

"So let's add another end goal then," I said. "Find a way to get rid of those other two commanders and their legions."

"And how–" Theo began, but Evander cut him off.

"Seven."

We all turned to stare at him. He had been pacing back and forth in front of the window while I recanted my meeting with Ellyda, Hadeon, and the other princes. But now his dark green eyes were locked on the Prince of Shadows.

"There are seven of us," Evander said.

A cold smile spread across Mordren's lips. "Since you do not actually have any skills to contribute, you do not count."

"Mordren," I interrupted and shook my head at him in warning.

"I can fight my own battles, Kenna," Evander snapped at me before turning back to Mordren and throwing his arms out. "What is your problem with me?"

"My problem is that I dislike people like you. You just leech off everyone else and never contribute anything of your own." Mordren raised his eyebrows. "What have you done since Kenna freed you? Since Kenna fought Volkan Flameshield in the arena and killed him to free you and everyone else? What have you done since then? What have you contributed to her rule?"

Anger and embarrassment flushed Evander's face. "I... I haven't figured out what I want to do yet."

"*Want* has nothing to do with it. What you want to do is irrelevant. I asked what you have *contributed* to Kenna's rule. You have lived in her home and eaten her food for months. What have you done to earn your keep?"

"I have a lot of information."

"Information that Kenna, as a former spy, most likely already knows. What else?"

"Well, I..."

Mordren slashed a hand through the air and shot him a disgusted look. "And that is my problem with you. Everyone here pulls their weight. Start thinking of what you can bring to the table." Without waiting for a reply, he turned back to us. "We will need a distraction."

"I agree," Eilan picked up smoothly. "We can't just waltz in and free the other princes. We need to create some kind of distraction so that the High Elves are occupied elsewhere when we make our move."

While they started bouncing ideas off each other, I glanced at Evander. He had taken a seat on the windowsill. Arms crossed, he glared at the wall above Valerie's head while his cheeks were still flushed with anger and embarrassment. Conflicted emotions bloomed in my chest.

He had informed me, in no uncertain terms, that he hadn't wanted me to defend him against Mordren, so I hadn't said anything. But in truth, that wasn't the real reason I had kept quiet. If I was being honest, I actually agreed with Mordren more than I wanted to admit. I had also experienced a time when I felt lost and uncertain about my future, so I knew how difficult those kinds of feelings could be. But even during that time, I had kept working. Kept fighting. Kept providing for myself. I had never just lived off someone else's generosity. And I did find Evander's moping around a bit frustrating at times.

"Oh!" Valerie suddenly exclaimed, startling me out of my musings. Jumping up from the couch, she landed on the floor and waved her arms around like a deranged windmill. "I've got it! What about an uprising?"

"Seriously?" Idra gave her a flat look from her position by the wall. "Where would we get an uprising from?"

"The humans, of course!" Her brown eyes glittered in the candlelight as she turned to grin at everyone in the room. "The High Elves are so focused on you all that they've forgotten our side of the population. None of the humans have been conscripted into being walking pools of magic, and none of them would believe that they're gods because we already have our own gods."

Theo shifted his gaze from his fellow thief to us, and shrugged. "She's right."

"Ha!" Valerie brushed her shoulders in a cocky gesture and wiggled her eyebrows. "Told you I'm the brains of the operation."

"More like an endlessly spinning spatula that keeps throwing food at the wall to see what sticks."

Eilan choked and slapped a hand in front of his mouth to stop the rest of his surprised laugh from escaping his throat. His chest shook, making his night-black hair ripple along his back.

"You think that's an insult, but I'll have you know that I would make a fantastic spatula."

Wheezing noises came from Eilan at that point.

Dropping into her seat again, Valerie flashed him a satisfied grin and winked. "I'd make a fantastic little spoon too."

I laughed out loud. Pressing a hand against my mouth, I shook my head at her while Theo did the same on her other side. Even Idra's lips twitched in the hint of a smile. Valerie, looking very satisfied with herself, raked her eyes up and down Eilan's body in a way that made him clear his throat and glance away while a faint red color seeped into his cheeks.

In his armchair next to me, Mordren massaged his temples. "Shall we get back to the proposed uprising?"

Eilan cleared his throat again. "Yes, let's."

"If we are going to persuade the humans to create a big enough distraction we will need to speak with the highest-ranking nobles from every court." Mordren swept an authoritarian stare around the room until everyone quieted down. "I can summon the human nobles from the Court of Shadows. And Kenna, I assume you can do the same in the Court of Fire?"

"Yeah," I replied. Turning towards the window, I met Evander's gaze. "Could you talk to the ones in the Court of Trees?"

His face lit up at that. "Of course."

"I have… an in," Eilan began vaguely, since Mordren and I were the only ones in the room who knew that he was a shapeshifter, "with the nobles in all the courts, so I can take either one."

When he shifted his gaze to Idra, she shrugged. "You can take Stone. I'll handle the Court of Water. They're the easiest to scare."

Several people exchanged glances. From her tone and the blank expression on her face, it was impossible to tell if she was making a joke or not.

"We need allies," Evander said into the silence. "Not for them to fear us."

Idra's dark eyes slid to him, which made him flinch, but her expression stayed as blank as ever. "One does not exclude the other."

"True that," Valerie chimed in. A wicked grin spread across her face as she rubbed her hands. "A little fear goes a long way to make sure someone cooperates."

Both Mordren and Eilan raised their eyebrows at that.

"Convince them however you like," I said with a diplomatic nod at both Idra and Evander. "Just make sure they come because…"

Before I had even finished the sentence, Theo and Valerie were already scrambling out of their seats.

"Where are you going?" I asked, bewildered.

"To find a location for the meeting, of course," Theo tossed over his shoulder while continuing forwards.

"Duh," Valerie added with a short shake of her head as if I really should have figured that out on my own. "Told you I was the brains of the operation. Spatula or otherwise."

Evander scrambled out of the way as they strode straight towards the window behind him. With matching grins on their faces, the two thieves fired off a mock salute and then disappeared out the window.

Chuckling, I stared after them into the dark night.

The blackened heavens were dusted with silver and the bright moon illuminated the white stone city outside. Clearing my throat, I pushed to my feet and spread my arms.

"Well, let's get to work then."

CHAPTER 22

Murmuring voices filled the grand mansion that had lain dark and deserted only hours before. Mirrors blackened with age lined the walls on one side of what looked to have been a ballroom long ago. A broken chandelier hung in the ceiling and cracks spidered through the white marble floor. I swept my gaze across the crowd of nobles standing before us.

"How did you even find this place?" I whispered to Valerie and Theo while we waited for the rest of the human lords and ladies to arrive.

It had been three days since we came up with this plan back in the Hands' former headquarters, and we had managed to reach most of the influential human families in every court. And out of those, at least a majority had agreed to come.

"Oh you know," Valerie answered. "We were just wandering through the wide-stretched landscapes of the Court of Stone some time ago and we just happened to come upon this completely deserted mansion sitting here in the grasslands looking all sad and alone."

I snorted. "Uh-huh."

"We might have burgled it at one point too," Theo added from her other side.

"That sounds more like it."

"But there really wasn't all that much to steal." Valerie smacked her lips and glared at the lonely chandelier as if it was its fault that all the valuables had already been looted. "A disappointment, really."

The doors boomed closed on the other side of the ballroom. A moment later, Evander became visible behind the sea of colorful dresses and suits. Raising a hand, he signaled that everyone had arrived. I nodded to him before exchanging a glance with Mordren.

Drawing in a soft breath, I stepped onto the small platform that I assumed the musicians had used long ago. Mordren followed.

"Thank you all for coming," I said in a voice that carried through the dusty hall. The nobles quieted in response. "As you must know by now, the High Elves who have invaded our lands have murdered King Aldrich and set themselves up as gods."

Worried murmurs started back up.

"I heard Princess Syrene is now the Queen of Elves," a dark-haired lord from the Court of Trees blurted out. "Is that true?"

"Syrene helped High Commander Anron murder the king in exchange for a position of power in the High Elves' new world order," I answered. It was almost true, anyway. I didn't want the nobles to know that the High Elves were planning to leave on their own as soon as they had enough magic. "Which means that she has allied herself with our enemies."

"Lady Firesoul," a lord from my own court began. He

inclined his head but there was a measure of hesitation on his face. "We understand that the murder of the king is terrible, but what exactly is it that you want from us?"

"We need your help." I spread my hands. "We need to get these High Elves away from our lands so that–"

The doors banged open. Clothes rustled as the whole crowd whirled around to see what had caused it. My hands shot towards my weapons, but then I froze. Anger and dread seeped through my bones as I watched a man with brown hair and pale blue eyes set into an angular face stride into the ballroom.

Lord Elmer Beaufort, my adoptive father, came to a halt in front of the crowd opposite me. Surprised whispers swept through the nobles. They were looking between the two of us, but Elmer's eyes were locked on mine.

"Kenna," he said, deliberately ignoring my title. "It seems you forgot to invite me to this meeting."

"Oh, not at all." I gave him a cold smile. "I am simply not interested in anything you have to say."

"I see," Lord Beaufort scoffed. "Well, you shall hear it anyway." Drawing himself up to his full height, he attempted to look down on me even though I stood on a raised platform on the other side of the room. "Why? Why do we need to get the High Elves away from our lands?"

Out of all the things I had expected him to say, out of all the insults and threats I had been preparing for, that statement had not even crossed my mind.

"Are you serious?" I frowned at him. "They have invaded our lands, captured our princes, and *murdered our king*. What part of that is difficult for you to grasp?"

"The part where this is of any concern to us."

The sea of nobles between us stirred in surprise, but then only turned to me as if waiting for an answer.

"How could it not be your concern as well? This is your home too, is it not?"

"Yes, it is. But you elves have ruled us humans for centuries now, as High Commander Anron and his friends have been pointing out." Elmer's eyes glinted in the torchlight. "Perhaps it's your time to be ruled."

Glass shattered. I threw my arms up over my head as the windows exploded throughout the ballroom. Nobles screamed and ran for cover while tall figures flew in through the now open windows and landed on the white marble floor inside.

My heart dropped into my stomach.

Lord Beaufort had sold us out to the High Elves.

Yanking out my blades, I called up a shield of fire around me. Dark shadows swelled beside me as Mordren did the same. From across the stampeding nobles, I locked eyes with Eilan. Valerie and Theo were trapped halfway down the ballroom by the panicking crowd, but Evander was right next to the shapeshifter.

"Go!" I screamed.

Eilan's eyes flicked to Mordren, who nodded. Just as a burst of wind barreled towards them, Eilan's arm shot around Evander and they worldwalked away. Neither of them would have been much help in a fight against the High Elves anyway.

Beside me, I felt Mordren breathe a small sigh of relief that his brother was out of harm's way. But it was short-lived.

Lightning crackled through the white hall.

The nobles screamed and threw themselves on the ground as a sizzling bolt cut through the air right towards us. I dove to the side. A *wham* echoed through the room as the lightning hit the back wall at the same time as a wave of water slammed into the dais where Mordren and I had been only moments before.

Rolling to my feet, I came up at the edge of the panicking crowd.

Sharp blue eyes locked on me.

For a moment, the rest of the world didn't exist as High Commander Anron and I stared at each other from across the chaos.

Then reality snapped back again.

Captain Vendir shot a second lightning bolt at us while the blond High Commander, Lester, threw another wave of water towards us. On the other side of the room, Anron and the black-haired commander, Danser, advanced as well.

Throwing up a wall of fire that singed the ceiling, I leaped aside to avoid the lightning bolt while the crashing water hissed into steam as it hit my flames. Alarm bells blared inside my skull as all four High Elves raised their arms for a simultaneous attack.

They stumbled a step back.

Covered in black shadows, Mordren sent another pulse of pain magic through the entire room. The nobles who were standing too close and got caught in it screamed in response, and the High Elves faltered.

I didn't have enough control over my fire magic to attack single targets in a room full of innocents, so I abandoned the idea of helping Mordren attack and instead darted towards Valerie and Theo.

The two thieves had ended up right behind High Commander Lester. Fear flickered on their faces as they tried to edge around him without drawing attention. To my left,

Idra was already wading through the chaos in their direction as well.

Roaring flames shot towards her.

I shoved a hand forward. Keeping the fire well above the humans stampeding towards the exit, I sent a wall to intercept the attack about to hit Idra. It was far from elegant, and it hit part of the marble behind too, but it smacked into the yellow flames coming for Idra's body and cancelled them out in an explosion of dark red and pale yellow.

A burst of air slammed into me.

Pain crackled through my side as I flew across the room at breakneck speed. Right before I could crash into the stone wall, black shadows shot out and broke my momentum. I bounced against the cool silken mass of darkness and instead rolled to a halt on the floor.

The involuntary flight had taken me farther away from Valerie and Theo.

Cursing under my breath, I leaped to my feet and started towards them again. Idra, on the other hand, had almost made it through.

High Commander Lester clearly knew that she could kill with a single touch because he backed away when she got closer and instead focused on throwing magic attacks at her. Moving with incredible speed and agility, she dodged the attacks as she sprinted towards him and the two thieves who had finally managed to maneuver around him.

Anron hurled another blast of air at me. This time, I saw it coming and managed to throw up a wall of flame to block it. Fire hissed and embers whirled through the air as the wind slammed into my shield.

Lightning crackled towards me.

I whipped around to see where it came from, but I already knew that I was too late.

Suddenly, the sizzling bolt flickered out as all four High Elves doubled over in pain from an attack by Mordren.

In the moment of stillness, Idra reached Theo. Her arm shot out and wrapped around him and then they were gone.

Mordren and I exchanged a glance, hoping that Idra had the same idea as we did, and then we raised a layered wall of shadows and fire between Valerie and the High Elves.

In shifting his attention to the shadow shield, Mordren's pain magic lost some of its intensity and our enemies regained control of their bodies.

Water, lightning, fire, and air roared to life from all four sides.

My heart pounded in my chest.

Keeping the shield around Valerie, I braced for impact.

Idra materialized next to the brown-haired thief. With a darted glance in our direction, Idra yanked Valerie to her just as the High Elves released their power.

Death screamed towards me and Mordren from all sides.

Valerie and Idra disappeared.

I let go of my flames and threw all my power into an escape.

Air and lightning crashed into the white marble floor.

But I was already gone.

CHAPTER 23

A three-story building made of dark wood loomed before us. I didn't recognize it, but I was in no mood to ask questions so I just stalked after Theo in sullen silence as he led us to the door.

"What is this place?" Eilan asked from behind me.

"It's a tavern," Valerie answered. "It's called the Black Emerald."

"Yeah," Theo said as he picked the lock on the door and then swung it open. "The Hands have safe houses in every court now. Including the Court of Water."

Since Lord Beaufort had sold us out, we couldn't risk staying in the Court of Stone anymore. So after a quick meetup at our previous safe house, we had gathered our things and worldwalked to the Court of Water instead. At this point, the adrenaline from the battle had begun to fade from my body, leaving only anger.

Glaring at the beautiful booths and tables of dark wood, I simply stopped in the middle of the deserted tavern and waited for Valerie or Theo to tell me where to go.

As if sensing my frustration and need to be alone, Theo cleared his throat and motioned towards a stairwell on the right. "There are lots of rooms up there. Pick any you like."

I gave him a nod and stalked towards the indicated staircase. However, before I could escape the eyes of my friends, someone grabbed my arm.

"Kenna," Evander said as he turned me back around. "Are you okay?"

"No, I'm not okay." I yanked my arm out of his grip. "If it hadn't been for all those stampeding nobles unknowingly shielding us, the High Elves would have taken us out within the first minute."

"Yes, but they didn't."

"That's not the point! We almost lost *everything* today."

Reaching out, he placed a hand on my arm. "Alright, calm down. There is no point in getting worked up about something that didn't happen."

"Don't tell me to calm down!" I slapped his hand away and then stabbed two fingers to my chest. "*My own family* sold us out. And all of you almost paid the price for that. I have every fucking right to be angry."

"But–"

"Don't," I cut him off and whirled around again before stalking up the stairs.

Rage burned through my soul and dark red flames flickered in my hair. Stomping up the wooden steps, I had to actively keep myself from hurling a firebolt at the smooth walls. Thankfully, Evander at least didn't follow me.

Picking a room at the end of the corridor, I stalked inside, lit the candles with a flick of my wrist, and then slammed my bag down on the floor. The soft thump it made as it hit the floor wasn't nearly loud enough to satisfy my anger, so I yanked out my blades and threw them down on top of it. Their metallic clanking was a bit more satisfying. Tipping my head back, I raked my fingers through my hair and forced out a breath.

The door creaked open behind me.

I whirled around, prepared to fend off another volley of calming words from Evander, but was met with an elf in a sharp black suit instead.

Mordren Darkbringer leaned his shoulder against the doorjamb.

"Are you here to tell me to calm down too?" I spat out.

He arched a dark eyebrow at me. "Why would I do that?"

"Because that seems to be the normal response when I dare to get angry."

"Suppressing feelings, and anger in particular, is never a good idea. It only makes it worse. If you feel angry, then be angry. You will feel better afterwards." Pushing off the doorframe, he took a step into the room and closed the door behind his back. "So, no, I am not here to tell you to calm down. I am here to provide you with someone who you can take out your rage on."

A humorless laugh slipped my lips. "Oh."

"So, let it all out."

"I don't even know what to say." Throwing my arms out, I shook my head. "I'm just so angry. And tired. Why does everything have to go to hell all the time? Every time I try to do something, I get my legs cut out from underneath me. Why do I always have to *fight* for everything all the time? Why can nothing ever just go my way? I'm so tired. I'm just so, so tired. I swear, I'm one more setback away from just setting it all on fire and watching everything I have built burn to the ground."

Mordren took a step closer to me.

"And I want to just scream out all my anger in an inferno of rage and flame." Throwing out my arms again, I gestured helplessly around me. "But I can't even burn anything down without actually, you know, burning it down."

"Yes, you can."

Shadows gathered inside the room. Swelling outwards, they filled the whole room with darkness until I was standing alone in the middle of what had become thick swirling black fog. I couldn't even see Mordren anymore.

"Let it all out." His midnight voice drifted through the shadows and caressed my skin. "Let it all out, Kenna. I can take it."

Relief and gratitude and... love bloomed inside me. I trusted him. I knew that if he said he could take it, then he could.

Drawing in a deep breath, I tipped my head back.

And then I screamed.

Not with my voice, but with my soul.

Dark red fire shot out all around me, searing into the darkness. It burned away the shadows in its path, but Mordren kept feeding the black mass and patching up the holes.

I poured all of my rage, all of my frustration and exhaustion and hatred for the cruel whims of fate, into the fire and I let it burn. And burn. And burn.

The shadows consumed it all.

After a while, the terrible pressure that had been trapped inside me lessened. And second by second, I could feel it all draining from me until I could finally breathe again. Until my soul felt empty. Cleared.

My long curls fell around my face as I let my head drop

forward. The fire around me flickered out, and at last, I blew out a long shuddering breath.

Gentle fingers appeared under my chin. I just drew in another deep breath while Mordren tipped my head back up. Glittering silver eyes met me.

"Do you feel better?"

I looked around the room. It looked exactly like it had when I arrived. No scorch marks. No blackened boards. It was completely untouched by the inferno I had unleashed.

"Yes." A smile blew across my lips as I looked up at Mordren. Raising a hand, I drew soft fingers along his sharp cheekbone. "Have I told you recently that I love you?"

An answering smile slid home on his face. "You have. But I might need to hear it again."

Grabbing a fistful of his dark shirt, I pulled his lips to mine and closed my eyes.

"I love you," I breathed against his mouth.

He brushed his lips against mine. "I love you too, my little traitor spy."

Wrapping his arms around me, he held me tightly. Candlelight cast dancing shadows over the walls as a warm summer breeze fluttered in through the window and brought with it the scent of sea air and blooming night flowers. I rested my cheek against Mordren's shoulder and let out a sigh.

"We almost got captured today because my family sold us out," I said at last. "And I could barely do anything about it. I'm not improving fast enough. I'm not good enough to take on the High Elves and win."

"Neither am I."

"But we have to be. Otherwise, we'll never get our friends back. Get our courts back."

"I know."

"So, what do we do?"

"We will eventually need to make a new plan for how to throw the High Elves into chaos." Mordren drew back slightly so that he could meet my gaze again. "As for what to do at this very moment? I am open to suggestions."

A small laugh escaped my throat. "Good. Then right now, I want you to distract me. I want you to make me forget that we are currently trapped in a war we cannot win."

Lifting his hand to my face, Mordren brushed his thumb over my cheek while a sly smile spread across his lips. "I see. Any particular preferences on how I should accomplish that?"

"I'll leave that entirely in your..." I raked my gaze up and down his body, "*capable* hands."

"Entirely at my mercy, huh? You may come to regret that, Lady Firesoul."

"Is that so?"

"Yes." His eyes glinted as he moved his thumb from my cheek to trace over my lips. "Because I am in the mood to hear that sweet mouth of yours moan my name and beg me for release."

A dark laugh slipped my lips. Holding his gaze, I arched one eyebrow in wicked challenge. "Well, I suggest you get started then, my prince."

Leaning down, he smiled against my mouth. "Gladly."

Lightning crackled through my skin as Mordren's lips met mine while his hand trailed down my chin and then snaked around the back of my neck. With a firm grip on my hair, he forced my head back. Candlelight gleamed in his eyes as he tilted my head and then kissed his way over my jaw and down my throat. A shudder coursed through my body.

Mordren's other hand caressed the curve of my hip and

pushed the dark fabric of my shirt slightly upwards. While his lips brushed my collarbones, his hand found its way from my waist to my stomach. I sucked in a gasp as his fingers traced the skin just above my pants, but the iron grip on my hair forced me to keep my head thrown back.

"We need to do something about these clothes," he murmured against my skin while his fingers pushed my shirt up higher.

"Yes," I gasped out.

He finally released my hair, but moved both his hands to my hips instead. Heat pulsed through me as he slid his hands down and grabbed my ass.

"Start with your shirt," he ordered as he kissed his way back up my throat.

Forcing out a shuddering breath, I gripped the hem of my dark shirt and started drawing it up my stomach while Mordren's hands followed it up my now bare skin. His distracting touch was enough to make me temporarily forget how to operate my muscles, so when his fingers brushed the bottom of my breasts, I lost my grip on the shirt and moved my hands towards his chest instead.

Strong fingers wrapped around my wrists and trapped them before I could touch him.

"Did I say you could stop?" Mordren demanded.

Holding my wrists in an iron grip, he stared me down until I started moving my hands back towards my own body. Only then did he let go.

"Finish the shirt," he ordered as he placed his lips in the crook of my neck and kissed my skin.

It sent another shiver through me. I drew in a steadying breath to force my mind back on track. With a renewed grip on my shirt, I pushed it up over my breasts. Mordren drew back only enough to allow me to pull the black fabric over my head. The shirt rustled faintly as it fell to the floor.

I raised my hand to pull Mordren back to me, but dark shadows snaked around my wrists and ankles, trapping me in place.

"Oh, I am not done with you yet," Mordren promised as he raked his gaze up and down my body. "You are still wearing far too many clothes. I want them all on the floor."

"How about a shirt for a shirt?" I bargained, and cast a hopeful look at his impeccable suit jacket.

A dangerous smile slid across his lips. "That is not how this works."

It was getting increasingly difficult to focus on anything except the way Mordren's lean muscles shifted under his clothes, but I still tried to burn away the shadows keeping me trapped. A wave of darkness washed over me in response, snuffing out the flames.

Mordren arched an eyebrow at me. I narrowed my eyes at him in response, but didn't try to use my fire magic again. After all, only minutes ago, I had seen exactly what his shadows could do to the full power of my fire.

With a smirk on his lips, Mordren walked slowly around me until he was standing behind my back. The silken black tendrils were still keeping me rooted in place, but I felt his body brush against mine as he moved into position. Reaching over my shoulder from behind, he traced his fingers over my collarbone. I shivered with pleasure.

His hand wrapped around my throat. With a firm grip, he forced my head back and then placed his lips against my ear. Faint pulses of pain flickered through my body.

"I could always make you."

After sucking in an unsteady breath, I grinned up at the ceiling. "Then make me."

A dark laugh caressed my skin. With one hand still wrapped around my throat, Mordren forced me backwards until my back was pressed against his chest. Starting at my hip, his other hand traced lazy circles over my skin.

I let out a small moan as his hand teased my breasts. My heart slammed in my chest. Just when my mind was threatening to leave reality, a flicker of pain pulsed through my body. I sucked in a gasp and my vision snapped back into focus.

"The more you disobey, the harder I will make this for you," Mordren whispered against my ear.

His fingers worked their way down my stomach and then teased the skin just underneath the top of my pants. Another shudder coursed through me. Flexing my fingers, I tried to pull my hands out of the shadows that were holding me prisoner. The hand around my throat tightened. Mordren kissed that sensitive spot below my ear at the same time as his fingers slipped below my waistline again. I trembled.

Another pulse of pain flickered through me and shattered my hazy mind.

Reality snapped back into place and I let out a pitiful moan.

"Are you ready to follow my orders?" Mordren breathed into my ear.

"Yes," I pressed out.

"Say it."

Flexing my fingers against the restraints again, I sucked in a shuddering breath. "I will follow your orders."

He smiled against my skin. "Good."

The cool silken shadows around my limbs disappeared as

Mordren released my throat and took a step back. There was a wicked smirk on his lips as he moved over to the desk. Wood scraped against wood as he pulled out the chair and lowered himself into it.

Lounging in the chair as if it were a throne, the Prince of Shadows flashed me a smug smile and raised his eyebrows expectantly. "Then strip."

Heat washed over me at his demanding voice and the hunger in his eyes. Holding his gaze, I dragged my hands down my body. When I reached the top of my pants, I paused for a second before slowly unbuckling the belt. While still keeping my eyes locked on Mordren, I slid it out of the belt loops.

It produced a soft thump as it hit the floorboards next to me.

As soon as the belt left my fingers, I started undoing the fastenings on my pants and then shifted my hands back to my hips.

With slow deliberate movements, I slid the dark fabric over my ass and down my legs.

Mordren bit his lip.

I toed off my boots before finally freeing my legs from my pants. Warm night winds blew in through the open window and caressed my body, but that was not the reason my skin prickled. It was the glittering silver eyes that raked over my now almost completely naked body. In only my underwear, I remained motionless on the floor while Mordren's gaze drank in the sight of me.

Then he looked up.

A villainous smile spread across his lips. "All of it."

My eyes widened.

In response, he leaned one elbow against the armrest,

keeping the hand raised in the air. Black shadows snaked around his wrist and twisted between his fingers as if to remind me what he could do if he wanted to.

I shook my head at him, but in the end, I slowly stripped out of my underwear too.

My cheeks flushed as I stood there, completely naked before him, while he sat fully clothed in his chair and watched me with eyes that had gone dark with desire.

"You really are beautiful," he announced.

The red on my cheeks deepened. After dragging his gaze over my curves one last time, he rose from the chair and advanced on me. I let him back me towards the wall.

As soon as my back hit the smooth wood, I reached out and yanked him the final bit to me. His graceful hands roamed my naked body while his lips at last met mine again. I wrapped my hand around the back of his neck and crushed his mouth to mine. He responded by planting a hand at the small of my back and pressing my hips to his. I moaned into his mouth.

Drawing my hands downwards, I traced the muscles of his chest before attempting to push the suit jacket off his shoulders.

Shadows sprang to life.

Mordren stole the vicious curse from my lips as he kissed me while moving my hands back and pinning them to the wall above my head. When I was firmly trapped against the cool wood, he tore his lips from mine.

"You have not begged yet," he informed me.

I yanked uselessly against the silken restraints. "I think your power trip has been quite extensive already, wouldn't you say?"

Wicked satisfaction glittered in his eyes as he leaned

forward and placed his lips against my ear. "Oh, but you will still beg."

Dark tendrils slithered around my ankles. I narrowed my eyes at the smug prince before me as he drew back enough to watch the expression on my face.

He yanked the shadow wrapped around my right ankle, forcing my legs into a wider stance. Shaking my head, I braced myself against the wave of pleasure that rolled over me as he traced his hand up over the inside of my thigh. I was *not* going to beg him.

His fingers reached my throbbing entrance.

I sucked in a gasp and yanked against my restraints.

"Beg," he coaxed.

Bucking my hips, I squirmed against the wall while drawing ragged breaths. But there would be no mercy from the Prince of Shadows. His clever fingers continued their expert movements. Lightning crackled through me, drawing moans from my treacherous lips and making my knees tremble. I yanked desperately against the shadows keeping me trapped against the wall, and a plea almost slipped out. My body shook.

Mordren's other hand shot out and grabbed my jaw in a firm grip. "Beg!"

The force of his command slammed into me and vibrated through my bones.

"Please," I gasped out. My body was trembling so hard from pleasure that I thought I was going to pass out. "Holy fuck, Mordren. Please. I beg you. I'm begging you. Please."

A midnight laugh swirled over my heated skin. Finally easing up on his mind-blowing torture, he leaned forward and stole a savage kiss from my lips. I opened my eyes to find a pair of silver eyes staring down at me.

Mordren Darkbringer smiled like a villain. "Oh, I do so love it when you beg."

"You—"

The door was shoved open.

"Kenna, I…" Evander began before abruptly trailing off.

His dark green eyes widened as he took in the scene before him. Since we were standing by the back wall, Mordren's body was thankfully blocking my nakedness. But the sight of my bare arms pinned to the wall by Mordren's shadows, and his hand around my throat, was apparently enough to transmit the gist of what was happening.

"I…" Evander began again.

"Do you fucking mind?" Mordren growled over his shoulder.

Before Evander could answer, a wall of shadows smacked into him and shoved him back into the hallway. A second later, the dark mass slammed the door shut in his face.

I let out an embarrassed laugh. Mordren released my throat and spat out a curse vicious enough to make the candles splutter in fear.

"I should cut out his bloody eyes," Mordren ground out, but he pulled back his shadows and let them disappear.

We both knew that Evander's interruption had already killed the mood. Taking a step away from the wall, I rubbed my arms.

Mordren's rage wavered as he caught the gesture. Slipping out of his suit jacket, he draped it around my naked body and then brushed a soft kiss over my lips.

"I'll let you get dressed," he said.

For a moment, he only continued leaning his forehead against mine. Then he stole one final kiss and opened his eyes before turning and making his way towards the door.

"Hey," I called.

He trailed to a halt with his hand on the door handle and turned to face me.

"I'm going to consider this a tie." I flashed him a grin and shook the black fabric around me. "Since I did manage to get you out of your suit jacket in the end."

A surprised laugh ripped from his throat.

Shaking his head, he looked me up and down while his eyes glittered with mischief. "Keep telling yourself that, darling."

Then, with one final wink, he was gone.

CHAPTER 24

*A*fter hanging Mordren's suit jacket on a hook in my room like a war trophy, I strode back into the hallway fully dressed once more.

"Hey," came Evander's voice immediately from a few doors down, as if he had been waiting for me. Stepping out into the corridor, he blocked my way to the stairs. "I'm sorry for just barging in like that, but can I talk to you?"

I blew out a sigh as I stopped in front of him. "Okay."

He glanced to the side before meeting my gaze again. "Outside?"

"Fine."

Only our footsteps broke the silence as we made our way down the stairs and towards the front door. Theo and Eilan were sitting in one of the booths on the ground floor. They looked up at us as we passed, but then went back to whatever discussion they had been in the middle of. Idra, Valerie, and Mordren were nowhere to be seen.

Warm air smelling of the sea filled my lungs as I followed Evander into the dark night.

He led us to the side alley right next to the tavern and then stopped. I came to a halt before him. The awkward silence stretched on for another few seconds.

"Are you okay?" he asked at last.

"I'm not angry about my family's betrayal and the ambush anymore, if that's what you're asking."

"No, uhm. It's not." Furrowing his brows, he scratched the back of his neck. "I..."

"I wasn't hurt in the attack," I offered since I wasn't sure where he was going with this.

"That's not..." He cleared his throat. "I mean, good. That's good. But what I was worried about was actually..."

My patience was running dangerously low so I raised my eyebrows and prompted, "What?"

He must have heard the hint of irritation in my voice because he blew out a harsh breath and threw his arms out. "I don't understand!"

"Understand what?"

"Why are you letting him do that to you?" His green eyes were wild as he stabbed a hand in the direction of the tavern. "You're the ruler of a court now."

It took me a second before I realized what he was talking about. That he was referring to the private moment between me and Mordren that he had interrupted. Another wave of irritation washed over me.

"So what? Because I rule a court now, I'm not allowed to have sex? Is that what you're saying?"

"No." Evander blushed at the directness of my words. "That's not what I meant at all. It's how he treats you."

"What are you talking about?"

"I saw what he was doing in there. Having you... pinned to a wall like that. It's not right. It's not... decent."

Blinking, I jerked back a little. "It's not *decent?*"

"No, it's not." Apparently mustering his strength, he drew himself up to his full height and crossed his arms. "You should be with someone who treats you right. Someone who is a gentleman."

"Are you saying that Mordren is not a gentleman?"

"Exactly. Because if he was, then he would be treating you with respect."

Staring at him in disbelief, I was momentarily at a loss for words. Was it just him? Or did other people also believe that Mordren didn't treat me with respect? It was such an absurd thought that I was having difficulty grasping it. If there was one person who *was* treating me with respect, it was Mordren. Sure, we had threatened and blackmailed and made each other beg on numerous occasions. But Mordren never tried to hold me back. He never tried to curb my ambition or talk me out of things, no matter how dangerous, because he trusted me to handle it. And to me, *that* was respect.

"I'm just trying to protect you," Evander said when the silence had stretched a little too long.

"I don't need protection."

"Yes, you do." He threw his arms out again while a look of genuine concern and desperation flashed over his face. "You can't see it, but he is leading you down into darkness. I'm just trying to pull you out of it."

Anger bubbled up inside me. "I have no idea what you're talking about, but who and how I choose to fuck is none of your damn business."

Evander jerked back at the harsh words. Shaking his head, he stalked past me and towards the open street. "I need some air."

Spitting out a curse under my breath, I dragged my fingers through my hair and tried to get my anger under control.

"Wow," came a voice from above. "He's really invested in your love life, huh?"

I whipped my head up and squinted against the darkness to find Valerie sitting on one of the windowsills above me. "What the... What are you even doing up there? Lurking?"

"I'm a thief," she replied, as if that was explanation enough. Which, I suppose, it was.

Letting out an exasperated laugh, I shook my head at her.

She grinned. "Come inside. We're gonna start plotting."

"Alright."

After casting one last glance towards where Evander had stalked off, I took a step right through the wall and into the tavern.

"Gah!" Theo yelped and leaped away while flapping his hands at me.

He had been on his way to the table where the others had gathered when I had materialized a mere step in front of him. Landing on the wooden floor several strides away, he stared at me with wide gray eyes before drawing his brows down.

"Gods, woman," he spluttered. "Would it kill you to give a guy a heads-up before you decide to go around appearing out of nowhere?"

Cackling echoed between the polished walls as Valerie sauntered down the stairs. "Ah, I wish I could forever save the view of you leaping away like a startled frog."

"Oh, shut up," Theo grumbled. Crossing his arms, he shot her a glare while closing the final distance to the table and throwing himself down on a chair. "You would have reacted in the exact same way."

"Bah." She swaggered over and dropped into the chair next

to him before slapping his arm with the back of her hand. "I have the heart of a wolf."

Eilan wiped a hand over his mouth to hide his smile while Idra just shook her head. I let out a soft chuckle while claiming the seat next to Mordren.

"So, how close are we to finding a way of getting those bracelets off?" Valerie asked, changing the topic before Theo could retort.

"I'm not sure," I admitted. "I haven't been back to the castle to see Ellyda since that first meeting three days ago."

When I had snuck into King Aldrich's castle, I had tried to give Ellyda and Hadeon a traveling book so that we could communicate while they were trapped inside. But it hadn't worked. Apparently, the book's magic was too weak on its own, so when Ellyda tried to use it, the bracelet sucked the magic out of the book right alongside Ellyda's powers. Which meant that I would have to physically go there every time we needed to talk.

"So I should probably go there and check on them soon," I continued. "But I'm not sure where we're at with the bracelets since we don't really know anything about them."

Valerie flashed us all a conspiratorial smile and then pulled out something sleek and black from somewhere in her clothes. "Would this help?"

We all blinked in shock at the black bracelet that dangled from her fingers.

"That's one of the High Elves' bracelets," Idra said. Her pale brows were furrowed but the tone of her voice suggested that it was more of a statement than a question.

Valerie answered anyway. "Yep."

"Where did you even get that?" Eilan asked, surprise still flickering in his eyes.

"I pickpocketed that blond High Elf Commander earlier."

"We were under attack!" I stared at the smirking thief in disbelief. "How the hell did you find the time to *pickpocket* someone?"

A victorious grin spread across Valerie's lips as she winked at us. Theo matched it and then held up a hand, which she promptly high-fived, before both of them leaned back in their chairs and crossed their arms while satisfied expressions slid home on their faces. I laughed out loud.

Amusement sparkled inside me as I shook my head at the two incorrigible thieves. I felt the final remnants of the irritation that had been swirling inside me drain away, as I pushed Evander's words from earlier out of my mind and instead focused on the present. While he had no right to comment on my sex life, we had made an effort to become friends again, so we would need to find a way to have conversations like that without both of us getting angry. I just wished that my friendship with Evander could be as effortless as my friendship with the people around this table.

"Alright," I said and held out my hand to Valerie. "I'll head to the castle tomorrow and give that to Ellyda to see if it will help her figure something out."

Valerie dropped the black bracelet into my palm and then rubbed her hands together. "Awesome. That's part one. Should we start plotting part two?"

"She's right," Eilan said. "Since we can't rely on the human nobles anymore, we need something else to distract the High Elves."

"Why can't we just kill them all?" Idra said. Impassive black eyes swept over our faces. "You get me within touching range and they'll be dead before they know it."

"I believe getting into touching range is the exact problem we cannot seem to solve," Mordren said.

"Yeah, with their ability to control all the elements," Eilan began, "and with far more power than any of us, we won't be able to get close enough to all of them for that to work. Before we can even try, we need all the other princes. And for that, we need a distraction."

"Fine." Idra flicked a lazy hand and leaned back in her chair. "We do it your way. But I will not become a slave to yet another master."

Pain stabbed into my heart at her words. No, she would not become a slave yet again. I would make sure of it.

The door swung open before anyone could reply to Idra's statement. Warm night winds whirled inside and made the candles flicker. They were followed by Evander. His green eyes found mine. I gave him a small smile and pulled out the chair next to me before motioning for him to come and sit down.

"What if we released those air serpents?" Theo blurted out while Evander made his way to the table. "That should create some chaos."

"Ha!" Valerie slapped his shoulder. "I like the way you think."

"How would that work, though?" Eilan asked.

Wood scraped against wood as Evander sat down and moved the chair a little closer to the table. I turned to face him.

"I'm sorry for getting angry before," I whispered while the others continued discussing the air serpents. "The topic just took me by surprise. I'm not exactly used to discussing my sex life with others."

A slight blush crept into his cheeks, but he nodded. "I'm

sorry too. I am worried about you, but I went about saying it the wrong way. I shouldn't have brought up... *that* like that."

"Then let's put this behind us and focus on something more important." I let a smile spread over my lips. "Like how to take down the High Elves."

"Yes, let's."

Turning back to the table, I found Mordren's silver eyes searching my face. I gave him a small shake of my head to tell him that it was nothing. If he said something, Evander would just get irritated again and I didn't have enough energy to deal with another conflict right now. So instead, I just shifted my attention to the others.

Valerie was waving her arms around and explaining some convoluted plan that would never work while Idra moved her glass out of the way and Theo shook his head. Looking at their faces, I smiled.

The High Elves had almost won today.

But now, it was time to strike back.

CHAPTER 25

Morning sunlight streamed in through the windows and illuminated the white marble table. Light glinted off the crystal goblets and pristine plates that had been set down the entire length of it, while platters containing everything from fruit to steaming meat pies were arranged along the center. From behind a smooth pillar, I watched the three spies seated together by one of the edges.

"Oh, I will never get tired of this," Monette said as she filled her glass with some kind of sparkling pink liquid. "Felix, could you pass me the strawberries?"

Felix, the copper-haired half-elf who also worked for Prince Edric, reached out to grab a small metal bowl before setting it down next to Monette.

"Imagine living like this all the time," she continued. Her turquoise eyes glittered in the sunlight as she spread her arms to indicate King Aldrich's castle. "Luxury, comfort, and no hard work to be done."

"It's—"

Ymas banged his fist down on the tabletop before Felix

could reply. Dishes rattled all along the table. The people from the Court of Trees who were sitting farther down started and cast nervous glances at the muscular elf who had caused the disruption. Even with the black bracelet blocking the magic that enhanced his strength and speed, Ymas was still strong.

"We are prisoners!" he snapped at Monette. "Not house guests."

Monette pursed her lips and swept her long blond hair over her shoulder. "For you, this might be quite the change since you have always considered yourself a free agent. But for us, this is exactly the same as living in Prince Edric's castle. Except here, our rooms are better, the food is better, and we don't actually have to work. Right, Felix?"

"Uhm..." Felix cleared his throat and cast an uncertain glance between the glaring Ymas and Monette, who raised her eyebrows expectantly. "It's... similar."

"Our prince is being held captive, our court is now a puppet state, and our magic has been stolen." Ymas shook the black bracelet on his thick wrist as if to emphasize the point while his dark eyes were locked on Monette. "If this keeps up, the High Elves might as well be gods and then we will be entirely at their mercy forever. You would do well to remember that."

"Don't talk to me as if I'm a child, Ymas. I am perfectly–"

Her sentence got cut off as I snuck to the final pillar and then phased through the wall. Silence enveloped me as I reappeared in a deserted hallway. If I was lucky, Ellyda and Hadeon would still be in their rooms. I needed to drop off the bracelet Valerie had pickpocketed and ask about the air serpents without any of the High Elves realizing that they had a spy sneaking through the castle.

Slipping through another couple of walls, I made my way towards the wing that housed their bedrooms.

Noise came from up ahead.

I edged closer to the corner and stole a glance at the corridor.

Alarm pulsed through me.

High Commander Lester sent a savage kick right into Hadeon's ribs. The force of it made the red-eyed warrior slide across the floor and crash into the wall behind him. When Hadeon tried to push himself off the floor, a High Elf soldier kicked his arm aside. Hadeon slammed back onto the marble floor. Two strides away, Ellyda thrashed in a third elf's grip as he held her firmly trapped against his bronze armor.

Placing his boot against Hadeon's shoulder, High Commander Lester forced him to stay down on the floor. "You forget yourself, *Low Elf*." He spat the final two words with venomous disdain. "You people have gotten arrogant since you fled from our lands with your tails between your legs."

Fury and panic tore through me. Every muscle in my body was screaming at me to do something. To attack. To help. But my mind was desperately trying to smother those instincts. If I intervened now, the High Elves would catch me too.

"Perhaps it's time to remind you who your masters really are," Lester continued. "And what we can do to you if you displease us."

"Don't," Ellyda called. Her voice cracked a little and her violet eyes were wild as she flicked them between her brother and the blond High Commander. "Please, don't."

"Your pathetic begging doesn't work on me."

"Please. I can... I can make you weapons," she blurted out and yanked against the hands keeping her trapped. "I'm magically gifted at forging. Please. I can make you weapons. Just... just leave him alone."

Lester's boot stayed firmly planted on Hadeon's shoulder, but his attention shifted to Ellyda. "You're gifted at forging?"

"Yes."

"What's going on here?" a powerful voice came from around the other corner.

My heart started up a nervous thumping when High Commander Anron and Captain Vendir came into view and came to a halt a few strides before Lester.

"We were just settling a disagreement," High Commander Lester said, but he took his boot from Hadeon's body. Turning, he nodded towards Ellyda. "And this Low Elf has just offered to make us weapons. Apparently, she is gifted at forging."

"Has she now?"

Hadeon had pushed himself to his feet and now opened his mouth, but a sharp glance from Ellyda made him shut it again.

"Yes," she said, her voice hard as steel. "If you leave me and my brother alone, then I will make weapons for you."

"Well, who am I to refuse such a generous offer." Anron gave her a cold smile and then snapped his fingers. "Vendir, escort Ellyda to the smithy and stay with her while she forges us something. If she can back up her claim, we will indeed honor her terms."

Captain Vendir's face was blank, as usual, but he dipped his chin to his commander and then shifted his attention to Ellyda. The High Elf soldier who had been holding her released his grip on her arms and gave her a shove in Vendir's direction. Anger flashed in Hadeon's red eyes, but he kept silent and still by the wall.

Stumbling a few steps, Ellyda shot the soldier a glare sharp enough to draw blood. But then she just straightened and came to a halt in front of Vendir.

The blond captain raised an arm to motion in the direction they had come. "This way, please."

"In the meantime," High Commander Anron said as he turned back to Hadeon, "I have a few questions for you. Come."

Without waiting for a reply, he spun on his heel and strode away in the same direction as Ellyda and Vendir. Lester and the two soldiers stared Hadeon down until he ground his teeth and followed the already retreating High Commander.

Worry flitted through me. And indecision. Ellyda was about to be stuck with the captain while she proved that she was indeed magically gifted at forging, and Hadeon was about to be interrogated by Anron. I wanted to make sure that Hadeon was alright. But I also needed to talk to Ellyda. Neither of them was in any position to speak to me right now, but I had to gamble and hope that an opportunity would present itself.

Making a decision, I snuck down the halls after Ellyda and Captain Vendir.

The route they followed did indeed lead to a rather spacious, but deserted, smithy. By phasing in and out of walls, I managed to remain undetected as I trailed them to their destination. When I knew where they were headed, I plotted a course that would take me to a small ledge up in the ceiling.

Age-old dust and metal shavings coated my clothes as I crawled forward on my stomach before stopping at the edge. A pang of nostalgia hit me. It felt as though I was back on that ledge above the kitchen, spying on Mordren's staff, while I plotted a way to blackmail him into paying off my debt for me. So much had happened since then.

"I don't know anything about forging," Captain Vendir began. "But I hope you will find everything you need here."

Ellyda only nodded in reply while surveying the forge with scrutinizing eyes.

"Hold out your hand," he said.

While still finishing her sweep of her new workstation, Ellyda held out her left hand. Vendir didn't do anything other than stare at it, but suddenly, the dark glow from the bracelet disappeared.

Ellyda snapped her gaze to it. Lifting her other hand, she rubbed her wrist. The bracelet was still locked around it, but the magic-draining effect had apparently been turned off.

"Please don't do anything stupid," Vendir said, as if Ellyda would now try to escape. His eyes were steady as he looked at her, but he sounded very tired.

Silence fell for a few seconds as she looked back at him. Then she simply turned towards the tools along the wall. "I never do anything stupid."

A surprised chuckle escaped Captain Vendir's lips. Shaking his head, he sat down on a nearby chair and watched as Ellyda began her work. From atop my ledge, I did the same.

Hissing flames and metallic clanking filled the room and lulled me into a daze as hours passed while Ellyda continued working. I shifted my position several times, but stayed where I was. To my surprise, Captain Vendir did the same. He never interrupted Ellyda. Never started up some meaningless small talk or attempted to make her explain what she was doing. All he did was sit there and watch her with his observant brown eyes.

Just when I was beginning to think that waiting him out was a lost cause, the door creaked open.

"Captain," a soldier in bronze armor said as he strode inside. "I need to speak with you."

Vendir flicked his gaze between him and Ellyda. Then he rose from his chair. "Outside."

My heart skipped a beat. This was it.

I tracked Captain Vendir as he moved across the floor. As soon as the door had swung shut behind him, I opened my mouth to call out to Ellyda. But she beat me to it.

"Kenna," she said, and her sharp eyes locked straight on me. "What news?"

"We have an unused bracelet," I said without preamble. Pulling out the black bracelet from my pocket, I tossed it to Ellyda. "It might help in figuring out how they work and how to get them off."

She caught it in both hands and glanced at it for all of one second before slipping it inside her own pocket. "What else?"

"We're going to create a distraction using the winged serpents. What do you know about them?"

"They're bred in captivity. The High Elves use command words to control them, but it's in a language I don't understand, so I don't know which words do what. There seems to be some sort of hierarchy among them, and I think Anron's is at the top. They don't like enclosed spaces, and as far as I can tell, they can get hurt." Her eyes flicked briefly to the door. "What else?"

"That's it." Worry crept into my voice as I asked, "Are you okay?"

She once more glanced towards where Captain Vendir was standing just outside the door. "I can handle him."

"And Hadeon?"

"I think his ego is more hurt than his body." She snapped her gaze to me. "You need to go. Now."

Right as the door creaked open again, I crawled backwards until I reached the wall. Ellyda had already gone back to work, looking as if she had never stopped, while Captain Vendir walked into the room again. His brown eyes searched her face for traces of trouble, but when he found none, he lowered himself into the chair once more.

I cast them both one last glance before disappearing through the wall again.

CHAPTER 26

"This is a bad idea."

"I know," I whispered. "But just hoping that it will work when we need it instead of actually testing it beforehand is an even worse idea."

Evander furrowed his brows but said nothing, as if silently admitting that I was right.

The forest lay dark and still around us. Only the occasional hooting of an owl broke the silence as we snuck between the thick tree trunks and towards the clearing farther in. Bright light from the moon painted the grass with silver streaks and illuminated our way.

Dark shapes formed a mound up ahead.

I slowed to a halt.

"They're not tied up," Idra announced as she stopped next to me.

"So there goes our plan of simply freeing them," Theo added.

"Ellyda said that there's a hierarchy." I motioned towards

the pile of sleeping air serpents. "When we do this for real, it will be Anron's serpent we're targeting. In this group, though, I'm not sure yet. But if we can figure out who the leader is here, and make that one bolt, the others should follow."

"There are a lot of ifs and shoulds in that sentence," Evander pointed out.

"So let's get rid of some then," Eilan said.

His pale green eyes swept across the sleeping air serpents. Their bodies moved slightly as they breathed, but other than that, they remained in place. Even though the moon illuminated the area, it was difficult to make out any details that could provide a clue for which animal was the leader.

"That one," Eilan announced, and pointed at one halfway across the clearing.

"How can you tell?" Valerie asked.

"See how they've positioned themselves? All of the others have formed overlapping circles around that one. They're protecting it."

"You're right," Valerie mused.

"Of course I am. Now, how about an acknowledgement of my tremendous skills?"

She snorted and slapped his chest with the back of her hand. "Don't push it."

Eilan threw her a sly smile and then turned to his brother. "Mordren, if you please?"

"Are we seriously doing this?" Evander interrupted.

"We need to know how they react," I said.

"What if they can breathe fire? Or shoot water?"

Valerie jerked her thumb in Evander's direction. "He's got a point. We should probably spread out so everyone doesn't get hit by the blast."

"That was *not at all* what I meant," Evander hissed, but everyone was already spreading out along the tree line.

"Ready?" Mordren's voice drifted through the dark woods.

The rest of us signaled that we were. Well, almost everyone, at least.

My heart pounded in my chest.

From across the grass, I watched as Mordren turned towards the group of sleeping air serpents.

And then he sent a pulse of pain magic straight at the leader.

A roar split the night.

Chaos erupted as the other winged serpents answered the cry and darted up from the ground, wings snapping in the air. Something whizzed through the night.

"Look out!" I screamed.

The tail of a long green serpent slammed into our flank. Evander and Idra went flying through the air as the hit flung them across the grass. Before I could do anything to help them, a group of beasts charged us.

Fire sprang to life around me as I yanked out my blades.

Snapping jaws and slashing claws filled the air before me as the serpents attacked.

Mordren sent another wave of pain, this one directed at all of them, but it only made them angrier. And none of them fled. All of the ones in the center just swarmed around their leader while the others went on the offensive.

I hurled a fireball at the closest one to force it back.

At the last moment, it turned its head so the flames exploded against its side.

All around me, roars and clashing blades and exploding shadows jumbled. I was vaguely aware of Mordren holding back three air serpents somewhere on my right while Eilan and Valerie were dodging between the trees on his other side. I couldn't find Theo. Or Idra and Evander.

Then the winged serpent I had attacked swung back around. Rage burned in its eyes. I threw up a wall of flame before me but it charged right through it.

Panic screamed inside me.

It was too big to fight with blades and it ran through my fire as if it were a curtain of summer rain. Leaping to the side, I narrowly managed to evade the jaw that had tried to snap me in half.

Grass crunched underneath me as I rolled to my feet and whipped around right as the beast lunged at me again. In a desperate move, I threw up my sword to shove its claws away.

The force as it struck snapped my arm to the side and I cried out in pain.

The creature roared and swung its neck around. My hand was out of position, so I couldn't block it. On instinct, I dropped down and pressed myself flat against the ground as the rows of gleaming teeth whooshed over me. The ground shuddered as the serpent stomped its feet, trying to trample me instead.

Alarm bells were blaring inside my skull as I rolled over and over to escape.

When the starlit sky was finally visible above me again, I jumped to my feet and whipped around. The beast sprang towards me. I ran.

Sprinting through the trees, I tried to escape the lethal claws and teeth coming for me. The animal let out a growl. And then it gave chase.

Feet pounded against the ground behind me with impossible speed. Wood groaned and cracked as the air serpent hurtled after me, knocking into tree trunks as I zigzagged through them. Its long tail smacked into a tree right next to me.

A scream tore from my throat and I skidded to a halt before taking off in another direction.

Fast-paced thudding sent the ground beneath my feet trembling as the great beast chased me through the dark woods. Terror crawled up my spine. That sound of something huge hunting me made my heart pound so hard that my chest ached. Blood roared in my ears.

I threw myself around another thick tree trunk right as a gigantic maw cleaved the air where I had just been. Suppressing the panic that flashed through me, I rolled forward and then leaped to my feet again before taking off in the opposite direction.

Pain shot through my side.

The far end of the serpent's tail slammed into my ribs. Night air rushed in my ears as I flew through the dark woods before crashing into a tree farther away.

A gasp ripped from my lips at the impact. I slid down the rough bark and crumpled down on the ground. Pounding feet echoed into the silence.

Fear surged up inside me. Grabbing my dropped weapons again, I struggled to my feet. My head rang and a dull ache was spreading through my ribcage.

The thudding feet sped up.

With terror fueling me, I threw my arms up. Walls of dark red fire shot up from the ground all around me until I was hidden from view by the writhing flames.

A roar came from outside as the air serpent ran towards the closest one, but I was already moving. Sprinting in the direction of the clearing, I pushed myself to go faster than my legs could carry me.

Dancing flames lit up the night behind me. Sounds of battle rose up ahead.

My lungs burned as I ran with everything I had to escape before the air serpent could figure out which direction I had picked.

A wall of shadows rose before me. My already pounding heart constricted painfully as I took in the scene.

Mordren and Idra were keeping a host of winged serpents away from the two of them and Theo and Evander. Throwing up another fire wall to aid their efforts, I skidded to a halt on Mordren's other side.

"Where's Eilan and Valerie?" I pressed out between ragged breaths. Sharp needles stabbed into my lungs with every word spoken, but I needed to know where they were before we could leave.

"We don't know," Idra called back as she dodged a swipe from a beast while trying to get her hand into position.

"They–" Theo began, but he was cut off by a yell.

"Mordren!" Eilan came sprinting out of the darkness with Valerie in his arms. "Where is everyone? We need to go. She's hurt."

My heart skipped a beat as I saw the pained expression on Valerie's face. Her shirt was soaked through with blood.

"Everyone is here." Mordren shoved a thick wall of shadows towards the attacking air serpents. "Go. Now. Imelda's."

Eilan disappeared into thin air almost before he had finished speaking.

Darkness surged up and blocked off the forest on all sides as Mordren raised even more shadows. "I said, go!"

Grabbing Theo by the arm, he worldwalked out. Idra blinked out of existence a second later.

"Evander!" I called.

He skidded to a halt next to me right as Mordren's shadow wall fell. Gleaming teeth and slashing claws rose up before us. I threw my arm around Evander.

A wave of fire roared through the woods.

And then we disappeared.

CHAPTER 27

Footsteps echoed between the walls of the small sitting room. Lingering fear and panic still bounced across everyone's faces, but it was slowly giving way to exhaustion. From my seat by the table, I watched as Eilan paced back and forth across the wooden floor.

"Brother," Mordren said, his voice gentle. "Please sit down."

Either Eilan didn't hear him, or he didn't care, because he just kept stalking up and down Imelda's sitting room. I wrapped my hands around the mug of hot tea before me in order to stop them from shaking. The sound of that air serpent thundering after me through the trees still rang in my ears.

From across the table, Idra watched me intently. Her face was an impassive mask, as it so often was. As if we hadn't just had to fight a horde of winged serpents, and were now waiting for Imelda to heal Valerie after she had gotten her back slashed up by a set of sharp talons. It was at times like these that I envied her ability to center herself. I gave her a weak smile.

Ceramic clattered as Evander almost dropped his tea cup when he tried to put it back in its saucer. Dark liquid sloshed over the edge and formed a small pond that covered the yellow flowers painted onto the white background. Clearing his throat, he dragged a trembling hand through his short brown hair.

Eilan kept pacing.

"It's not your fault," I said.

"Yes, it is." Eilan's light green eyes were haunted as he turned towards me. He was spinning a knife in his left hand. "She pushed me out of the way. We were fighting and I didn't see it coming behind us and she... pushed me out of the way. Why did she push me out of the way? Why?"

I wasn't sure if he knew that he was repeating himself. In fact, I wasn't even sure if he was talking to me or himself. He spun the knife faster in his hand.

"She'll be fine, Eilan," I said. "Imelda is healing her right now. And Theo is with her."

"She's human. I could have taken it. I *should have* taken it."

"None of us should have taken it." Prying my fingers from my tea cup, I raked them through my hair and then rested my head in my hands for a few moments. "This isn't working." I looked up and met each of their gazes. "What are we doing? We don't know enough about the High Elves to take them on."

A hint of guilt flickered in Idra's dark eyes, but she said nothing. Mordren brushed a hand over my arm. I squeezed his hand while a wave of exhaustion washed over me.

"Every time we go up against them, we only escape by sheer luck." I shook my head. "Sooner or later our luck is going to run out."

Evander pushed his cup around the small pool of tea he had spilled. "It almost ran out today. And we weren't even fighting the High Elves." He let out a bitter laugh. "We were fighting their mode of transportation."

Another wave of guilt exploded in Eilan's eyes and his step faltered as he glanced up towards the room upstairs where Valerie was being healed.

"Shut up," Mordren snapped.

Evander cut him a glare. "I have as much right as…"

He trailed off as footsteps sounded from the stairs. Everyone whipped around to face the dark-haired elf as she descended the stairs and smoothened down her apron.

"Valerie will be fine," she announced.

The air seemed to leave Eilan in a whoosh and he collapsed onto the nearest chair.

"It looked worse than it was," the healer continued. "The slashes across her back weren't too deep, but they bled a lot. I have healed them all now. She will have no permanent scars or damage from it, but she will need rest. I would recommend at least two days. Three, if you can manage to go that long without battling what looked like a gigantic beast."

We exchanged a glance, but didn't comment on how Valerie had gotten her wounds.

"Thank you," Mordren said. "I will come back with payment tomorrow."

Something like regret crept into her eyes. "No. No need, my prince."

"I insist. If you…" he trailed off. Shock flooded his eyes. "*No.*"

Wood crashed against stone.

A wall of black shadows shot up before it and blocked both

the gust of wind that had blown in the door and the people who followed it.

"Take the back," High Commander Anron snapped.

Wood scraped and clattered as all five of us shot to our feet and scrambled towards the staircase at the back of the room. I threw up a wall of flame to strengthen Mordren's barrier. Lightning crackled and boomed into our shields while the windows exploded. Shattered glass rained down over the floor.

"I'm sorry, my prince," Imelda blurted out from where she had taken cover in a corner. "I didn't want to betray you. I never would have betrayed you. But they have my daughter."

But Mordren wasn't listening. He was sprinting up the stairs after Eilan.

"Get Valerie and Theo!" Evander called and shoved me after them. "I'll hold them off for a few seconds."

Grabbing a chair, he threw it with impressive strength towards the High Elf who was climbing in through the window. As soon as the chair had left his hands, he snatched up another piece of furniture and did the same. Grunts of pain and surprise ripped from the High Elves as Evander hurled whatever he could get his hands on.

"Go!" he called.

I sprinted up the stairs. Mordren and Eilan were thundering up the steps at the front, while Idra had hung back slightly. When she saw me racing towards her, she took off as well.

The sounds of crashing furniture echoed from below. I was pretty sure that this was about Evander proving something, either to me or to Mordren, but I didn't let myself dwell on it because he was right. We needed a few seconds' head start to reach Valerie and Theo before the High Elves caught us.

Glass shattered.

On instinct, I raised a wall of fire as the window on the second floor exploded inwards as well. Mordren shoved a mass of shadows towards the flash of bronze armor that had become visible beyond it. Dropping my flames at the last second, I let it pass through. It slammed into the High Elf outside.

Up ahead, Eilan threw open the door to a small bedroom. Theo was already standing up, and he brandished a chair in front of him like a weapon, while Valerie was still lying on her stomach across the bed.

"We need to go," Eilan called.

Tossing the chair aside, Theo stepped back to allow Eilan room to get to Valerie. A moan slipped her lips as Eilan lifted her into his arms.

"The Black Emerald," he said.

And then he was gone.

Idra sprinted into the room after him right as a lightning strike crackled through the house. A moment later, the whole building rocked as hurricane winds slammed into it. I stumbled to the side and smacked into the wall. My shield of flames spluttered out.

Yanking the blond thief towards her, Idra worldwalked out with Theo.

Footsteps pounded up the stairs.

"Go! Go! Go!" Evander screamed from inside the stairwell.

"Go," I snapped to Mordren, and then sprinted towards the stairs to meet Evander.

Blood ran down the side of his face from a cut above his eye and there was an angry red bruise forming on his cheek.

The wall of shadows disappeared along with Mordren right as I slammed into Evander. He slipped and toppled backwards.

Throwing an arm around his back, I grabbed him but he pulled me with him.

Evander and I fell into the space between worlds.

CHAPTER 28

Pain shot through my side as I slammed into a table inside the Black Emerald. I sucked in a sharp breath between my teeth. Letting go of Evander, I pushed myself upright and whirled around to face the rest of the room.

A strangled moan came from Valerie. Her eyes were drooping and hazy with the aftereffects of the wound and the healing. Her torn and bloody shirt had been cut from her body and she was currently naked from the waist up. Eilan had draped his own shirt over her to shield her and was already moving towards the stairs. After checking to make sure that everyone had arrived, Theo hurried after him.

While they carried Valerie to a bedroom upstairs, I collapsed into the nearest chair. Idra drew her fingers through her silky white hair and blew out a deep breath while Evander sat down by the table where I had left him after I worldwalked us here.

Both he and I jumped when Mordren banged his fist into another table.

"Imelda," he growled out the name. "Is there no one we can trust?"

"The High Elves have her daughter," Evander said once he had settled down in his seat again.

"The High Elves have *everyone*," Mordren snapped. "Soon we will not even be able to move outside during the day without someone betraying our location to Anron."

"He's right," Idra said. She was leaning against the wall with her arms crossed. "We need to move up our timeline."

"What timeline?" I countered. "We don't even have a plan anymore. Our last two ideas were just shot to hell."

Her eyes were like bottomless pools of black water as she looked back at me. Then she gave me a small nod. "Yeah, you're right about that too."

Wood creaked as Eilan stalked down the stairs. "The plan will have to wait for another few hours. Mordren, let's go. We need to go get some supplies for Valerie. She's still in shock from everything that has happened this past hour. She needs medicine to help her sleep, and I don't trust myself to make rational decisions right now."

"Of course." Mordren fell in beside his brother as they moved towards the door. "Whatever you need." His silver eyes met mine. "Keep an eye on them. We will be back soon."

Not being able to muster enough energy to speak, I simply nodded. A warm night wind smelling of sea air whirled in through the door as Eilan shoved it open and stalked outside with Mordren on his heels. It swung shut with a soft click.

Bracing my forearms on the table, I let my head slump forward and rest against them. After two battles in one night, my nerves were raw. Panic and fear and anger were still bouncing around inside me, and I couldn't decide whether I wanted to pace around the room like a skittish horse or sleep for a week.

Evander placed a hand on my back. "Are you okay?"

"I can't even tell anymore."

"I'll take that as a no." He squeezed my shoulder. "Maybe you should get some rest."

"Yeah, I probably should." Heaving a deep breath, I lifted my head and met his gaze. "Thank you, by the way. For buying us those extra seconds to get Valerie and Theo out."

An embarrassed expression flashed across his face as he reached up and scratched the back of his neck. "Of course. Anytime."

"How did you–" Idra began but was cut off by the crashing of wood.

I shot to my feet right as a horde of elves and men poured across the threshold with weapons raised. For a moment, I could only stare, dumbfounded, at the group of assassins that faced us down. Disbelief rang inside me like a gigantic bell. The Ghosts were back.

"Oh you have got to be fucking kidding me," I pressed out at last.

Wooden splinters, sharp like blades, shot out from a blond elf's palm. I yanked out my blades and threw up a wall of fire in front of me.

"You have got to be fucking kidding me!" I screamed again.

The splinters were incinerated in the flames, but the floorboards were starting to blacken too so I extinguished the fire. Evander scrambled towards the back of the room while Idra and I stalked forward. The assassins fanned out until they formed a half-circle before us.

I gripped the handle of my blades so hard my fingers ached. Flames flickered in my hair. I wanted to burn them all to hell, but Valerie and Theo were upstairs, and I couldn't destroy this whole tavern with them in it.

Fire whooshed down along my blades.

A ripple went through the group of killers before us in response to it. Idra cast me a glance from the corner of her eye since I had never used my magic like that before, but she only continued to advance along with me.

"This is the third time someone has tried to kill me tonight," I ground out. "The third time. Tonight! My patience is at an end. So if you want to take your shot, then take your shot!"

Another volley of sharp splinters shot towards me. I slashed my sword through the air. A precise line of fire shot out and incinerated the wooden projectiles midair.

The assassins exchanged a glance.

And then they attacked.

I spun around. My blades whooshed through the air. Arcs of fire pulsed from my weapons and tore through the room towards the attackers. Beside me, Idra broke into a sprint.

Panicked screams rang through the dark wooden building as Idra Souldrinker plowed her way through the ranks of assassins while they were busy ducking the flaming scythes I threw at their heads. Using my blades was like a cheat code that helped me focus my fire magic in a way I hadn't been able to do before. I couldn't believe that I hadn't tried it sooner.

A human collapsed to the ground, unseeing eyes staring up into the ceiling, after one touch from Idra, while an elf fell screaming as a fiery blade cleaved his chest in two. Ducking under a strike from behind, I shoved out my knife. It sailed towards the attacker's stomach and a thin spear of flame shot out before it. The blade would have missed. The fire didn't.

The smell of burnt flesh clouded the air as the spear seared through his stomach, but I was already moving towards the next target. A human woman with short red hair threw a hand axe at my chest. I slashed my sword through the air. A razor-sharp band of flames shot out and split the axe handle in two. Losing its momentum, it clattered to the ground while I cut my dagger through the air as well.

Another arc of flames shot towards the stunned axe-thrower and carved a burning gorge into her chest. She fell screaming.

Whipping around, I slashed my arms through the air again and again.

Idra had left a trail of dead bodies behind her as she danced through the group of assassins.

The air was turning sour with the stench of sweat, fear, and panic. I shot concentrated bursts of fire at the attackers while circling around so that I blocked the door. Before they realized what was happening, Idra and I had trapped them between us.

Heavy thuds echoed as their bodies hit the floor one after the other.

Dark red flames flickered in my hair, lifting it up around me like a burning waterfall. My sword connected with a man's ribcage at the same time as a lance of fire shot from my knife. The elf who had been focused on Idra screamed in pain as it tore a hole through his chest.

I yanked out my sword from the other man's ribcage. It produced a wet squelching sound as it slid free. Strangled gurgling followed it.

"Not him," I called to Idra as she moved towards the last man standing. "I have questions."

Now that I knew that High Commander Anron needed me so that he could drain my magic, I knew that he couldn't have been the one who was also trying to kill me. It would be incredibly counterproductive to his goals. Which meant that someone else was behind these assassination attempts.

Spinning my blades, I advanced on the assassin.

He was lean and wiry, with sandy blond hair and a vicious look in his eyes. Raising his blade, he prepared to go down swinging. I had no intention of allowing him to do that, so I sent a scythe of fire that cut his sword off at the handle.

Shock slammed home on his face as the blade fell to the floor, producing a metallic clattering. His moment of stunned surprise cost him dearly as Idra rammed a fist into his stomach. He doubled over, gasping for air, but she was already dragging him towards a chair.

Still holding on to my burning blades, I stalked after them.

The assassin struggled against Idra's grip, but she hit him again before tying him to the chair using a decorative rope from the green curtains.

"Who sent you?" My voice came out cold and flat. "And this time, don't give me some bullshit about not knowing. I might have fallen for it last time, but there's no way you would accept this kind of contract without knowing who's behind it."

The glaring assassin struggled against the restraints but said nothing.

"I have already played this game with one of your people." Stopping before him, I stared him down with eyes that burned with dark flames. "I tortured him quite extensively before I killed him. People have tried to kill me six times since then. Six. You have one chance to answer, or this is going to get really ugly, really fast. Because my patience ran out five hours ago." I placed my burning sword against his shoulder. "So I will ask again. Who sent you?"

Hesitation flickered in his pale eyes.

I pushed the flaming blade through his shoulder.

Deafening screams bounced between the dark walls, and the assassin thrashed in his chair. I looked down on him with cold eyes. Then I yanked the sword back out.

Another cry ripped from his throat.

"The fire instantly cauterizes the wound, which means that you won't die of blood loss," I informed him. "So we can do this for a while, if you want."

Hate filled his eyes as he stared up at me.

"No?" I shrugged. "Well, let's just skip ahead then." Raising the sword, I positioned it in front of his right eye. "Tell me who sent you, or I will burn out your eyes one at a time."

Pure terror flooded his face.

"Have it your way," I pressed on before he could answer.

"No!" he screamed. "Please, no. I'll tell you. I'll tell you whatever you want."

Pausing with my fiery blade right in front of his eyeball, I cocked my head. "Then answer. Fast. Who is paying you to kill me?"

"Lord Beaufort," he gasped out. "It's Lord Elmer Beaufort."

Silence so loud it was deafening descended over the room. I stared at the sandy-haired assassin. Fire hissed from my blades.

"Lord Beaufort?"

He yanked against his restraints but nodded. "Yes."

"You accepted a contract *from my adoptive father* to kill me?"

"Yes."

"Why?"

"He didn't say."

My hand dipped, lowering the sword from his eye to his throat. "I meant, why did you accept the contract?"

Lifting his shoulders awkwardly against his restraints, he shrugged. "Because it was money."

A humorless laugh slipped my lips. "I see. Well, I hope it was worth it."

I studied the expression on his face as I slowly pushed the burning sword through his windpipe. He choked. Hissing flesh and gurgling mingled as the blade burned its way through while also cutting off his air. My red eyes were cold and distant as I watched him die.

When his eyes at last glassed over, I stood there for another few seconds before pulling out the sword again and extinguishing the flames.

Ringing silence filled the tavern.

I was vaguely aware of Theo watching us from the stairwell as I turned to Idra. "I have to go."

She only nodded in understanding and stepped aside.

"Kenna, wait," Evander called.

He had taken cover behind a table farther in, but now took a step towards me. I looked back at him with impassive eyes. My soul felt numb.

"Wait," Evander said again. "We need to talk about this."

"No," I said simply.

And then I worldwalked away.

To the Beaufort family's mansion in the Court of Stone.

My former home.

CHAPTER 29

The white marble mansion sat like a pale jewel in the dark countryside. Warm night winds ruffled the grass and brought with them the scent of soil and summer flowers. Halfway to the front door, I noticed that I was still holding on to my blood-smeared blades and that my hands were stained red as well. But then I realized that I didn't care, so I just walked through the door without doing anything about it. My boots left footprints of dirt and blood on the shining white floor as I stalked into the living room.

Everything looked exactly like it always had. Clean. Pristine. And unwelcoming.

Coming to a halt in the middle of the open floor, I just stood there and took in the house that had been my first home. Where I had been taught to always put other people's needs ahead of my own. Where I had been taught to always read every shift in the mood around me to see if I had upset someone. Been taught that love was not unconditional. That I was not enough. Standing there, I let the memories of this house wash over me.

I hadn't quite decided yet if I was going to burn it down.

"Elmer Beaufort!" I bellowed at the dark and silent mansion. "Your day of reckoning is here. Come down and face me."

Exclamations of shock came from upstairs. Furniture banged and items clattered to the floor. Then, running footsteps sounded.

Without even turning to look, I lit every single candle in the room. Light flooded the space and reflected off the shining marble surfaces.

"Kenna, what is the meaning of this?" Lord Beaufort demanded as he stomped into the living room.

My mother hurried after him. Both of them were dressed in their nightclothes. Impeccable gowns of white fabric fluttered around them as they moved.

"Kenna, dear, why are..." Lady Adeline Beaufort trailed off as her dark blue eyes fell on the blood-stained weapons in my hands.

"You tried to kill me," I said simply.

Patricia, my half-sister, scurried inside the room as well and took up position next to her father before saying, "We have been sleeping. Not running around town like some kind of outlaws."

"Oh, I know. You would never deign to get your own hands dirty." I swept my gaze over the three of them. "Instead, you paid a group of assassins to kill me."

"Clearly they did a shit job of it," Lord Beaufort spat out.

"It's true?" The stunned voice that came from the hallway belonged to my half-brother Elvin. He had somehow found the time to put on a pair of pants and a shirt before going downstairs, but his pale blue eyes were wide with shock as he moved into the living room. "You tried to have her killed?"

"Of course we did." He scowled at his son. "What did you expect?"

"We didn't want to burden you with it," my mother added.

"You knew?" Elvin gaped at his mother before sweeping his gaze over his father and sister as well. "Did all of you know about this?"

Adeline had the good grace to look apologetic, but Patricia only mirrored her father's look of disdain and crossed her arms as if she wasn't at all embarrassed to admit that she had known about it.

"Why, Father?" Elvin raked his fingers through his short red hair and shook his head. "Why would you do something like that? There is absolutely no logic in it."

It wasn't exactly a declaration of love, but I hadn't been expecting one either. My half-brother had never been one for feelings. Facts and statistics had always been more his thing.

Since I actually wanted to hear how Lord Elmer was going to justify this to his son, I only cocked my head and watched the Beaufort family as they faced off against each other with three on one side and Elvin on the other.

Lord Beaufort raised his chin and flicked a dismissive hand in my direction. "Because we can't allow someone like her to have the kind of power she has."

"It's nothing personal, Kenna dear," my mother added, as if that would soften the blow of finding out that my own family had hired assassins to kill me. Wringing her hands, she sent me a pleading look. "It's just... if we let it continue like this, our social standing will be damaged beyond repair and the other noble families would eventually ostracize us."

I frowned at her. "Because your daughter is now the Lady of Fire?"

Elmer slammed his fist down onto the table, making my

mother jump. "Because my wife's bastard is now bossing us around!"

"*That* is the reason you tried to kill her?" Elvin stared at him. "Father, how could you possibly think that this was the best course of action?"

"My son, always the pragmatist," Lord Beaufort spat. Drawing himself up to his full height, he shook his head. "When will you learn that sometimes you have to do what feels right, and not what is most logical."

Next to him, Patricia looked down her nose at her brother as if she agreed. Adeline flicked nervous eyes between Elmer, Elvin, and me. Or more precisely, the blades in my hands.

"You're wrong," Elvin said. It sounded like he had just come to that realization himself. An expression of sudden understanding and regret drifted over his face as he looked at his father and shook his head. "I used to think that you knew everything. When you told me that Kenna was dangerous, I believed you. I helped you drug her and tie her up so that you could give her back to Prince Edric when she was on the run, because you said that it was the best course of action. But just because you're my father it doesn't mean that you know what is best."

"Yes, it does. I have lived much longer than you and I always know what is best."

"No." Tiredness blew across Elvin's face as he shook his head again. "You never did know when to walk away. Your gambling is the reason we almost became homeless last year."

"That has nothing to do with this."

"It has everything to do with this! Because if Kenna hadn't bailed us out, we would have ended up on the street. But still you told me that she was dangerous. That she couldn't be trusted. And still I believed you."

"Because she is dangerous!" Spit flew from his mouth as he stabbed a hand towards my bloody weapons. "Because she can't be trusted."

"And then you started gambling again," Elvin pressed on as if he hadn't said anything. "And you lost. Again. Because you acted on feeling. You can't act on what feels right, Father. You have to act on logic, reasoning, odds."

"Don't lecture me, boy."

"If I hadn't started counting cards, we would have been homeless again right now!" Elvin screamed back. Frustration shone in his pale blue eyes as he swung out his arm to motion at me. "And now, I find out that you've used the money I've won back for us to try to kill Kenna. She's an elven prince in all but name. She killed Volkan Flameshield, for gods' sake! And now she *rules the Court of Fire*. She could make our lives a living hell if she wanted to. She could burn down our home with a snap of her fingers. And there is nothing we could do to stop her. And quite frankly, after what we've done to her, I'm surprised she hasn't already. We should be trying to get back into her good graces, not trying to kill her!"

"Burn down our home?" Lord Beaufort scoffed before turning to me with a vicious look in his pale blue eyes. "She can try. It has withstood centuries and it's made of the finest marble."

A razor-sharp smile slid home on my lips. "Everything burns if you try hard enough."

He spit out a scornful laugh, but Adeline and Patricia cast nervous glances at the dark red flames that played in my hair. Grabbing Patricia by the arm, Lady Beaufort pulled her daughter with her as she edged a step backwards towards the door. I shifted my gaze to them.

A wall of fire roared to life.

Both of them yelped in shock and fear as a flaming barrier appeared in the doorway, cutting off the way out of the room. It didn't touch them. And it wasn't hot enough to do any real damage to the marble floor and walls, but it served a psychological purpose. They wouldn't leave. Unless I allowed it.

"All you have ever done is bring misery to my family." Lord Beaufort puffed his chest up and looked at me as if I were an insect. "And I am not sorry for trying to kill you."

A gasp ripped from my mother's lips. Her scared eyes darted between me and her husband while she dragged Patricia towards one of the pale blue sofas. As if that would protect them if I decided to act on the rage burning in my soul.

Lord Elmer Beaufort held my gaze. "My only regret is that I didn't kill you when you drew your first breath."

The saddest part of all was that his words didn't even hurt. A calm sense of certainty spread through my cold heart. I was done with abuse. Done with being made to feel worthless. Done with literal assassination attempts. He might have been my adoptive father, but enough was enough.

"Well, I suppose you should have." Fire whooshed down my blades as I took a step towards him. "But now, it's too late."

"No." Elvin's voice was gentle as he stepped out in front of me and blocked my way to his father. Pleading blue eyes met me. "Please."

"Don't you dare try to bargain with her," Lord Beaufort growled from behind his back.

I kept my eyes on my half-brother. "He doesn't deserve your protection. Or my mercy."

"I know. After everything he has done, after everything *we* have put you through, your revenge is more than justified. But I will still ask you..." Elvin swallowed. And then he lowered himself to his knees before me. "I will still *beg* you to show mercy."

"He has tried to kill me too many times."

"I know. I know that you hate him. To be honest, I think I hate him too right now." He looked up at me with desperate eyes. "But he is still my father. And I know that he doesn't deserve it, that none of us deserve it, but I'm still begging you to spare his life. And if not for his sake, then please do it for me."

"If I let him live, he will just try to kill me again."

"No. No, he won't. I will make sure of it. I will make sure that he never does anything like this ever again. And if he ever were to try it, I would deliver him to you myself. Him and me. And then you can take your vengeance on both of us."

Only the crackling curtain of fire from the doorway broke the silence that fell over the white marble room as I looked down at Elvin.

"Please." He sat back on his heels and rested his palms on the floor before bowing his head. "Please, Lady Firesoul."

I dragged my gaze from my half-brother and took in the rest of the room. Tears ran down my mother's cheeks where she stood with one arm wrapped around Patricia's shoulders. My half-sister, on the other hand, looked back at me with a mix of hatred, envy, and fear on her face.

Behind Elvin's back, Lord Beaufort was staring at the two of us. He looked truly horrified by the sight before him.

I locked eyes with my adoptive father.

"If you ever do anything against me or my friends again, I will come back and burn this house down with you in it."

Without even bothering to wait for a reply, I strode towards the doorway and walked out right through the curtain of flames.

CHAPTER 30

"Are they dead?"

Striding in through the door to the Black Emerald, I found three people turning to face me. Mordren and Idra stood in the middle of the now empty floor while Evander, who had been sitting on a chair by the door, shot to his feet as soon as I entered. Before I could reply to Evander's question, the air vibrated slightly and then Eilan materialized next to Mordren and Idra. Presumably after having helped them worldwalk all the dead bodies away, since the only thing that remained of the battle were the bloodstains on the wooden boards.

I dragged my impassive gaze to Evander. "To me? Yes."

Horror flashed on his face.

"But they're still breathing, if that's what you're asking," I finished.

"You didn't kill them?"

"No."

"Why not?" Idra asked.

There was absolutely no judgment in her voice. In fact, it

sounded more like... professional curiosity. And that thought was enough to jolt me out of my numbness.

When that sandy-haired assassin had confessed that it was Lord Beaufort who was behind the attacks, my heart had taken a savage blow. And without me even realizing it, my mind had tried to protect me the way it usually did. By shutting off my emotions. But the notion that Idra was genuinely curious, from one killer to another, why I hadn't murdered my family was so ridiculous that it snapped me out of the dazed state I had been in. So I let the feelings back in.

My heart started cracking again. But I let it. I had every right to feel hurt. So I allowed myself to feel all the pain of yet another betrayal. And I recognized it. Recognized that broken-hearted little girl deep inside me who had been desperate for someone to love her, and who still hurt when her family once more showed her how much they hated her. I felt it. I recognized it. I accepted it. And then I moved on.

Feeling my usual self return, I shifted my gaze to Idra and flashed her a sly smile. "Because now Lord Beaufort has to live knowing that the only reason he is still alive is because of my mercy. Because I decided to show them mercy after his only son and heir got down on his knees before my feet and begged me to spare his father's life. They're worried about their social standing? Let's see them try to survive that shame."

A slight smirk played over Idra's lips. "Smart."

"Right?" I shrugged while closing the distance to her and the two black-haired brothers. "I also told them that if they ever crossed me again, I would burn down their house with them in it."

Mordren let out a dark chuckle. "Effective." Wrapping an arm around my shoulders, he kissed my temple. "I like it."

"No," Evander snapped from by the door. "No! Not smart. Or effective. Or good." Taking a step towards me, he stabbed a hand at the bloodstains on the floor. "Can we talk about what happened here tonight?"

"What's there to talk about?" I stepped out of Mordren's embrace and frowned at Evander. "My family sent a group of assassins to murder me. We killed them. And then I went to my family and threatened them into never trying to assassinate me again."

"You tortured someone! Again. And then threatened to burn out his eyeballs."

Mordren glanced down at me. "You did?"

"Yeah. It was very effective."

"Sorry I missed it."

"You tortured someone," Evander repeated even louder, as if to drown out Mordren's interruption. "And then you worldwalked away to *murder your own family.*"

"I know. Isn't that what I just said too?"

"You seriously don't see anything wrong with that?"

"They tried to kill me! How was I supposed to have reacted?"

"I don't know. But not like *this.*" Fury flashed in his green eyes as he stalked straight for Mordren. "This is all your fault!"

It took me by surprise, so all I did was watch as Evander advanced on Mordren. Both Idra and Eilan only stared at him in silence as well. Lifting his arms, Evander made as if to shove the Prince of Shadows backwards.

Dark shadows shot out.

Evander's movements froze halfway through as black tendrils wrapped around his wrists.

Tension crackled through the room.

Taking a single step forward, Mordren Darkbringer leveled cold eyes on the elf before him. "Put that hand on me and your pain receptors will feel the full power of my magic. And then I will stand here and watch as you writhe on the floor in agony until your mind shatters."

A hint of fear flickered over Evander's face, but it was quickly replaced by anger. "This is what I'm talking about!"

Trying to take a step back, Evander yanked against the shadows around his wrists. Mordren stared him down for another few seconds before finally releasing him. I was just about to intervene when Evander pressed on.

"This is all your fault," he growled at Mordren and then stabbed a hand in my direction. "When I met her, she was selfless and kind. But then she met you. And now she does things like *this*." Swinging his arm around, he motioned at the bloodstained floor. Hatred burned in his eyes as he shook his head. "She was perfect. And you ruined her."

Utter disbelief clanged through me. For a moment, I only stared at him while my mind refused to process what he was saying. Then it caught up.

Rage roared inside me.

"This is who I am." Dark red flames flickered in my hair as I threw my arms out. "This has always been who I am."

"No, it's not," Evander snapped back. "When we first met, you cared about other people. You helped Monette and your family even though you didn't have the time or money to do it. You did good things."

"And then I realized that they were just using me without actually giving something back."

"That's what I'm trying to say! You only started thinking like a selfish and cruel person after you met *him*." He pointed an accusatory finger at Mordren. "No, Monette and your family might not always have deserved your help but that's what makes someone a truly good person. They help regardless of whether the other person deserves it or not. And you used to do that. When we first met, you were *a good person*. But now he is turning you into someone you're not."

"He's not turning me into anything. I have already told you. This is who I am!"

"No, when we first–"

"Don't you get it? When we first met, I was playing a part. Come on, Evander, we've already been through this. We were both playing each other to get information."

"I know, but it doesn't matter. This person he's turning you into isn't the real you."

"Yes, it is." Massaging my forehead, I forced in a deep breath to calm myself before continuing. When I met Evander's gaze again, I shook my head at him. "That girl who giggled and stumbled so that you would catch her with your strong arms and who boosted your ego by letting you teach her how to throw darts... She isn't real. *She* is the fiction. Yes, I might have helped everyone who asked for it at the expense of my own health and happiness, because that was how I was raised. But I also spent most of my teenage years blackmailing ordinary people for money. I have always been this ruthless."

"It's so sad that you can't even see it. If you would just step out of his shadow then–"

"Evander," Eilan interrupted, speaking for the first time since I got back. His voice was calm and smooth, but there was a sharp glint in his pale green eyes. "Perhaps it would be best if you took a walk so that everyone has a chance to clear their head. I don't think this conversation is getting anywhere right now."

For a moment, it looked like he was about to argue, but

then Idra crossed her arms. Evander flicked his gaze from Eilan to her.

"Fine," he spat out. "But you know I'm right."

And with that, he stalked out the door and disappeared into the dark night.

I collapsed into the nearest chair and, to my horror, felt tears sliding down my cheeks. Reaching up, I angrily wiped them off. Wood scraped against wood as the three lethal elves around me sat down at the table as well.

It was only then that I noticed the dark red flames still flickering in my hair. I extinguished them. I would have to do something about that. It was a dead giveaway for when I was angry or upset.

"I have had enough of confrontation for one night," I muttered to no one in particular. "In the past few hours, we have fought *three* battles. Air serpents. High Elves. Assassins. And then I had to face my family. And now this." Dragging a hand through my hair, I blew out a frustrated breath. "I need a fucking glass of wine."

Eilan leaned back in his chair and casually twirled the knife in his left hand. "I could stab him for you."

"I could torture him," Mordren offered.

"I could kill him," Idra added.

"Did someone say wine?" Valerie called from the stairwell.

Surprised laughter echoed between the smooth wooden walls as we all turned to face the two thieves who were descending the stairs. Valerie was holding on to the railing instead of sauntering down as she usually did, and Theo watched her with an expression that was half exasperation and half worry.

Making her way to the table, she dropped into the chair next to Eilan while Theo disappeared towards the kitchen.

"Man, I'm not even gonna ask." She chuckled and winked at me. "Because, you know, I already heard everything. You guys are *loud*."

Another ripple of laughter went through the room, draining the lingering tension.

"I mean, she has a point," Theo announced as he returned and deposited a mass of glasses and bottles on the table. "Though, given the topic, I think not using your indoor voice was kind of justified."

"Thanks." I chuckled and then picked up one of the bottles. My eyebrows rose as I studied the label. "This is some really expensive whiskey."

"Well, yeah. We're thieves." Valerie grinned at me from across the table. "Did you really think we wouldn't have top-shelf liquor lying around in every safe house?"

Theo dropped into a chair as well and tipped his head in Valerie's direction. "What she said."

"So…" She rubbed her hands. "What's the new plan?"

"What plan?" Eilan stared at her in bewilderment and then waved a hand in her direction. "And what are you even doing up? You're supposed to be resting."

"I'm sitting down, aren't I?" She gave him a small shake of her head as if that was the silliest thing she'd ever heard. "And I'm talking about the plan for how to distract the High Elves since the air serpents will apparently bite our heads off, literally, if we try to disturb them."

When Eilan was about to protest, Theo leaned towards him and mumbled, "Trust me, this is her version of resting."

"Yeah, unless you wanna handcuff me to the bed," Valerie said and wiggled her eyebrows at Eilan.

The shapeshifter's face flushed an alarming shade of red. From his chair next to Eilan, Mordren snickered, which made the blushing elf smack him in the ribs with the back of his hand. Pretending to be entirely unaffected by the blow, Mordren only continued to smirk while Idra shook her head.

Eilan cleared his throat. "So, the plan?"

"Oh!" Valerie blurted out. "What about our original plan?"

I frowned at her. "What…?" Then realization dawned. "Oh. *Ohh*. That might actually work."

"Care to fill in the rest of us?" Mordren prompted.

While Valerie launched into a rather convoluted explanation that I would definitely have to clarify later, I tried to keep my attention on the five people around the table and not on the one that had stormed out the door.

Evander's words bothered me more than they should. I meant what I had said to him. I had always been this ruthless. The only difference was that I had never before been put in *this* many extreme situations one after the other. Situations that required me to be ruthless. Over and over again. So I wasn't changing into a different person. I was only showing my true self more often.

And as for his claim that I had been a good person before, but that I wasn't anymore… that was wrong. I still cared about people, I would still do everything I could to protect my friends, and I never killed or hurt others just to be cruel. Evander was wrong.

I could be both ruthless and a good person at the same time.

Couldn't I?

CHAPTER 31

The door vibrated as someone rapped their knuckles on the dark wood. I already knew who I would find on the other side, so I blew out a long sigh and rolled out of bed. Another knock came. After pulling on a pair of pants and a shirt, I closed the final distance to the door and swung it open.

"Kenna, I..." Evander trailed off as his eyes drifted from my face to the bed behind me.

Twisting slightly, I followed his gaze.

Bright morning sunlight streamed in through the window and fell across the lethal body of Mordren Darkbringer. His lean muscled chest and chiseled abs were visible above the white sheets where he lay propped up on one elbow. A slight smirk played over his lips.

"Am I interrupting?" Evander finally asked.

"No," I answered at the same time as Mordren said, "Yes."

I shot him a glare before moving into the hallway with Evander and closing the door behind me. Without the light from the window inside the room, the corridor was suddenly gloomy. From downstairs, the sound of clanking pots and clinking plates drifted up and disrupted the silence.

For a moment, Evander and I only watched each other. Then I opened my mouth, but he beat me to it.

"I'm sorry," he blurted out. Raising a hand, he scratched the back of his neck while a sheepish look flashed over his face. "I feel like all we ever do is fight and apologize to each other."

"Yeah, I've started to feel that way too."

"But you were right last night. I have been trying to hold on to a version of you that doesn't exist. I was so convinced that Mordren was turning you into someone you're not. That he was making you do things and doing… things to you that you didn't want. But now I've realized that you actually like it. That this is actually who you are. And I'm just sorry it took me so long to realize it."

"Thanks." I gave him a small smile. "And for what it's worth, I don't actually like torturing and killing people."

"No, I know." He cleared his throat while his eyes darted towards my door and the Prince of Shadows who waited in my bed behind it. "I meant the other… *things* we've fought about before."

"Oh. Right. Well, thanks. And I'm sorry too. For yelling at you last night. I know this past week hasn't been easy."

A brittle laugh escaped his throat. "No, it really hasn't. Being on the run, moving from place to place," he gestured at the building around us, "sleeping in a thief's safe house, being hunted and attacked, waking up every morning wondering if this is the day I die… It's just not something I'm used to."

I was about to say 'me neither' but then stopped myself when I realized that this actually wasn't my first time being in a situation like this. So instead, I gave him my most reassuring smile. "I know. But hopefully, it will soon be over. We're breaking into the castle tonight."

He jerked back and blinked at me in shock. "Tonight?"

"Yeah, we received word that Anron and the others will be in the Court of Fire to… well, take over my court more firmly, I suppose. So we're going to use that opportunity to meet up with the others inside and properly explain what the plan is now." When hesitation drifted over his face, I added, "But you don't have to come if you don't want to. I realize that breaking into the High Elves' stronghold probably is one more thing that you would rather not be doing. So I understand if you want to stay here with Valerie and Theo. The rest of us can handle it."

"I…" Evander flicked his gaze up and down the corridor and chewed his lip. Then he apparently made up his mind because he stood up straighter and gave me a decisive nod. "No, I'll come too. I want to help make sure this all ends soon."

"Okay, good." I hiked a thumb towards my room. "We fought three battles yesterday, so I'm going to use the time until tonight to rest. If I were you, I'd do the same."

His eyes drifted to my closed door again. "Rest… Right, yeah, that sounds like a good idea."

Reaching out, I gave his arm a squeeze as I moved back to my door. "I'll see you tonight then."

"Yeah, see you tonight."

The distracting sight of a half-naked Prince of Shadows met me when I finally closed the door behind me again. Mordren was sitting up in my bed, his back resting against the headboard, the sheets only covering him from the waist down. I released a long breath and ran a hand through my hair.

"Do you want me to torture him into showing some

manners?" Mordren's eyes glittered mischievously as he arched an eyebrow at me. "Or would you like me to watch while you do it?"

A surprised laugh slipped my lips. I made an effort to shake my head at him, but couldn't quite hide the grateful smile on my mouth, as I stripped out of my clothes again and climbed back into bed.

"No, he, uhm..." Wood creaked slightly as I maneuvered myself into position next to Mordren, who scooted down from the headboard and lay down as well. "He apologized."

"Good." Mordren wrapped an arm around me and pulled me closer so that my cheek rested against his chest. "Then he gets to keep his tongue."

"I would laugh but I know you're serious."

"I am. I know that you are perfectly capable of taking care of yourself, which is why I have not intervened, but being forced to stand by and watch as someone makes you feel bad about who you are is growing increasingly difficult."

"Based on what he said in the hallway just now, I don't think he'll do something like that again."

"Like I said, good. Because then he gets to keep his tongue."

That time I did laugh. Lifting a hand, I gave his annoyingly chiseled abs a swat that he pretended not to feel. Instead, he leaned down and kissed my forehead.

"Do you think he was right, though?" I asked, not meeting his gaze. "That I'm too ruthless to be a good person?"

Mordren brushed a loose curl from my cheek and hooked it behind my ear. "I think the world is far too complicated to be divided into simply good and bad people. Take us, for example. You, me, Volkan, Syrene, Anron. Have you noticed that, at the end of the day, we all want the same thing?"

"Power," I filled in.

"Yes. Volkan wanted to stay in power, so he murdered my parents to make sure that the Court of Shadows would not be too much of a threat. You wanted power, so you killed Volkan. I want power, so I have Eilan find out people's secrets and then I use that and my pain magic to make people fear me. Syrene wanted power, so she made a deal with the High Elves and helped them kill King Aldrich. Anron wants power, so he steals our courts and forces us to wear those bracelets so that he will have enough magic to overthrow the emperor in his homeland. When it all comes down to it, we are all the same. So who is to say which side is good and which is evil?"

Tracing the muscles of his chest, I was silent for a while. "You're right. That actually makes a lot of sense."

His hand found my chin and tipped my head up so that I finally met his gaze. Then he arched a dark brow at me. "What is with the tone of surprise?"

I laughed, feeling the heaviness in my chest disappear, and then winked at him. "Well, after all the times I've outsmarted you, I keep forgetting that you're actually pretty intelligent."

"Is that so?"

"Hmm."

The bed creaked as he released my chin and rolled over. Pushing me down against the mattress, he straddled my hips while taking my wrists in a firm grip. His muscles shifted as he forced my arms down and pinned them to the bed on either side of my head.

"Then perhaps I need to remind you what exactly I can do when I put my mind to it," he said, his voice dark with both desire and threats.

"Do you really think that's wise?" I flashed him a wicked

smirk. "After we have just established that I'm a ruthless person too?"

"Yes. Because you see..." Mordren leaned down and placed his lips next to my ear before finishing in a whisper. "I think your ruthless streak is hot as fuck."

A shudder of pleasure coursed through my body. Biting my lip, I arched my back and pulled against the strong hands keeping my wrists trapped.

Mordren's lips brushed over my jaw as he kissed his way towards my mouth. I bucked my hips against him. When he reached my lips, he drew back and locked eyes with me.

The seriousness of his gaze made my breath hitch.

Then a wicked smile spread across his lips and he spoke words that vibrated into my soul.

"You are perfect just the way you are, my ruthless little traitor spy."

CHAPTER 32

*O*nly a few High Elves had been left to guard the king's castle and the numerous people who were kept there as involuntary guests. Though given the fact that the only way off the mountain was by air serpent or worldwalking, and everyone who was able to do so already had their magic blocked, it didn't pose any great risk to Anron and his ilk. It did, however, make it easier for us to sneak inside.

"I'll watch this side of the hallway," Idra whispered as we reached the corridor that housed Hadeon and Ellyda's rooms.

"I'll take the other side, then," Evander said and motioned in the opposite direction.

"Alright, we'll be quick." I gave them both a nod. "If anything goes wrong, warn us and then run. The same way we got in. First priority is getting out. We can meet up afterwards." While following Mordren and Eilan towards Hadeon's room, I briefly met Evander's gaze. "Evander, make sure to stay with someone who can worldwalk."

He nodded. "Yeah."

We didn't expect the High Elves to attack us tonight. After all, we already knew that they were currently in the Court of Fire. But none of us had survived this long by being careless either, so it was always best to be prepared in case things went sideways.

Torchlight flickered over shining white walls as we crept closer to our target. Nothing moved apart from the three of us and Evander, who settled into position at the far end of the hall, but I still suddenly got a bad feeling about the whole thing. Perhaps we shouldn't have risked coming here. I knew that Mordren and Eilan wanted to, no *needed* to, see Ellyda and Hadeon to make sure that they were okay, but I suddenly couldn't help feeling that this was a mistake.

My heart was thumping in my chest when Eilan pushed down the handle and cracked open the door to Hadeon's room.

There was a beat of silence.

"He's not here," Eilan whispered at last.

"Shit," I swore under my breath. "Check Ellyda's room."

We snuck farther down the corridor. When we reached the door to Ellyda's room, we all paused outside it for a moment. No movement. After exchanging a glance with us, Eilan pushed down the handle and edged it open.

"Are you serious? It's Mordren *and* Kenna," Hadeon's voice hissed from inside. "Of course they have a plan."

"But how is that going to help us if we don't know what it is?" Prince Edric grumbled back.

"I'm telling you, they'll be here. Anron and the others are gone for the night, there's no way they won't take that opportunity."

"Well, you're right about that," Eilan announced as he pushed open the door and strode inside.

Furniture scraped against the floor as the room's occupants shot to their feet and whirled towards the door. I rolled my eyes at Eilan's dramatic entrance, but followed him and Mordren into the room.

"Told you," Hadeon said in a smug voice.

He was standing next to the Prince of Stone in front of a couch they looked to have been sitting on only moments before. Ellyda was curled up in an armchair by the wall, reading a book about forging techniques. Where she had gotten that, I had no idea. Prince Iwdael and Rayan had probably been sitting opposite them but they now stood facing us as we moved inside.

"This is very risky," Prince Rayan said.

Mordren ignored him completely as he strode straight for Hadeon and drew him into a crushing embrace.

Drawing a hand over my mouth, I wiped the smile off my face and shifted my attention to the Prince of Water. "I know. But we need information and we also need to explain what's happening on the outside. And…" I flapped a hand towards where Eilan was now hugging Hadeon. "Well, *that*."

"Ellyda," Mordren said as he moved closer to her armchair.

She snapped her gaze up. Her eyes went in and out of focus a few times as she blinked, but then they settled on the two black-haired brothers before her. "Mordren. Eilan. Are you okay?"

"Yes." Mordren couldn't quite hide the concern on his face as he studied her. "Are you?"

She was silent for a while. Then she gave him a single nod. "Yes."

"And we're all fine too, thanks for asking," Prince Edric grumbled. "So, what news?"

"First, we need to know what you know about the other two commanders," I said.

"Oh, uhm…" Rayan furrowed his dark brows. "I haven't spent much time with them, so I'm not sure what they're like."

Iwdael shrugged. "They're both pretty serious people. And have no sense of humor."

Mordren heaved a sigh. "That was not exactly what–"

"They both follow Anron's orders," Ellyda interrupted. Setting her book down on her lap, she met each of our gazes in turn. "Anron, Lester, and Danser all command a legion each. But Lester and Danser are not the decision makers. They know about Anron's plans to overthrow their emperor and they're backing him because he has promised to give them powerful positions in his new rule. But they would never try to challenge the emperor on their own because they're terrified of him. Lester, the blond one, has a cruel streak. He enjoys making people feel powerless and afraid, probably because he feels afraid and powerless against the emperor. Danser, the dark-haired one, is pretty nonchalant. He doesn't care what the others do as long as it doesn't impact him." She frowned. "Oh, and Danser really hates potatoes for some reason."

All seven of us blinked at her. She just continued staring at us for another few seconds. Then she nodded to herself and went back to her book.

"That was a great assessment," Eilan said, even though we weren't sure if she was still listening. "Thanks, Ellyda."

Iwdael was staring at Ellyda with his mouth slightly agape. Raising a hand, he pointed at her. "Is she always…?"

"Yep," Hadeon answered.

"Huh."

Edric cleared his throat. "Yes, well, now to your side. What has been happening on the outside, and what exactly is the plan to get us all out?"

Silence fell. Mordren, Eilan and I exchanged a glance. Then they both motioned at me to take the lead. After taking a deep breath, I launched into an explanation of what had happened on the outside this past week and what we had already tried.

Everyone listened intently. Even Ellyda put her book down as soon as I started, and she only interrupted to either ask for clarification or to explain something that she had worked out on her end that would impact our plan.

"... but the air serpents apparently don't panic and fly off when something happens," I said, reaching the end of the story. "They attack. Which means that we can't use that as a distraction. But, we think we might have another idea. We just need–"

The door crashed open.

CHAPTER 33

"They're coming!" Evander yelled in a frantic voice. "The High Elves are back and they're coming here!"

Wood clattered against stone as the princes shot up from their seats.

"Already?" Edric snapped. "They just left. They shouldn't be back for hours."

"We need to go!" Evander urged from the doorway. "Now."

My heart leaped into my throat. Shoving Eilan and Mordren in front of me, I took off towards the door as well.

"Do not engage," Mordren ordered when Hadeon got ready to follow us. "Protect each other until we return."

Hadeon's curses were cut off as the three of us skidded into the hallway behind Evander.

Clanking armor came from the end of the corridor.

We ran.

Idra whirled towards us as we came charging down the hallway. After taking one look at our faces, she sprinted towards our exit point as well.

All we had to do was make it through the corridor, into another, across one of the deserted ballrooms, and then we could climb down from the balcony. From there, we could worldwalk out.

Shouts rose behind us. It was followed by the thudding of boots on marble.

With my heart slamming against my ribs, I pushed myself to run faster. We had to make it. Torches hissed in the draft as we flew through the corridor and into the next one. As long as we could keep the High Elves behind us, we'd be able to make it out.

Relief fluttered through my chest as the doorway leading into the ballroom became visible before us. Almost out.

We threw ourselves around the corner.

And screeched to a halt in a vast marble ballroom filled with High Elves.

Wood creaked as the ranks of soldiers drew back their nocked arrows. At the front were two people I recognized well by now. High Commander Anron and Danser.

"Here we were, searching the Court of Fire for you," Anron said with a sharp smile on his lips. "And you decide to do our job for us by just strolling into our castle."

"Yes, well, we were just leaving," I called back.

"And how do you plan on doing that?"

As if on cue, all the soldiers shifted position so that the arrows pointed straight at us.

"You won't kill us," I challenged. "You need us alive to drain our magic."

Interest flickered in Anron's blue eyes. It was quickly replaced by smugness as he raised a hand. "You and Mordren, yes. But those other three are perfectly acceptable losses."

He jerked his hand down.

Evander sucked in a gasp and crouched down on the floor with his arms above his head, as if that would stop the rain of arrows speeding towards us.

I yanked up my arms.

Fire roared to life and cast the whole room in flickering red light as a curtain of flames rose from the floor all the way up to the ceiling. The arrows disintegrated as they met the fiery barrier, but before we could counter, all hell broke loose behind us as well.

High Commander Lester and his soldiers, who had been pursuing us from behind, crashed into the ballroom. With a cry, Evander tried to duck out of the way but a High Elf in bronze armor shoved him into the wall and put a sword against his throat before he could escape.

Somewhere to my right, Idra charged at the closest soldier but my attention was forced back to the front of the room when a wave of water crashed over my flames. Hissing steam filled the room. And then a great wind slammed into our group.

Dark hair fluttered in the air as Mordren and Eilan flew across the room before Mordren managed to break their fall with a wall of shadows.

That terrifying hum of magic, the one we had all felt on the plains, filled the room. It made my survival instincts scream in panic, but I forced myself to remain where I was. After throwing up another flame shield, I hurled a firebolt at Danser.

He knocked it aside easily with a blast of wind.

Dark red flames exploded against white stone as my attack hit the wall behind them instead.

The power gathering in the room grew even more. The sounds of Idra fighting behind me were almost drowned out by whatever forces Anron and Danser were calling up. Magic crackled through the room.

My mind was screaming at me to surrender.

I threw another useless attack at Anron and Danser.

The hair on the back of my neck stood up.

And then they attacked.

A blast of water shot towards Eilan and Mordren, who had just climbed to their feet again, while hurricane winds slammed straight into me.

My fire was useless against it.

It smacked into me with the force of a hammer blow. Pain shot through my body as I flew backwards and crashed into the ranks of High Elves behind me who had been busy fighting Idra. I sucked in a gasp as I collided with a soldier and we both went down in a tangle of limbs.

Everything ached and my head spun.

Trying to figure out which way was up, I pushed against whatever I could find.

Strong hands wrapped around my wrists. I blinked furiously to clear my head while ramming a knee into what I hoped was my attacker's stomach. A grunt sounded. The pressure on my arms let up momentarily.

"Stop!" Mordren screamed.

Shoving against the soldier above me, I managed to shift him enough to get a brief glance at what was happening on the other side of the room.

Dread crawled up my spine.

Eilan was twitching in the air. Inside a ball of water. With one hand around his own throat, he looked like he was desperately trying not to drown.

The elf above me renewed his attack. One hand shot down and grabbed my wrist again while the other aimed for my throat. I kicked up a knee and twisted my head to the side.

My knee missed.

His hand didn't.

Fingers wrapped around my throat.

"Stop!" Mordren screamed again, and this time his voice broke. "Please."

"Then surrender," Anron commanded.

The High Elf above me squeezed my throat. I struggled against his superior weight and tried to force him off but it was useless.

"Alright, I surrender," Mordren called. "I surrender. Just please… Let him live."

Throwing up my one free arm, I placed it against the High Elf's chest and pushed. Nothing happened. My vision was growing dark at the edges.

Sounds of battle still came from above me where Idra was fighting Lester's force on her own. The other side of the room had gone eerily quiet, but I couldn't see what was happening.

Rage roared up inside me. It couldn't end like this.

I planted my palm firmly against the soldier's bronze breastplate. And then I called up the fire.

Dark red flames spread from my hand and poured against the metal of his armor. I added more heat. And more.

He jerked back. Scrambling to get out of his now melting armor, he finally released the pressure on my throat. I gasped in a deep breath and threw up a ring of fire around me in case any of the other soldiers would try to take his place.

Black spots swam before my eyes, but I struggled to my feet just as a loud splash echoed across the room.

I whipped my head towards it.

Eilan was lying on the white marble floor, coughing up water. And Mordren...

My blood froze.

Mordren was on his knees before High Commander Anron.

A black bracelet that glowed with dark light encircled his wrist.

"Enough!" Idra bellowed from behind me.

Whirling around, I found that most of the soldiers were dead. And the ones who weren't had all backed off and were staring between their commander and the other side of the room.

Idra was standing behind High Commander Lester and her hand was wrapped around his arm. "You let us all go right now, or I will kill your precious commander."

Outrage flickered in Lester's eyes, but he remained motionless.

Across the room, Anron snapped a bracelet shut around Eilan's wrist as well while he was vomiting water from his lungs.

"I don't think so," the smug High Commander said as he straightened.

"You think I'm bluffing?" Idra's dark eyes flashed. "I've killed more people than you've even met, boy."

Utter disbelief slammed home on Anron's face at the way she spoke to him. But then a sharp smile spread over his lips. "No, I don't think you're bluffing. But I don't think you understand the consequences of your own actions. Kill a few of our soldiers, sure." He nodded towards the dead bodies around us before shifting his gaze to Lester. "But kill *him*. Kill a High Commander of one of the Ten Flying Legions and a

Wielder of the Great Current... and Valdanar will send its entire might here to wipe your whole continent off the map."

Idra only continued to stare him down, but I could see the hint of hesitation in her eyes. Anron might be spinning the world's most convincing lie. Or it might be the truth and we would condemn everyone in our lands to death if we killed this one person. And there was no way to know if he was bluffing.

"Let them go," Idra said. "And I'll let him go too."

"No."

My eyes darted around the room. High Commander Danser was standing next to Mordren, holding a sword across his throat. A short distance away, Eilan had pushed himself to his knees next to Anron. And by the opposite wall, a soldier in bronze armor kept Evander pinned against the wall with a blade to his neck as well.

"Idra," Mordren began, his voice calm and steady.

Edging closer to Idra, I cast a glance at her. I could see her assessing the odds as well. Anron wasn't going to let the others go. But he probably wasn't keen on letting Lester die either, so he wouldn't stop us if we dragged the blond commander with us as we left.

"Kenna," Mordren continued as his silver eyes slid to me. "Run."

And so we did.

With Idra's lethal grip on Lester's arm, we used him like a shield as we left. High Commander Anron and the other High Elves watched us as we moved across the now messy ballroom, but no one tried to stop us. Tense silence was our only companion as we walked all the way out of the castle and into the open air.

Guilt and fear swirled inside me as Idra and I at last stepped into the cold night with Lester next to us.

She wrapped her other arm around my waist. Then she let go of Lester.

And worldwalked us out before he could even whirl around.

So we escaped.

But the problem with running away was that you had to leave people behind to do it.

CHAPTER 34

Cool night air smelling of damp soil and pine trees filled my lungs. Stepping out of Idra's embrace, I looked around at the dark forest spreading out on three sides.

"Where are we?" I whispered.

Idra's eyes had taken on a haunted look as they fell on the dark ruin barely visible in the starlight up ahead. "Somewhere no one will think to look."

After drawing in a shuddering breath, she started towards it. I stared after her for another second before hurrying to catch up.

Only the crunch of pine needles beneath our feet and the mournful singing of nocturnal insects broke the stillness as we made our way towards what looked to have once been a great castle. Now, moss and lichen covered the walls and the pale stones were partially blackened as if by fire. Majestic mountains formed a formidable backdrop to the abandoned palace, and with the vast forest around it, it would probably have been a beautiful place before it was left to decay.

The grand gates were scorched and crooked, and had been left leaning awkwardly against the defensive walls.

Idra trailed to a halt just shy of crossing the invisible line that marked the threshold to this place. Silver light from the moon fell across her face and drained all color from her features. I came to a halt next to her, but said nothing. Her dark eyes flicked over the castle that awaited us inside while she absentmindedly rubbed her forearms.

"I never thought I would come back here," she said, her voice barely more than a whisper.

Understanding drew its icy fingers down my spine as I realized what this place was. But before I could say anything, Idra sucked in a deep breath and stepped across the threshold. A chill that had nothing to do with the cool night winds coursed through my body, but I followed her towards the castle entrance in silence.

Those double doors had also been left open. Old leaves and pine needles that had blown in from the woods lay like a carpet across the entrance hall. Sweeping my gaze around the grand space, I studied the blackened chandelier in the ceiling and the scorched walls and paintings around us.

"Is this...?" I finally dared to ask.

"Yes."

Idra cast one look at the ruined hall and then strode straight through it until she reached a door made of metal bars. This one, like all the others, had also been left open. There was a dark stairwell waiting on the other side.

A small shaky breath escaped Idra's lips.

Then she squared her shoulders and stalked down the stairs.

I summoned a small flame to light the way before

following her, but she moved as if she would have found the way in the dark as well.

The stone stairwell twisted around and around until it finally reached the bottom. There were no windows here, so I assumed we were far below ground level. With a flick of my wrist, I lit the torches that still hung mounted on the dark walls.

Yellow light bloomed.

And my heart almost stopped.

We were standing in a rectangular room made of the same pale stone as the rest of the castle. Along the entire right side of the room was a row of cells. No solid walls. Only metal bars that separated the small spaces from each other and also formed a long barrier between them and the rest of the room. Bookshelves lined the wall on the other side. Thick tomes as well as various pieces of equipment still filled them. And in the middle of the room was one more thing. A stone table.

Idra's eyes were fixed on the metal restraints that were still attached to the stained slab of stone. Ice sluiced through my veins as I realized that the dark stains on the table weren't from age. It was blood.

Moving carefully, I placed a hand on Idra's arm and then spoke in a gentle voice. "We don't have to be here. There are other places we can hide. We really don't have to be here if you don't want to."

The sound of my voice seemed to break the trance she had fallen into. Drawing in a deep breath, she gave her body a few quick shakes as if casting off the horrible memories of this place. Then she turned and met my gaze.

"I lied to you."

I blinked at her in surprise.

Drawing a hand through her shining white hair, she tipped

her head to the side. "Well, not really lied. But I didn't exactly tell you the truth either. Do you know what this place is?"

"It's the place where you were kept prisoner and experimented on," I answered carefully.

"Yes. But that is only part of the truth. Do you remember that I only vaguely referred to him as an elven *ruler*?"

"Yeah?"

"He was actually an elven prince." Spreading her arms, she gave me a mirthless smile. "Welcome to the enlightened and glorious Court of Light."

Shock clanged through me. "The Court of *Light*?"

"It was tiny compared to the others, but yes, there used to be a sixth court. The last Prince of Light was André Truthseeker. My first master." Moving towards the row of cells, she brushed her fingers over the bars of the second closest one. "This was mine. For so, so many years, this was my whole world. This cell." She turned back to me and then nodded towards the blood-stained slab of stone. "And that table. And endless, endless pain."

"I'm so sorry," I breathed.

"Yeah, me too. But to be fair, I should have seen it coming. You see, the Court of Light, and Prince André in particular, was obsessed with knowledge. He believed that everything could be explained and replicated if we only had enough knowledge about it. Like our magic. No one really knows how it works. Why some people are born with magic and some not. Why they receive a specific power and not something else. What the limits of that power end up being. But he thought that if he could just study it enough, he could find the answers."

"Did he ever find any?"

"No. Because apparently, there is no system. Our magic is

like a chaotic force with a mind of its own. Except for the pure elemental magic that the princes can absorb when they drink from one of those two sources." When I frowned in confusion, she waved a hand in front of her face. "We'll get back to that. But Prince André still thought he could find answers, and that it was his life's mission to bring knowledge to the rest of the world. To pull the other courts out of their ignorance and into enlightenment."

"He did all this in the name of enlightenment? He tortured you and..." I glanced at the row of cells, "others?" When she nodded, I shook my head in disbelief. "Because he thought it would bring enlightenment that he could then spread to the other courts by using your death magic to conquer them? By all the gods and spirits."

"That was his goal, yes. But since the Court of Light was so small, and he hadn't actually succeeded with his experiments, the kings and the other princes that rose and fell while I was here didn't bother doing anything about it."

"Wait, what? Everyone... Everyone knew that Prince André was doing all of this?"

"Yes."

"And no one intervened?"

"No."

I shook my head. "Why not?"

"For the same reason that no one intervened when Volkan enslaved people. What happens inside a court is that court's business. As long as it doesn't affect any of the other lands, they're free to do what they want with their own court." Idra shrugged. "For all of Volkan's faults, he was the only one who actually did something about it. Granted, it was to wipe out a potential threat to his own court. But still."

Firelight danced over the walls. I didn't even want to

imagine it. Idra lying shackled on that table, screaming her lungs out beneath a scalpel for years on end, until finally Volkan Flameshield, of all people, barged inside and put an end to her suffering.

"But I don't understand," I began, shifting my gaze back to Idra. "Why doesn't anyone talk about this? Why doesn't anyone know that there was a sixth court?"

"For two reasons. When Volkan attacked, he didn't just kill Prince André. He wiped out the whole court." She shrugged again. "Like I said, the whole Court of Light was obsessed with knowledge at this point so Volkan didn't want anyone else picking up André's torch and starting the research back up again. So he killed everyone in the court. Well, everyone except me, I suppose."

The delayed realization hit me like a blow to the chest. *Idra was from the Court of Light.* In fact, she was the last surviving member of the Court of Light. Pressing a hand to my temple, I tried to stop my head from spinning.

"And the other reason," Idra continued, "is that the king wiped that whole chapter from our history books after Volkan had finished destroying the whole court. He didn't want people to know what André had been doing. Either because he was embarrassed that he had let it continue, or because he didn't want anyone else to try to do the same thing. So he forbade everyone to speak of it. Pretended like the Court of Light had never existed. And because he was the king, everyone followed his decree and never spoke of it again. So the children growing up afterwards were never taught that there had been a sixth court or what had happened there."

"He just erased a whole court from our history?"

"Yes. Mordren, Rayan, Edric, even Iwdael... They're too

young. They were all born after this. But Volkan knew. And King Aldrich."

My gaze had been drifting to the stone table, but now it snapped back to Idra. "King Aldrich? This was during his reign?"

"No. But he was the Prince of Stone at the time when Volkan launched his attack." She drew a hand through her hair and stared at the wall at the far end of the room while her eyes took on a faraway look. "I think he came to regret it. In the end. That he didn't do anything about it, I mean. I think that was why he never went after Volkan, even after he did some pretty awful things. Because he was grateful to Volkan for actually doing what no one else dared to do. Wipe out the Court of Light."

King Aldrich had always seemed like such a kind and wise person, so it shocked me to learn that he had known about all this but never done anything about it. But perhaps we all had secrets. Maybe this was one of his defining moments. The thing that had made him become the kind and wise ruler that everyone came to love. I supposed Mordren was right: the world was far too complicated to be divided into simply good and bad people.

"But that's not why we're here," Idra said. After motioning for me to follow, she moved towards the stone wall at the far end of the room. "We're here because I have been keeping more secrets. You've said for a while now that we don't know enough about the High Elves to beat them."

Torchlight flickered over her face as she stopped in front of the stone wall. For a brief moment, I swore that I could see a hint of guilt in her dark eyes. But then she cleared her throat and pressed on.

"What Prince André was able to figure out was that our

magic comes from the High Elves. Or is connected to the High Elves in some way. Which means that he did extensive research on them." Turning, she ran a hand over the stone wall. "And it's all still here. No one knows about this, except me, because I watched him open this door a million times. And I didn't tell anyone. Not Volkan. Not King Aldrich. Not you." She blew out a soft breath. "Because I didn't want to come back here. I didn't want to think about this place ever again."

"We can still leave, if you want," I offered gently.

"No." Shaking her head, she gave me a mirthless smile. "Because now, I'm about to become a powerless slave drained of my magic again. And I would rather face this place and the horrors of my past than have my future taken away from me. Again."

Determination settled on her features as she turned back to the wall and pushed a few random stones in a seemingly haphazard order.

Stone groaned.

And then part of the wall swung open to reveal a small room behind. Idra reached up and removed one of the torches from the wall before taking a step into the doorway.

Holding out her arm, she motioned towards the room beyond. "Here it is."

I leaned forward and peered into the darkened space. Light from the torch flickered over a series of bookshelves packed with ancient tomes. My heart started thumping in my chest.

"Here is everything the Court of Light knew about the High Elves."

CHAPTER 35

Paper rustled into the silence as I turned the page in one of the thick tomes Idra and I had brought up from Prince André's secret library. Moonlight streamed in through the panorama of windows in the deserted dining room and bathed the table we currently occupied in bright light. I still pushed one of the candles closer as I squinted at the pyramid drawn on the page in black ink.

My heart skipped a beat.

"Look at this," I said and glanced up at Idra before pointing to the page in front of me. "This is their hierarchy."

Idra pushed aside her own book to peer at mine. It had taken most of the night to just sort through all the books to find the ones that had information about the High Elves, and even then, we had to scour them to find information that would actually be useful to us.

"Both the emperor and empress are at the top?" Idra said as she frowned down at the drawing. "That's odd. I wonder if that means that they're ruling together with equal power."

"Maybe. But look who's below them." I traced my finger

over the words written in flowing script. "The High Commanders of the Ten Flying Legions. That's Anron and the other two. And below them?" I moved my finger again. "The Wielders of the Great Current. And Anron, and at least Lester as well, belong to both of those groups."

The pyramid continued with a layer of soldiers, then common people, and then at the very bottom was one more group. Low Elves.

Idra sat back in her chair and expelled a huff. "So, he really wasn't bluffing, huh? Anron, Lester, and Danser belong to the very top of High Elf society. And if we just killed them, the emperor and empress would probably send the other seven legions here to either wipe us all out or take us back to their land as slaves." Lifting a hand, she massaged her brows. "Shit."

"Yeah. Well, one problem at a time. First we need to figure out a way to free the other princes so we can start taking back our courts." I slapped the book before me with the back of my hand. "And what even is a *Wielder of the Great Current*?"

Silence fell as Idra shrugged and went back to flipping through the pages of her own book. I rubbed the back of my neck and turned to stare out the window. An owl hooted from the trees somewhere outside.

"How do you feel about hunches?" I suddenly asked.

Glancing up at me, she threw me a frown. "I can tell that you're dancing around another question, so just cut to the chase and ask what you really want to ask."

A surprised chuckle escaped my throat. But then I shook my head. She was right. And besides, Idra never was one who sugarcoated and minced words anyway.

"My gut is telling me to do something."

"If your gut is telling you something, it's usually right."

"But if I do it, and it turns out that it *isn't* right, then I will just be proving to everyone that I really am a shitty person."

Paper rustled as Idra turned another page. For a moment, she said nothing as she continued to scan the page before her. Then she looked up and met my gaze.

"Can you live with being a shitty person?"

Now it was my turn to fall silent. Drumming my fingers against the dusty tabletop, I considered for a while. Idra kept her eyes locked on mine.

"Yes," I said at last. "Yes, I can."

"Can you live with not following your gut if it turns out that it was right?"

That one was easier. "No."

She nodded. "Then you have your answer."

"Yeah, I suppose I do." Lifting up a cluster of pages, I started quickly flipping through them and letting them fall back down. "I just wish that life wasn't so complicated all the time. The thing is, I think that..." I slammed my hand down on one of the pages. "Great Wielders of the Current! Here it is."

Idra snapped her gaze back up to me. My heart pounded as I read the page written in the same flowing black script as the rest of the book.

"Oh, by all the gods and spirits," I said as I finished. "No wonder we can't beat them. The High Elves... Their magic system. It works like a... like a hive mind. Every High Elf is born with magic, but not everyone can use it. Most people are just conduits. Or... maybe more like storage vessels." I snapped my fingers and looked up. "Like what those bracelets are doing. But it's all organic."

"Kenna, you're rambling."

"Right." I cleared my throat and pushed together a cluster

of books so that they were all gathered on my right. "Most of the High Elves are conduits." I pointed at the mass of books. "They have magic inside them, but they can't use it." Picking up a thick tome, I moved it so that it sat alone on my left. "And then a small part of their population is what they call Great Wielders of the Current. They also have magic, but the difference is that they can use it. *And*, they can use everyone else's magic too!"

"So Anron can draw on the magic of every soldier in his legion," Idra summarized.

"Yes! And Lester and Danser and Captain Vendir, and those other squad captains who started levitating and throwing magic around on the battlefield." Throwing myself back in my chair, I pressed a hand to my head. "They're not born with specialized powers like we are. They have access to a whole current of raw magic that they can draw from while also using the non-wielders as conduits to boost their power. That's why they can use all the elements. And why their power is so much greater than ours."

Idra stared at me in silence for a moment. Then she blew out a long breath. "By all the demons in hell."

"Yeah."

"And they have *three legions* to draw from and an unknown number of wielders within those. Not to mention the air serpents."

"Yeah," I repeated.

Shifting her gaze to the window, she stared out into the dark night for a while. It looked like she was in deep thought so I didn't want to interrupt her. Besides, my mind was spinning through a jumble of schemes and options too.

A sharp thud rang out.

It was so sudden that I almost jumped.

Idra, who had snapped her book shut, slid her gaze back to me. There was something heavy, defeated, and far too serious in it for my liking.

"We can't win this," she announced. Raking her fingers through her hair, she let out a bitter laugh, as if she couldn't quite believe it herself. "Against these odds, there is no way in hell we can win."

"No," I agreed. Then an idea struck me like a lightning bolt. Flipping frantically through the book before me, I searched for an earlier page. "Unless..." When I finally found the page I was looking for, I spun the book around so that it faced Idra and then stabbed a finger at it. "*This*. This is how we even the playing field."

She frowned in confusion as she looked down at the page. Then realization dawned. Raising her eyebrows, she stared at me in disbelief. "You can't be serious."

"Of course I am." I stabbed at the page again. "This is so within my wheelhouse. Not to mention that it's probably our only chance."

For another few seconds, she only continued staring at me in stunned silence. "You are, without a doubt, the craziest person I have ever met."

"I thought we already established that after I shoved a sword through my own chest to kill Volkan."

"We did. But I thought that was a one-time thing."

"Nope."

"This is insane." Leaning back in her chair, she tilted her head back and dragged her hands through her hair again. "But... It probably is our only chance." She blew out a deep breath and shook her head before meeting my gaze again. "Alright, talk me through this. How would that even work?"

Anticipation bounced around inside me as I launched into

an explanation of the slightly insane scheme I had come up with. Anron thought that he had won. That he could just invade our lands, drain our magic, and then leave us all powerless in the hands of Syrene while he went home to steal another throne.

That he could take my court.

My power.

My throne.

Oh he had no idea who he was dealing with.

CHAPTER 36

"That is insane." Mordren stared at me from across the room. "And brilliant."

I grinned. "Right?"

After Idra and I had finished scheming in what had once been the Court of Light, we had worldwalked back to the Black Emerald to fill in Valerie and Theo on the plan, sleep for a few hours, and then get ready for the next stage. When night had fallen, I had once more snuck into King Aldrich's castle. And without being slowed down by people who actually needed to walk around the walls instead of through them, it had been fairly easy to get into Mordren's bedroom. It probably helped too that Anron didn't think I would have the balls to break in again so soon after we had been caught. But as previously mentioned, he really had no idea who he was dealing with.

"So, tomorrow then?" Mordren said.

"Yeah. Tomorrow, we will all either be free or prisoners together. Or I will be very dead. That's a possible outcome too." I motioned towards his closed door and the hallway outside it. "Where are the others? We need them all here so that we can explain the plan."

"Eilan and Hadeon are in their rooms. As are Rayan, Iwdael, and Evander. But Ellyda is in the smithy with Captain Vendir, and Edric is somewhere in the Court of Stone with Anron and his friends."

"In the Court of Stone? What are they doing there?"

A sly smile drifted over Mordren's lips. "I might have let slip that your family could be sheltering you."

I gaped at him. "You did not."

"While you might have refrained from killing them, it does not mean that I have suddenly forgiven them for everything they have done to you." He smoothened out an invisible crease in his dark suit while a wicked glint shone in his eyes. "So after pressuring them for a while, I assume Anron and the others will be spending at least a few hours scouring the countryside with Edric's help."

"You didn't need to do that."

"No. But I wanted to."

I inclined my head in his direction. "Well, I have to admit, I do approve of your methods. But how did you even get Anron to believe it? After all, my family sold us out to the High Elves earlier."

Mordren sauntered across the floor until he was standing right in front of me. Drawing soft fingers along my jaw, he tipped my head back. "Oh, I can be very manipulative."

A dark laugh slipped my lips. "Yes, I'm aware."

He flashed me a satisfied smirk and then dropped his hand. "So, Ellyda and Edric will not return for at least a few hours. Would you like me to explain the plan to them instead?"

"No, I think I need to be the one to explain it."

"I believe so too." He cast a glance at the door. "At least Anron, Lester, and Danser are away. And Vendir is occupied elsewhere. So there is no risk of you being discovered." Sliding his gaze back to me, he let another sly smile spread across his lips. "At least as long as you stay in my bedroom."

"In your bedroom, huh?" I matched his smirk. "Well, seeing as this might be my last night of freedom and possibly my last night alive, I might as well enjoy it to the fullest."

Mordren took a step forward, backing me towards the desk by the wall. I let him. The pale wooden piece of furniture produced a soft thud as my thighs connected with it and pushed it back the final bit against the smooth marble behind.

A small shudder coursed through me as Mordren drew his fingers over my collarbones. "Well, in that case, I really should make you do something about these clothes."

Tilting my head back, I met his gaze. And then a ball of fire whooshed to life above my palm. "Oh, I don't think so."

The dark red flames danced as I lifted my hand and flexed my fingers. Mordren raised his eyebrows. I only continued staring him down, daring him to do something about it. A midnight laugh dripped from his lips. Then he leaned forward until I could feel his hot breath on my skin.

"Careful now," he whispered against my mouth. "Remember what happened last time you tried to blackmail me?"

A cocky grin slid across my lips. "You mean when I poisoned your wine and made you grovel at my feet for the antidote?"

He wrapped a hand around my throat and forced my chin up. "I was thinking more of the time when I used my belt to tie you to the ceiling, blindfolded you, and then stripped you of your clothes right before you ended up on your knees before me in your underwear."

I let the dark red flames spread from my hand and up my arm. Mordren's eyes flicked towards them. The fire licked its way across my skin and towards my throat. Challenge shone on Mordren's face as he looked between me and the flames advancing towards his hand. I stared right back.

The fire had almost reached my throat.

He snatched his hand back.

I let out a victorious laugh and drew my other hand across his jaw. "Yes, I remember that. Vividly. But now, it's time for revenge."

Letting the fire spread across my body, I took a step towards him, forcing him to retreat. Challenge, and awe, burned in his eyes. But he backed across the floor when I took another step closer. After three strides, we both came to a halt.

Mordren lifted his left hand and shook it slightly, making the black bracelet around his wrist shift. "I cannot help but notice that you waited until I did not have access to my magic to exact your revenge."

After snuffing out the fire covering me, I grabbed the front of his suit and pulled his face down to mine. "Oh, you know what they say. All is fair in love and blackmail."

Releasing him, I returned to the desk and drew myself up on it. A wicked smile settled on my lips as I crossed one leg over the other and waved an expectant hand in the air.

"Now, strip."

He let out a baffled laugh and shook his head. Flames flickered between my fingers. Narrowing his eyes, he stared me down for another few seconds. I only continued smirking at him.

Then he blew out a breath and removed his suit jacket. Holding my gaze, he demonstratively dropped it on the floor right next to him. I arched an eyebrow expectantly. He shook his head again but still complied.

Reaching up, he started slowly loosening his tie. I bit my lip as I watched the muscles in his forearm shift. Heat pulsed through my body as the thin piece of fabric slid out from around his neck and over his collarbone.

When he was about to drop his tie on the floor next to his jacket, I snapped my fingers. Mordren gave me an incredulous look. I held out my palm.

With a sigh that promised vengeance, he closed the distance between us and placed the smooth black tie in my hand instead. I ran the silken fabric between my fingers while arching an eyebrow at him again.

Mordren kept his eyes locked on mine as he reached up and started unbuttoning his black shirt. Slowly. Torturously. His clever fingers took their time undoing each button before moving down to the next one.

My heart thumped in my chest.

At last, he reached the final one.

Dark cloth fluttered in the air as he pushed the shirt off his toned shoulders and let it fall to the floor. I drew in a soft shuddering breath. Light from the candles danced over his lean muscles.

Clenching my fingers around the edge of the tabletop, I drank in the sight of Mordren's beautifully lethal body. The slopes of his chest and the ridges of his abs made me want to trace my fingers all over it. All over him. My breathing was growing heavier, but I dragged my eyes back to his face.

Mordren's eyes had never left mine. And they were dark with desire too.

His hands drifted down until they reached his belt.

Keeping his eyes locked on mine, he slowly unbuckled the belt and slid it out. Then he advanced on me. I raised my eyebrows in challenge, but he kept coming until he was standing right in front of me.

While still holding on to the belt, he grabbed my thighs and uncrossed my legs. After spreading them wide, he stepped in between them. Reaching up, he slid his belt around the back of my neck and then grabbed the edges with both hands.

With a firm tug, he forced me closer to him. Waves of heat pulsed through my body at the dangerous glint in his eyes as he leaned down.

"After tomorrow, when I am free of this bracelet," he whispered, his voice dark and husky, "you will pay dearly for this."

I laughed against his mouth. Releasing his grip on the belt, he let it fall down so that it hung around my neck. With that lethal glint still in his silver eyes, he moved his fingers to the top of his pants. I let a wicked smile spread across my lips.

"Oh, I am counting on it, my prince."

CHAPTER 37

Candles fluttered as the door was pulled open. I shifted in my seat to find Eilan and Evander sneaking in through the door. Ellyda, whose room we were once again occupying, was sitting in her usual armchair by the wall, but this time her eyes were clear and sharp. Spending hours in a forge was sure to exhaust other people, but it seemed to refill Ellyda's energy reserves and calm her mind. I swept my gaze over Hadeon and the four princes around me as well while Eilan and Evander took their seats.

"Alright, now that we're all here I will get straight to it," I said without preamble. "We're getting you out tomorrow."

Evander blinked in surprise. "Tomorrow? You've come up with a new plan?"

"Yes. When Idra and I escaped, she worldwalked us to... well, it's a long story but it's where she was before she worked for Volkan." Her story wasn't mine to tell, and I also didn't want to get into the whole Court of Light revelation, so I just glossed over that part and pressed on. "And she showed me a hidden library that had a lot of information about the High Elves, and about magic in general."

"Now that is interesting." Prince Iwdael sat forward on the couch. "What did you find out?"

"Don't interrupt, Iwdael," Edric Mountaincleaver grumbled. "She just has to say what she needs to, and then she has to leave before she gets caught. Anron came back with me, remember?"

Iwdael rolled his eyes and shook his head, but sat back again. I suppressed an exasperated sigh. Clearing my throat, I moved on before the Prince of Stone could say anything else.

"We found out a lot of things, but the two most important ones were that I found instructions for a really high-powered fire magic attack." I nodded towards Iwdael's wrist. "And Idra found a way to deactivate the bracelets."

"I understand the part about deactivating the bracelets," Eilan cut in. "But what are you going to do with the fire magic attack?"

"I'm going to attack the High Elf legions stationed in the Court of Water."

Silence fell across the room.

"I'm sorry, what?" the Prince of Water finally said.

"You are going to attack the Court of Water?" Eilan interrupted before I could answer, his dark brows climbing towards his hairline. "Alone?" When I flashed him a grin in reply, he raised a hand to massage his forehead. "This is insane."

On the couch next to me, Mordren lifted one shoulder in a casual shrug. "That is what I said as well."

"Yes, well, everyone seems to be saying that." I slid my gaze to Prince Rayan. "And besides, I'm not going to attack the Court of Water. Only the High Elves stationed there."

Rayan heaved a deep sigh. "Does it really have to be *my* court?"

"The High Elves are only stationed in two courts: yours and Iwdael's. And well, everything in your court is covered in water so my attack won't do any actual damage to the city. Iwdael's on the other hand... I really don't want to burn down his entire forest."

"Why thank you, Kenna," the Prince of Trees said, amusement tugging at his lips.

"Fine." Rayan rubbed a hand over his forehead and blew out a resigned breath. "I suppose you're right."

"Can we get back to the plan already?" Prince Edric snapped. "This meeting is already running far too long."

After shooting him a brief glare, I turned back to the others again. "The plan is this... I will attack the High Elves in the Court of Water. Since they'll be entirely unprepared for my surprise strike, Anron and the others will have to scramble the rest of their troops and hurry there to catch me. I'll wreak enough havoc at random intervals to make it seem like I'm there but just taking some time between attacks. So while Anron and the others are on their way to the Court of Water, Idra will worldwalk here and get those bracelets off you."

"Are you sure about this, Kenna?" Evander said. Uncertainty swirled in his green eyes. "It sounds awfully dangerous."

"With this new fire magic attack, and since the bulk of their army won't be there, I'm pretty sure that they won't actually be able to catch me."

"Pretty sure isn't actually sure."

"Have you forgotten that she rammed a sword through her own chest to kill Volkan Flameshield?" Hadeon interrupted. A rumbling laugh escaped his throat as he shook his head at me. "I think her playing-it-safe ship sailed long ago."

"I'm quite certain of that as well," Prince Rayan added before shifting his violet eyes back to me. "So, I assume we will be on the clock once Idra gets here. Where should we meet her?"

"Once you see Anron and the others fly away from the castle, head to the slopes below the balcony in the main ball room. It's outside the wards. Idra will meet you there and deactivate the bracelets so you can worldwalk out straight away." I met each of their gazes in turn. "Remember, we won't be able to get everyone out. So make sure that the ones you want to bring when we escape are ready and waiting along with you."

Seriousness washed over the room and they all gave me a somber nod.

"Now would you please get out, Kenna?" Prince Edric said in a stern voice, and stabbed a muscular arm towards the nearest wall. "Before this whole plan goes up in flames before it has even begun."

Scattered chuckles broke the tension that had settled over the room after my final words. I gave the Prince of Stone a small smile and a nod before pushing to my feet. Clothes rustled as the others stood up as well.

"Tomorrow afternoon. Be ready."

Sweeping my gaze over all of my co-conspirators, I gave them a decisive nod. And then I strode back out through the wall.

Tomorrow, we would free our friends and all the other princes.

Tomorrow, the resistance movement would either begin.
Or die.

CHAPTER 38

My heart slammed against my ribs. Standing atop a clock tower, I looked down at the rows of barracks below me. Water rushed over the great defensive wall to my right, marking the barrier between the castle and the flat stretch of land where the Court of Water usually kept their army. Now, it had been taken over by High Elves.

Tall figures in bronze armor moved between the one-story buildings below. Not a lot of them were outside at the moment. But I knew that there were no elves from Rayan's court here because I had staked the place out earlier that morning.

Hadeon had been right when he said that my playing-it-safe ship had sailed long ago, but I still didn't really want to think about just how dangerous this was going to be. Even if I had calculated correctly, there was so much that could go wrong. But the plan was already made. The pieces were set. Now, I just had to make the first move and hope that I would survive long enough to finish the game.

Drawing in a deep breath, I raised my blades.

Fire whooshed down over the sharpened steel as I held them out to my sides.

And then I flicked my wrists.

Scythes of fire shot out one after the other and sped towards the buildings below until the air was filled with burning arcs.

Shouts rose from the few High Elves outside. Sprinting away, they leaped through the nearest doorways and windows as death came for them from above.

Right before the flaming scythes reached the ground, I yanked up my blades in front of me and then rammed them back down again. Two sharp lines of fire flashed out from them and shot towards the ribbons of flames below, cleaving them in half.

A boom rocked the field.

The wide scythes exploded when they were split in two and shot sideways through the rows of barracks. Hissing water and steam rose as fire crashed into the walls with enough force to make them tremble.

Dark red flames flickered in my hair and a grin spread across my mouth as I looked down at the scene. Oh, I was definitely getting better at this.

Raising my blades again, I waited for the High Elves to come running out of their barracks. Fire still crackled along the side of several buildings. My heart continued thumping in my chest.

Nothing happened.

Just as I was about to turn around, a battle cry split the air behind me. I whipped around. Ranks upon ranks of High Elves, led by High Commander Danser, charged towards the clock tower from behind.

Alarm clanged through me.

Not hesitating a second, I leaped back through the wall and sprinted down the stairs.

A cold weight settled in my stomach as I hurtled down the twisting stairwell. They had been waiting to ambush me.

My head spun from going around and around at this pace, but I kept running. I had to make it to ground level and out of the clock tower before the High Elves surrounded me.

Boom!

The whole building shook as something slammed into the side with stone-shattering force. Thrown into the railing by the impact, I sucked in a gasp between my teeth and threw out my arms to steady myself. Metal clanged against metal as my blades connected with the railing, but I managed to get my feet back underneath me.

Chips of stone and mortar crumbled from the walls and rained down around me.

Keeping one hand brushing the railing, I sprinted downwards.

Another explosion echoed into the air.

This time I was more prepared for it, so I only rocked sideways as the blast hit the tower, and continued running. More stones crumbled and fell through the air before clattering to the floor. My pulse pounded in my ears.

With a leap, I cleared the final steps and then skidded across the debris-covered floor. In one fluid motion, I kicked open the door and shot a torrent of fire through the opening.

And then I darted through the side wall instead.

Screams split the afternoon air as the High Elves dove aside to escape the flames that I had shot through the door, but I couldn't spare the time to see if it had worked.

Golden sunlight gleamed against bronze breastplates to

both my left and right. I hurtled across the dusty stones and towards the cover of the barracks before me. Magic hummed in the air.

That primal feeling of fear and submission hit me like a physical blow as the strength of it increased. Danser or one of the other wielders was going to unleash a powerful attack any second.

Whipping my head from side to side, I found the dark-haired commander moving into position to my right. My feint with the fire at the front of the clock tower had bought me precious seconds. But it wouldn't be enough. The nearest barrack was too far away.

With panic screaming in my head, I slashed my sword through the air while continuing to sprint for cover.

Fire shot up from the ground and swept towards the commander like a great wall.

His gaze snapped from me to it and he flicked a hand. A tidal wave sprang to life, dwarfing my flames, and cancelling them out in a hissing cloud of steam.

Dread crawled up my spine. If I hadn't interrupted the attack he had been gearing up for, it would have been over. My only advantage in this was that they couldn't actually kill me. I, on the other hand, didn't have to show the same restraint.

Diving forward, I flicked my blades and shoved a pair of flaming scythes towards both Danser and the High Elves who had been closing in from the other side of the clock tower.

Shields of water flashed up to meet them.

Lightning crackled through the air from Danser's side.

And then silk brushed against my skin as I phased through the wall of a barrack and rolled to my feet inside it.

Barely breaking a stride, I took off towards the back wall and leaped through that one too. I veered left.

Arrows whizzed through the air.

Throwing up a wall of fire, I incinerated them. But thudding feet came from the left and another volley of arrows meant to wound was sure to come. Danser called out a command to cut me off from the right. Skidding around a corner, I changed direction. With blood pounding in my ears, I sprinted straight for the high defensive walls instead.

The castle was situated on top of a cliff, so I couldn't just phase through the wall from here. But there was an opening that led to a back entrance. According to Viviane, the elven thief I had gotten to know earlier this year, there was a door behind the rushing waterfall up ahead. If I was right about this, I could make my way into the castle and keep my plan on track.

Power crackled between the buildings.

I sent another flaming attack shooting towards both sides before ramming my blades back into their sheaths and focusing all my strength on running.

The small door that I knew was hidden behind the rushing waterfall and that led to the back entrance grew closer.

Danser called out for another volley.

Bows creaked from my left and magic hummed through the warm afternoon air to my right. I sucked in desperate breaths. The door was getting closer.

Twangs echoed from behind the buildings.

Pushing off the ground, I threw myself the final bit through the back door.

The feeling of passing through a curtain of sheets enveloped me.

And then I crashed down on the stones inside.

Pain flared up my shoulder.

A moment later, sharp thuds came from the other side of the wall as arrows hit it before being washed away by the crashing water. I scrambled to my feet. While rubbing the aching spot on my shoulder, I darted up a narrow set of steps that had been carved into the cliff.

Prince Rayan's castle loomed above me.

With my lungs screaming for air, I bounded up the final steps and in through the small door at the top. My leg muscles groaned when I found another staircase waiting for me, but I sprinted up that one as well. It wouldn't take Danser long to get through the back door I had used, and then he would be on my heels again.

Eerie silence pounded against my eardrums as I ran up the darkened stairwell and leaped through the next door. Now, all I had to do was–

I skidded to a halt.

The wide room with carved white walls and a painted ceiling that served as Prince Rayan's ballroom on the second floor stared back at me.

And so did a mass of High Elves.

"Shit," I breathed.

I couldn't go back, because Danser and his soldiers were already scrambling up the stairs behind me, and the other stairwell leading down to the ground floor was blocked by the bronze-clad army in front of me.

High Commander Anron flashed me a triumphant smile where he stood at the front of his very successful ambush. Next to him, Lester cocked his head and studied me as if he was genuinely curious what I would do now.

Feet pounded against the stone steps behind me.

My eyes flicked back and forth across the room, judging distances, as I carefully moved forwards to avoid being grabbed by Danser from behind.

When I reached the middle of the room, Anron held up a hand. "That's far enough."

Standing in three solid lines that blocked the entire front of the room, Anron and Lester's soldiers simply waited for their commanders to give them orders. Or to draw magic from them. Armor clanked behind me as Danser and his men spread out along the back wall.

"You knew I was coming," I said.

It wasn't really a question, but Anron answered anyway. "Yes."

I flicked a quick glance at Danser. "And you weren't really trying to capture me. You were herding me."

"We knew that you wouldn't go down without a fight," Anron answered in his stead. "So we figured that it was best to trap you somewhere you couldn't slip through our fingers." He shot me a knowing look. "Or through the walls."

My eyes darted around the room again. I was awfully far from any walls that actually led somewhere safe.

"Your best course of action now would be to surrender," he finished.

"Or you could try to fight," Lester added beside him. A wolfish grin spread across his mouth as he looked at me. "Make it interesting."

I blew out a calming breath that did nothing to actually calm me.

Then I threw up flaming barriers between me and the two forces, and darted towards the side wall on my left.

Steam hissed and washed over the room like gray waves as

Anron, Lester, Danser, and two of the squad leaders cancelled them out with a flash of water.

A block of stone rose before me to cut off my way to the wall. I ran straight through it. It boomed back into the floor as whoever had called it up slammed it back down again, right as a blast of wind took me in the side.

The force spun me around and almost threw me off my feet. I hurled a fireball to block something orange coming for me on the left. Flames exploded through the pale room as my desperate defense hit another attack of fire magic. The air vibrated with power.

Almost losing my balance, I stumbled to the side while trying to make it the final distance across the floor.

Lightning cut through the air.

My instincts screamed at me to duck.

Dropping to a knee, I threw my arms over my head right as a white streak of lightning flashed above me and then exploded against the wall with a deafening boom.

Another lightning strike cleaved the air right above my shoulder. It was so close that the energy from it crackled through my hair and made it stand on edge. With my arms still over my head, I crouched down deeper right as a third bolt cut through the room and barely missed me before exploding against the wall.

"Shit!" I blurted out. "Okay. Okay. I get it."

"Take one more step towards that wall," High Commander Anron warned in a voice dripping with threats, "and the next lightning bolt goes into your chest."

Still cowering on the floor, I lowered my arms enough to glance at the wall. Black patterns marked the spots where the lightning had struck. If I got hit with that, I would be twitching on the floor for half an hour.

"Do you understand?" he prompted.

"Yes. Yes, I understand."

Keeping my hands raised, I slowly stood back up again while shifting my gaze to Anron once more. Amusement danced in his eyes as he watched me.

All three High Commanders had moved to the middle of the room and were now standing side by side, studying me. Lester's eyes gleamed as he kept a shifting wall of fire hovering above the floor to my right. To my left, Danser had raised a mirrored wall of water. Lightning crackled around Anron's hand as he kept it pointed towards me.

I swallowed.

"I think she should apologize before being allowed to surrender," High Commander Lester said. When Anron slid his eyes to him, he shrugged. "She has wasted so much of our time. Running around. Us having to chase her. I want to hear her beg our forgiveness for that."

Ellyda's assessment of the blond commander's character had been right indeed. He certainly got off on making people feel powerless. I narrowed my eyes at him but said nothing.

"And she's a Low Elf," he continued with a disgusted sneer. "Causing this much trouble for us shouldn't even be possible for someone like her."

"I'm actually half human too," I sniped back.

Fire shot towards me. I leaped back and to the side to escape Lester's fiery blow. Lightning immediately cleaved the air next to me. I sucked in a gasp.

"Alright, alright," I said, edging back slightly. "I get it."

"No, I don't think you do," Lester challenged. "Or you wouldn't continue to be disrespectful."

Meeting his gaze, I gave him a cold smile. "Fine. You want me to beg, I'll beg."

With my hands still raised, I crouched down on one knee.

High Commander Anron glanced at the grinning Lester, but then shifted his sharp blue eyes to me. A satisfied smile settled on his lips as he took in my kneeling form.

"Ah, Kenna. Finally right where you're supposed to be."

CHAPTER 39

Three High Commanders stared me down and ranks of High Elf soldiers flanked them to cut off access to any walls that I could have escaped through. Glancing up from the floor, I met Anron's victorious gaze.

"Yes, finally right where I'm supposed to be," I said.

And then I phased through the floor.

My stomach lurched as I free-fell down into the room below, but before I passed through the pale stone floor, I managed to get one last glimpse of Anron's face. Shock and disbelief flashed across his features. I let out a wicked laugh.

It was cut short as I crashed down on the floor in the room beneath the ballroom. Rolling forward with the motion, I tried to soften the landing but the hit still jolted through my bones and sent flares of pain through my body.

Phasing through the floor was always ridiculously dangerous because there was no way of controlling the landing. All I could do was hope that I wasn't about to be impaled on something. Or break my legs.

Stone scraped against my shoulder.

I glanced at the inner wall that I had just barely missed.

If I hadn't managed to move this far back, I would have either not been able to phase through the floor at all because there would have been a wall right beneath me, or I would have ended up on the other side of that wall. In the main entry hall. Where Anron no doubt had more soldiers waiting.

But because I had jumped back and sideways after I provoked them into shooting lightning at me again, I had managed to end up on the right side of the wall. My ankles and shins throbbed, and my heart was still beating wildly in my chest, but I pushed to my feet inside the narrow corridor. And then I ran.

When I had broken into Rayan's bedroom all those months ago, this was the side exit that the guards had used when they escorted me out. If it hadn't been for them, and for Viviane, I would never have survived this.

Pain shot up my legs with every stride, but I sprinted towards the door at the end. Pounding feet sounded from upstairs. It wouldn't take them long to find me again, but this would hopefully give me enough of a head start.

Leaping through the locked door at the end, I burst out into the courtyard outside. Golden light from the afternoon sun shone down on the pale castle and made the ever-flowing waterfalls and fountains glitter like jewels. I barely spared them a glance as I hurtled straight for the water-covered defensive walls that would take me into the city beyond.

Warm winds ripped through my hair.

The ache in my legs from the hard landing pounded in tune with my thumping heart as I ran towards the walls ahead. Water crashed down before me. Only a little farther.

Doors banged open behind me.

"There!" High Commander Anron bellowed as he and his army poured out of the castle.

Fire roared and wind rushed and lightning crackled.

Pushing myself with everything I had, I dove right into the waterfall before me.

Instead of pounding water, silk whispered against my skin. Light exploded somewhere inside the defensive walls, but I was already through. My shoulder took another hit as I slammed into the stone street at an awkward angle before rolling to my feet and continuing my headlong rush.

Startled citizens jumped out of the way as I darted into the nearest alley. Hunting footsteps and clanking armor echoed behind me. I threw up a wall of fire that blocked off the entire street as I skidded around the next corner.

Steam hissed behind me as someone threw a wave of water at my flaming barrier.

Leaping over a small canal, I switched directions again and hurtled down another street.

"Left!" someone screamed behind me. "She went left!"

Wood clattered against stone as I slammed right into a set of chairs and tables outside a café that suddenly appeared out of nowhere around the next corner. Shrieking humans scrambled away from their overturned seats as I tried to untangle myself from the nefarious pieces of furniture.

A boom echoed between the houses.

Elves and humans screamed louder and ducked into the nearest doorways as a firebolt exploded against the wall next to me.

Shoving aside the final chair, I jumped through the wall of the café. The guests cried out in alarm as I materialized out of the dark wooden wall and pushed them out of the way.

Teacups shattered and biscuits flew as I forced myself through the crowded room.

"Out of the way!" I bellowed as I knocked tables aside on my way to the back wall.

A woman in a blue dress jumped out of my path and knocked into a huge potted plant in her hurry to get away. The plant wobbled precariously before crashing right into me, leaves flapping in terror. With an irritated shove, I pushed the suicidal plant back against the wall and then leaped through next to it.

Lightning exploded against the wood beside me.

Sucking in a sharp breath between my teeth, I ducked and hoped that it would be enough. Chips of stone flew through the air and rained down around me as another lightning bolt zapped over my head and hit the building on my other side.

"She's here!" Lester snapped.

Without a second look back, I jumped to my feet and took off down the street in the other direction. I zigzagged across the stones as more lightning cleaved the air around me. When one almost grazed my shoulder, I phased through the nearest wall.

A silent bedroom appeared around me.

The shock of the stillness was so jarring that I almost slammed into the set of drawers in front of me. Swerving at the last second, I navigated around it. With a palm on its smooth surface, I jumped over the narrow bed and then out through the next wall.

Ordinary citizens cried out in surprise, which of course immediately alerted the High Elves.

But I didn't have enough breath to spare for a curse so I just sprinted towards the next cross street.

A blast of air slammed into me.

The world spun as I flew through the air.

Right before I hit the stone wall with what would have been bone-breaking force, I phased through it.

Pain flared up my side as I crashed into a chair and then a dining room table inside the building instead. The force flipped me over and I slid across the tabletop before smacking into the chairs on the other side and tumbling to the floor. Everything hurt and my head spun, but I pushed to my feet and staggered towards the nearest wall.

Blinking against the sunlight, I stumbled into the street outside the building. Moving sent bursts of pain through my whole body but I whipped my head from side to side anyway to figure out where I was.

A wave of water came crashing around the corner.

My mind finally snapped back into place. After throwing up a thick shield of fire, I took off in the other direction. The countermove was of course a dead giveaway for my location, and shouts rose behind me.

I grabbed the corner of the nearest building and skidded around it.

Hurricane winds whooshed down the street I had just left. Sprinting down the next alley, I was vaguely aware of someone levitating above the buildings behind me, probably trying to keep track of my location.

Screeching to a halt, I yanked my arms up.

Fire screamed across the pale blue heavens and towards the dark-haired figure flying up there. High Commander Danser dropped quickly to evade it, but not before calling out my location. I whirled back around and hurtled towards the next corner.

A tidal wave of water hit the slanted roof next to me. It crashed into it with enough force to make the tiles rattle.

Screams rose from inside the building and water washed down over me like a torrent. I slipped on the wet stones and slammed into the statue outside the door. The woman made of stone glared at me as I pushed off her marble chest and staggered to the next corner.

Every part of me ached. Every step sent a jolt of pain through my body. Every inhalation was like breathing in shards of glass.

Lighting crackled through the air.

I dove forward on instinct as a white bolt zapped through the street where I had been moments before. Pushing back up to my feet almost made me cry, but I forced myself to do it.

A desperate scream tore from my lips as I shoved my hands forward and sent a firebolt back at the attacker from behind.

High Commander Anron pulled up a wall of water.

Steam exploded through the street.

I ran.

Lester appeared from a street on my left while Danser materialized from the corner on my right. Wind and stone shot towards me. I leaped to the left and let Lester's block of stone pass through the street as I phased through it. It crashed into Danser's wind with a deafening boom.

Behind me, Anron shouted at the two of them in anger and then fired off another lightning bolt.

Mustering every smidgen of strength I had left, I dodged the crackling strike and then sprinted towards the gigantic building up ahead.

Doors banged against stone as I threw them open and crashed inside right at the same time as explosions went off in the vast room as well.

Black smoke bloomed around me.

Shooting fire bolts high up at the walls, I dove behind the nearest cover just as Anron, Lester, Danser, and a whole slew of their soldiers poured into the room.

Blasts of wind whirled around to clear the smoke while lightning cracked into the smooth white walls.

People screamed.

An alarm went off. It sounded like a vengeful banshee screaming into the void of the dead.

And then power the likes of which I had only felt from the High Elves before tore through the building.

Still on my stomach behind an empty silver counter, I rolled through the wall unseen and into the street outside.

Dust and grime covered my wet clothes. While sending a wave of flame up and down my own body to dry it, I snuck off into the nearest alley and ran until I found a house with a green circle painted next to the door.

I phased through it and then took the stairs three at a time until I finally reached the rooftop terrace.

Warm summer winds blew across the lounge chairs, and the decorative plants rustled peacefully in the breeze.

It clashed so thoroughly with the booming sounds of battle from a few streets away that I almost laughed.

Three people turned to face me as I made my way towards the edge of the roof.

"You look awful," Idra announced.

That time, I did actually laugh. "I know."

"I've always wanted to see what would happen," Valerie said as I came to a halt between her and Idra.

"Good thing we're not the ones they're angry with," Theo supplied from her other side.

"Yeah," she agreed. "Even though we're technically the ones who dropped the bombs and the smoke vials."

Standing there in the golden light of the afternoon sun, the four of us watched for a few moments as High Commander Anron, Lester, Danser, and their small army of soldiers battled the full might of the bank in the Court of Water, who thought they were being robbed.

Before Anron had killed King Aldrich and forced our whole continent to its knees, back when we had only been dealing with the assassination attempts, our original plan had been to set up a break-in at the bank. More precisely, a break-in that was supposedly orchestrated by the High Elves and funded by that bank account that was paying the assassins. Then we were going to tip off the bank, so that they would shut down the bank account for us. But then Anron killed the king and everything went to hell before we could set that plan in motion, and I forgot all about it. Valerie, however, did not.

When she proposed that we should use our original plan, I could barely believe how clever it was. The banks all functioned as independent states. They didn't care who ruled as long as no one tried to mess with them. Or rob them. So all I had to do was get all three High Commanders, lead them to the bank, and then burst in under the cover of the smoke bombs that Valerie, Theo, and Idra had dropped through the windows. And that was it.

The bank thought that the High Elves were trying to rob them.

The High Elves thought that the bank was attacking them.

And just like that, we had our distraction.

Fire, air, water, lightning, and stone exploded from across the rooftops and mixed with magic I had never seen before. No one knew how the banks' magic worked. Only that it was ridiculously powerful.

A wicked smirk spread across my lips.

My lethal deception had worked. Anron and his High Elves were going to be busy for at least a few hours.

Drawing Valerie into a one-armed embrace, I planted a kiss on her temple. "You're bloody brilliant, you know that?"

She swatted at my arm but a wide grin flashed across her lips. "Oh, stop it."

After releasing her, I turned to face all three of them. "Thank you for covering me back in the bank. None of them had time to see my face before the smoke bombs went off. You timed it perfectly."

"Well, to be fair, it's not exactly our first burglary." Theo winked at me before a thoughtful look passed over his face. "Though it might be our first fake one."

"Fake or not," Valerie filled in and her brown eyes sparkled as she looked at the battle raging a few streets away, "I've always wanted to see what the banks are capable of."

I laughed and shook my head. "Thieves."

"You know you love us," she teased and flashed me a grin.

"Yeah, I really do."

Idra's dark eyes slid to me. "I'll make sure they're safe. Go get the others."

I nodded.

"See you on the other side."

CHAPTER 40

Scythes of flame shot through the air as I flicked my blades while materializing in the landing area right below King Aldrich's castle. The two lonely High Elves who had been left to guard the entrance to the palace died before they even realized that I had worldwalked up there.

Armor clattered against stone as they crumpled to the ground with burning slashes straight through their bodies. Since I already knew that the rest of the soldiers, along with Princess Syrene, would be waiting below the ballroom balcony on the other side of the castle to capture the princes as they attempted to flee, I didn't even bother to cringe at the noise and instead took off up the slope towards the grand doors.

My tired and aching body protested, but I darted through the open door and into the shining marble hallway beyond.

A strong hand yanked me to the side and threw me against the wall as soon as I set one foot across the threshold. My breath exploded from my lungs in a huff.

"Kenna?"

I blinked up at a pair of red eyes. "Hadeon."

"You're okay?" Releasing me, he took a step back as he scanned my body from head to toe. "It took longer than we thought it would."

"I'm fine. Are you ready on your end?"

"She's beginning to run out of excuses, but yeah."

Shoving my blades back into their holsters, I nodded. "Then let's go."

As we ran through the white halls, I couldn't help but feel like the whole castle was less... well, everything. Less magnificent. Less glittering. Less welcoming. When King Aldrich lived here, it had felt like both a home and the grandest piece of architecture I had ever seen. But now as I looked at the gleaming silver candelabras and glittering chandeliers hanging over sprawling carpets and beautiful paintings, I couldn't help but feel that it had all lost its glamor.

"I need you to be straight with me," Hadeon suddenly said as we ran down another corridor. "How injured are you?"

Flicking my gaze down, I realized that I had been limping. The fall through the floor and the subsequent chase through the city where I had been flung into walls and furniture and hit by magic had taken its toll. I cleared my throat and tried to force myself to run properly.

"I can manage."

"Kenna." His voice came out sounding almost like a growl.

I forced out a breath through my already raw throat. "Alright, yeah, I'm pretty hurt." As we started down a stairwell, I glanced over at him. "But I still have my magic."

"She will be next to him. Are you sure you can control it enough not to hit her?"

Only our boots thumping against the stone steps broke the silence as I tried to justify an affirmative in my current exhausted state. The stairwell ended and we arrived in an undecorated corridor.

"No," I finally admitted.

"Alright, I'll take care of it."

Whipping my head towards him, I opened my mouth to voice a protest.

Hadeon cut me off before I could. "Do you trust me?"

"Yes," I answered without hesitation.

Surprise flickered in his eyes for a moment. Then he gave me a small smile and nodded. "I'll handle it."

"Okay."

We had arrived at the door at the end of the corridor. Faint sounds came from within. Hadeon and I exchanged a glance. He nodded again. Drawing in a deep breath that burned my throat, I shoved open the doors.

"You need to hold it like this," Ellyda was saying. There was an urgent note to her voice. "No, not like that. Careful. Or this is going to ruin the whole thing."

Captain Vendir jerked up his head as the doors to the smithy banged open. Shock danced on his handsome features.

"You?" he blurted out. "But you're supposed to be—"

"In the Court of Water?" I finished for him. "Sorry to break it to you, but you've been played."

Magic started humming through the room as he leveled commanding brown eyes at me. "Surrender right now, or..."

A soft click sounded.

The power that had been building inside the room disappeared as if someone had blown out a candle.

"You..." Shock bounced across Captain Vendir's features as he stared from Ellyda's face, down to the glowing black bracelet she had snapped shut around his wrist, and then back again. "How...?"

It sounded more like a rhetorical question, but Ellyda answered anyway. "One of Kenna's thief friends stole it from your friend Lester a while back, and then gave it to me. When I studied it, I realized that they were very easy to put on. All I had to do was feed some of my magic into it and it would start to glow. Then I suppose it was just a matter of actually putting it on someone."

"But you..." He trailed off as his eyes fell on the black bracelet around her wrist.

"Yes." She shook the dull piece of jewelry. "You've been deactivating it so that I can work on the sword, remember?"

A hint of fear flickered in his brown eyes as he realized that he suddenly didn't have access to his magic.

"Give me the sword, El," Hadeon called from across the floor.

"No!" Vendir snatched the blade from Ellyda's fingers and dropped into a fight stance.

From a step behind him, Ellyda edged backwards but there wasn't really any more room for her to back away. Hadeon had been right. When I was this exhausted, my control was slipping again and I wouldn't be able to use my fire magic without the risk of hitting her as well.

Steel sang into the workshop as Hadeon reached out and drew another blade from a rack by the door. After a quick glance at him, I moved out of the way.

The two sword-wielding warriors advanced on each other.

Captain Vendir was more than a head taller than Hadeon. Not to mention that he had the godlike physique that all the High Elves seemed to possess. My heart thumped in my chest as I watched Hadeon square up against an opponent who had every physical advantage.

"I will give you one chance to put that sword down and

surrender willingly," Captain Vendir said to Hadeon, voice brimming with authority. "Otherwise, you will get hurt."

"You're awfully sure of yourself, aren't you?"

"Without your magic, you're helpless." He nodded towards the glowing black bracelet on Hadeon's wrist. "Even if I don't have access to my magic either, you don't stand a chance of beating me without yours."

Hadeon shot across the floor.

Steel clanged against steel as Vendir jerked up his sword to block the strike while jumping backwards. With a flick of his wrist, Hadeon shoved the weapon aside and jabbed at Vendir's ribs. The High Elf had to throw himself backwards again to evade it.

Pressing the advantage, Hadeon feigned to the right and then struck left. Panic flashed across Vendir's features as he tried to parry, but he didn't quite succeed. A sharp gasp ripped from his lips as Hadeon's sword nicked his arm.

In one fluid motion, the red-eyed warrior kicked at the captain's hip, forcing him back across the floor, while swinging his sword again. Vendir barely managed to twist aside.

Chips of wood flew through the smithy as Hadeon's blade slammed into the table instead. Seeing his chance, Captain Vendir rammed his own sword towards Hadeon. But he wasn't fast enough.

With one powerful pull, Hadeon yanked out the massive sword again and swung it at Vendir with impossible speed.

Metal clashed as their blades connected.

The force of the blow sent Vendir's arm wobbling to the side.

It left his chest wide open and Hadeon used the

opportunity to ram his shoulder into it. Air exploded from the High Elf's lungs and he staggered backwards.

Hadeon flicked his sword hand at the same time as he took out Vendir's legs from underneath him. A dull thud echoed through the silent forge as the captain crashed down on the floor. Scrambling for purchase, he pushed himself up on his knees.

But the battle was already over.

Hadeon was standing before him, holding both swords. With the blades crossed, he rested one on each side of Captain Vendir's neck.

The High Elf's chest heaved, but the red-eyed warrior didn't even seem winded. Locking hard eyes on the defeated elf, Hadeon stared him down.

"You think I'm helpless without my magic." An uncharacteristically cold laugh ripped from Hadeon's throat. "I'm not magically gifted, asshole."

Shock clanged through me. I hadn't known that. Since Hadeon's speed and strength in battle had always seemed so impossible, I had just assumed that he had been born with some kind of magic powers connected to that.

"None of my skills were just granted to me freely," he growled down at his captive. "I have paid for them with years of blood and sweat."

There was respect, as well as fear, in Vendir's eyes as he looked up at the warrior holding two swords to his neck. "I can see that."

Hadeon didn't take his eyes off the captain, but spoke over his shoulder to me. "Kenna. Let's go."

Jolted out of my surprise, I quickly made my way towards them while pulling out a small vial from one of my pockets.

To my surprise, Ellyda held out a hand as she moved into position in front of Vendir as well.

"How much?" she asked.

"Theo said a quarter of a bottle for a human," I replied as I placed the vial in her palm.

She nodded. "He'll probably need the whole thing then."

"Yeah."

"Don't do this," Captain Vendir bargained. Still on his knees, he flicked pleading eyes between the three of us. "You still won't be able to get the bracelets off. High Commander Anron only gave me control over yours." He looked at Ellyda. "I can't take off the rest."

A frown of genuine confusion creased Ellyda's brows. "You really haven't figured it out yet?" When he only looked back at her with uncertain eyes, she motioned at the ornamental sword in Hadeon's left hand. "That's what the sword is for."

"What?"

"I wasn't crafting a magical blade for you. Hadeon and I staged that confrontation with your friend Lester so that I could offer to make a magical sword for you without looking suspicious. But it was never meant for you. I was making one that could cut through the magic of the bracelets." She nodded at the bracelet Valerie had stolen that now encircled Vendir's wrist. "As soon as I had that, it was easy."

"But... but you said the sword wasn't finished. That you needed me to be here today, needed a set of extra hands, *today*, to help you finish it."

"I'm magically gifted at forging. Do you really think it takes me a week to make one sword?" Amusement flickered in her sharp violet eyes as she shook her head. Then it disappeared and she shoved the vial towards him. "Now, drink."

Captain Vendir eyed it warily.

"Drink that or I cut your head off," Hadeon growled.

A hint of fear flashed in Vendir's eyes again, but it chased out the uncertainty. Holding Ellyda's gaze, he opened his mouth.

She poured the whole vial down his throat without hesitation.

Nothing happened.

When we were coming up on half a minute, Hadeon glanced over at me and opened his mouth to say something.

Then Vendir's eyes rolled back in his head and he slumped down unconscious on the ground.

"Effective," Ellyda announced with an approving nod in my direction before snatching her magic sword back from Hadeon.

After placing her wrist on the nearest table, she wedged the blade underneath the bracelet and then pushed upwards with the sword. The bracelet shattered as if it were made of thin glass. I raised my eyebrows. Sometimes, I forgot what a genius Ellyda really was.

She snapped her fingers at her brother.

While putting the borrowed sword away, he held out his wrist. The sound of shattering glass filled the room as his bracelet broke apart and rained down in shards on the floor.

"We will take care of him," Ellyda said and nodded towards Vendir while she shoved the magical sword into my hands. "Go get the others."

I nodded. "I'll see you outside."

With a firm grip on the ornamental sword, I whirled

around and raced out into the corridor and up the stairs again.

Ellyda had finished the blade days ago, but since we didn't have a distraction that we could use in order to get the sword away from the watchful eyes of Captain Vendir, she'd had to bluff for several days. To be honest, I hadn't been sure she would have it in her. But maybe the fact that it all took place inside a forge had helped calm her mind enough to trick a High Elf captain for days on end.

Pain shot through every part of my body as I bounded up another flight of stairs and then sprinted down one more hallway before skidding into what had once been one of King Aldrich's meeting rooms.

A mass of people whipped around to face me.

CHAPTER 41

"It works," I panted.

Sighs of relief and a few cheers rippled through the crowd. I was too winded to smile so I only jogged up to Mordren and pushed the sword into his hands. He stole a kiss from my lips before wedging the blade under his bracelet and yanking upwards.

Shards clinked against the floor as it fell off.

Another round of relieved gasps went through the elves gathered in the room.

When Mordren passed the sword to Eilan, shadows flickered around the cuffs of his suit jacket. A smile tugged at his lips in response.

While Edric, Rayan, Iwdael, Evander, Princess Lilane, Augustien, Ymas, and several other elves that each prince had brought with them clustered around Eilan to wait for their turn with the sword, I collapsed onto the nearest chair.

Everything inside me ached. And we still weren't done yet.

"The guards at the main landing area are dead," I announced into the murmuring of voices and shattering of bracelets. "Once your bracelets are off, you can worldwalk out from there."

The people gathered in the room nodded.

Tension still clung to the air like a crackling storm waiting to happen. We didn't know for certain how long Anron and the others would be busy. They could return at any time. And then we would have to fight our way out instead. An elf from the Court of Stone, who I knew as one of Edric's chief administrators, fumbled with the sword as he tried to get the bracelet off. Another wave of nervousness washed over the room.

It slowly drained away as he handed the blade to the next person. Instead, a confident feeling took its place. It was almost cheerful. Victorious.

The room drew in a deep breath, and then the shattering of bracelets sped up with steady hands.

Iwdael Vineweaver winked at me from across the room.

I smiled back at him.

As soon as Prince Rayan's bracelet was gone, he stalked towards me. "You look injured."

"Well..." I began but he was already crouching down in front of my chair.

The ache pulsing through me lessened with every second as Rayan poured his healing magic into my body, fixing the sprained ligaments and cracked ribs and other various cuts and bruises. Closing my eyes, I drew in a deep breath.

"There," he said at last as he stood up.

My body felt like new again. A grateful smile spread across my lips as I looked up at him. "Thank you."

"No, thank *you*." He held my gaze as Princess Lilane and the rest of his people clustered around him. "Thank you. And good luck." His purple eyes slid over Mordren and Eilan's faces as well before returning to me. "We will see each other again."

Mordren and Eilan gave him a nod while I pushed to my feet and then did the same. "And when we do, there will be hope."

He smiled. And then the Court of Water walked out of the room and towards freedom.

"While dramatic goodbyes are usually my thing," Prince Iwdael said as he sauntered up to us with his court behind him. "I'll try to keep this short." His gaze darted to Augustien, the handsome golden-haired elf next to him, for a moment before it slid back to me. "Thank you for helping me and my people out of a mess I made because of a broken heart."

I swept my gaze over the now very calm people around the room before shooting him a knowing look. "I think you played your part very well too."

Iwdael chuckled and winked again. Threading his fingers through Augustien's, he started towards the door. "When you get back, you'll find us in the forest. Ready for a rebellion."

"We'll see you soon," I called after him as he and his court left as well.

The final bracelet clattered to the floor. I looked up to find Prince Edric striding towards the door with Ymas and the rest of his chosen few behind him. Right as he opened his mouth to say something to me, someone else spoke up.

"I'm staying," a shrill voice called out.

Edric whirled around.

Blond hair shifted over a turquoise dress as Monette crossed her arms and raised her chin. "I'm staying."

Stone rumbled beneath our feet. "What?"

"I am not going to spend the rest of my life hiding out in

caves while trying to fight some desperate resistance battle," she announced to the Prince of Stone. "So I'm staying."

Rage flashed over Edric's face and he took a step towards her. But then he seemed to think better of it. Raking a hand through his long blond hair, he shot her a contemptuous look. "You always were a slimy one. Ever since you ratted Kenna out, I've always wondered whether you'd betray me too if things ever got too uncomfortable for you. I guess I have my answer now."

A block of stone shot up from the floor and sped towards Monette. She threw herself down on the ground to escape it as it crashed into the wall behind her.

"Stay then," Edric said. "I have no use for turncoats. But if you ever betray my secrets, I will come back and kill you. And you still owe me money. Don't forget that. Because one day, I will come to collect it."

All the blood drained from her face as she climbed back to her feet, and for a moment, it looked like she was going to take it all back. But the Prince of Stone was already stalking away.

"Felix," he snapped.

The copper-haired half-elf, who was madly in love with Monette, stared between her and his prince. For a moment, I forgot that we were still in the middle of an escape that might go to hell any second. This was a defining moment for Felix. He had always done whatever Monette wanted, in the hopes that she would fall in love with him. Now he had to choose. Monette. Or his duty, and debt, to his prince.

Monette arched an expectant brow at him.

His brown eyes darted to Edric's broad back again before meeting her gaze. A disappointed sigh was building in my chest. *Of course he would never leave her.*

I blinked.

And so did Monette.

In fact, her mouth dropped open as Felix tore his gaze from her and hurried after the Prince of Stone. I wiped a hand over my mouth to hide my smile.

Prince Edric, who hadn't even seen this momentous decision happen, stopped briefly before me on his way to the door.

Placing a hand on my shoulder, he leaned in and whispered in my ear, "We will make sure the High Elves never find the magic."

I nodded.

He drew back and clapped my shoulder again before nodding to Mordren. "When battle comes, we'll be ready."

Boots thudded against the floor as the Court of Stone made their way out as well, taking Ellyda's magical sword with them. That only left five people in the vast room. Me, Mordren, Eilan, Evander, and Monette.

She seemed to realize who she suddenly found herself surrounded by and made a hasty escape through the door. I didn't even look at her as she passed. My eyes were locked on Evander's.

After a nervous glance at the disappearing Monette, he drew himself up to his full height and raised his chin. "I'm staying too."

Shadows flickered around Mordren's dark suit.

"I'll meet you outside," I said to him without taking my eyes off Evander.

"Yes, you will," Mordren said.

With a final vicious look at Evander, he jerked his chin at Eilan and then stalked out the door.

The vast room made of pale marble suddenly felt very

small. Standing only a few strides apart, Evander and I watched each other. Light from the afternoon sun fell in through the windows and made his dark green eyes glitter like emeralds.

"It was you, wasn't it?" I said at last.

He stared back at me in silence for a while before replying, "Yes."

"I figured as much. When did they turn you?"

"At Imelda's house. Anron overwhelmed me quickly, but he didn't capture me. He made me an offer, and then he let me go. A comfortable position here in the castle. In exchange for you and Mordren. Well, the offer was actually from Queen Syrene since, you know, we have history." He shrugged. "But I hadn't planned on actually going through with it."

"But you did."

"Yes." His face was devoid of all emotion as he looked back at me. "When did you figure it out?"

"I started suspecting it after we were attacked here that night Mordren and Eilan were captured. And that's when I started thinking about it. About your words. When you apologized to me that morning, you weren't apologizing to *me*. You were apologizing to yourself for not realizing sooner that I wasn't the person you wanted me to be."

"Fool me once, and all that, huh?"

"Something like that." I studied the way the light brought out the gold in his brown hair for a moment. "But it wasn't until today, when I found the High Elves already waiting for me, that I knew for certain that you had betrayed me."

"It could have been any of the others too."

"No. Because you see, you were the only one who didn't know the real plan. When Eilan came to tell you that I was there for a meeting, we had actually already had a meeting where I had explained the real plan." I lifted my shoulders in an unapologetic shrug. "The plan I explained when you were in the room was bait."

"I see."

"I have to admit, I was afraid you'd catch on because Edric is such a terrible liar. At least the others were better at playing along."

"So you wanted to have Anron and the other High Commanders waiting for you in the Court of Water?" He jerked his chin in the direction of the main ballroom. "And for Queen Syrene and the other soldiers to be waiting under that balcony on the other side of the castle? It was all part of the plan?"

"Yes."

"What would you have done if I hadn't told Anron about it?"

"I would have felt like a really shitty person for doubting your loyalty."

"That's not what I meant."

"I know." I shrugged. "In case it turned out that you weren't a traitor, we had a back-up plan where Rayan would tip him off on the pretense that he didn't want to see his court destroyed in a battle. But it really was much more convincing coming from you."

Silence fell over the room as we watched each other.

"Why did you do it?" I asked at last.

He huffed out an incredulous laugh. "You really don't know?"

"I want to hear you say it."

"Alright." Locking eyes with me, he gestured at the room around him. "Because this is what I want. A comfortable life where I don't have to worry about anything ever again. All I have ever done since joining your court is to face one horrible situation after another. If it isn't assassination attempts, it's High Elves who are attacking us, or giant air serpents, or you're torturing someone, or planning an entire resistance movement that will only involve more fighting and being hunted by people who are more powerful." A bitter look flashed across his handsome face. "And besides, you were never going to leave him for me anyway, so why should I spend my life helping you?"

At that, I actually raised my eyebrows in surprise. "You were only helping me because you wanted me to sleep with you?"

"I really don't understand it." He stabbed two fingers to his chest in frustration. "I am a *nice* person. How could you choose him over me?"

Even though he didn't really deserve an explanation, I answered anyway. "Because he loves me for who I am. Not some fantasy of who I might have been if I was less ambitious, less ruthless, less... me."

"Well," Evander scoffed. "I suppose you're right about that."

Oppressive silence fell over the room like a wet blanket. It had been less than half an hour since Anron was forced into a battle with the bank in the Court of Water, so we should have plenty of time. But I couldn't stay for that much longer either. Or perhaps it was that I simply didn't want to stay.

"So, what happens now?" Evander said at last, breaking the silence. Spreading his arms, he raised his eyebrows at me. "Are you going to kill me? That seems to be what you do to people who betray you."

I was silent long enough to let him know that I was thinking about it, before I finally said, "No."

"Why not?"

"Because I have finally realized that just because I think that what I'm doing is right, it doesn't mean that everyone else agrees with me. We all have different priorities in life. And at the end of the day, my priorities aren't better or worse than someone else's. So I shouldn't try to force other people's priorities to align with my own. I've tried to do that once already." I motioned towards the doorway. "With Monette."

"How so?"

"Her first priority is to live a safe and comfortable life. That's why she's staying here now. Last year, my first priority was freedom. And I tried to force her to make that her first priority too when I told her about my blackmailing scheme to buy my freedom from Prince Edric. And she betrayed me." I waved a hand towards Evander. "Now I tried to do the same with you. And you also betrayed me." Dropping my hand again, I shrugged. "So no, I'm not going to kill you. Because you were just doing what was best for you. Just like I am now."

"How magnanimous of you."

A cold smile dripping with threats slid across my lips. He flinched back a step.

"A piece of parting advice. When Syrene finally figures out that she was tricked into standing under that balcony while all their important prisoners escaped right through the front door, she's going to be looking for someone to blame. Not to mention what Anron will do. If I were you, I would've made myself scarce by then."

His gaze darted towards the door while a hint of alarm flashed across his face.

"Oh and Evander?" Dark red flames flickered in my hair as I locked eyes with him again. "This was a one-time act of mercy. If I see you across the battlefield, or if I find out that you continue to help my enemies, I will not extend the same courtesy twice."

He swallowed but then raised his chin defiantly. "Likewise."

"Goodbye, Evander." I cocked my head slightly. "I hope you get everything you wish for."

With one final smile that was sharper than my blades, I turned around and strode out of the room. Leaving Evander behind. For the very last time.

Because once a traitor, always a traitor.

I should know. Since I was one too.

Just ask Volkan Flameshield.

Oh right.

He was already dead.

CHAPTER 42

Waves crashed against the shore. Feeling the warm sun on my face, I drew in a deep breath of salt-tasting air and let the sound of the ocean calm me.

Then I turned back to the bound High Elf captain that Mordren was in the middle of torturing.

A scream ripped from Captain Vendir's throat as the Prince of Shadows sent another pulse of pain magic over him. But out here, there was no one to hear him. Twisting in the sand, he tried uselessly to get away. Mordren only sent another wave of agony through his body.

"Are you serious?" Mordren said and arched an eyebrow at the captain. "I have barely even begun the real torture."

Apparently, High Elves were so used to everyone else bowing and scraping before them that they were unaccustomed to being hurt themselves. Or perhaps that was just Wielders of the Great Current.

Fear shone in Vendir's brown eyes.

"But we can avoid all that," Mordren continued. "If you do as commanded."

"You're insane."

"Have it your way."

"No!" Captain Vendir flicked his eyes between the five of us. "What I meant was that even if I do this, you will never succeed."

"Let us worry about that," I said. "So, do we have a deal?"

"It's more blackmail than an actual deal." When Mordren only arched an eyebrow again, Vendir blurted out, "Yes. Yes, we have a deal."

"Splendid."

Bending down, he untied the disgruntled captain. Vendir brushed sand off his armor before trying to shake it out of his blond hair as well. It worked poorly, but he stood up straight anyway and blew a series of whistles into the warm afternoon air.

On Mordren's other side, Hadeon scanned the beach around us. "Didn't you say she should be here by now?"

"She's not late yet, but I..." I trailed off as the air vibrated next to me.

Suddenly, two people materialized on the pale sand. Valerie with a wide grin on her face. And Idra, with a scowl. She dumped a whole stash of backpacks on the ground next to her before flicking a hand towards the excited thief.

"You can explain this," she muttered before worldwalking out again.

"Uhm," I began, glancing at the backpack, *my* backpack, that Valerie was holding in an iron grip. "What are you doing here?"

Just before she could reply, Idra reappeared with Theo. Shaking her head, she dropped another couple of backpacks on the ground and then turned to glare at the two thieves.

"We're coming with you," Valerie announced.

My eyebrows shot towards my hairline. "You're doing what now?"

"Come on. You're going to the home of the High Elves to blackmail their emperor and empress. Did you really think we would sit this one out?"

"We're not going to blackmail–"

"Fine, you're going there to manipulate them." She waved her hands in front of her face. "Potato, *potahto*. The point is, there's no chance in hell we're gonna miss this."

Idra crossed her arms and directed her scowl at me. "You never should have told them our plan."

But I had. Because *this* had been the real plan. That absolutely insane plan that I had hatched that night we spent reading books in the Court of Light. There had never been any special fire magic attack that I had learned and that I would use against the High Elves while Idra supposedly deactivated the bracelets. That was what we had told Evander. But that wasn't the truth. The real plan was much crazier than that.

When I had seen that page detailing the hierarchy of the High Elves' society, I had realized what we had to do to even the playing field against Anron. If we killed him, or even Lester or Danser, then Valdanar would send the other seven Flying Legions to wipe us out because we killed one of their precious commanders and wielders. And besides, we couldn't even fight a battle against three High Commanders and three Flying Legions.

Wings boomed into the air.

A moment later, a green air serpent landed on the beach next to us. Sand flew into the air and drifted away on the ocean breeze while Captain Vendir placed a hand on his mount's neck and gave it an affectionate rub. A row of leather saddles spread across the serpent's back.

"Well, climb on then," he said, his voice resigned.

"Alright!" Valerie called and threw me my pack, that she had apparently been holding hostage until Idra worldwalked her and Theo here. "Let's go!"

Both Hadeon and Eilan chuckled and shook their heads, as did Theo and Idra. But in the end, they all bent down, picked up their own packs and followed the grinning thief towards the winged serpent waiting in the sand. Ellyda studied Captain Vendir with an intensity that made him glance away. Then she too grabbed the backpack that Idra had brought her and moved towards the saddle.

Mordren and I exchanged a glance.

Nervous anticipation bounced across the beach as our small group climbed into the row of saddles. Captain Vendir, his black bracelet still glowing and cutting off his magic, didn't cause any trouble. In fact, he helped direct people onto his air serpent with clear instructions. Perhaps he was just glad that he had woken up from the potion we had used to knock him out before transporting him here. Or maybe he had simply realized that without his magic, he was thoroughly outmatched in the present company.

My heart pattered in my chest as I settled into the saddle behind Idra and in front of Mordren. Adjusting the straps over my legs, I blew out a steadying breath.

Captain Vendir swung himself into the saddle at the very front with more graceful movements than the rest of us combined. After casting a glance behind at all of us, he shook his head as if he couldn't quite believe that he had managed to get himself captured by such a bunch of absolute idiots. Then he leaned forward and spoke in a language I didn't understand.

My stomach lurched as the air serpent shot upwards.

No, we couldn't fight three High Commanders and three Flying Legions and hope to win. So we had to do the one thing that Anron would never expect. Would never even dream of in his wildest nightmares.

We had to rat him out.

We had to expose his treachery to his sovereign leaders.

And then we had to manipulate the Emperor and Empress of Valdanar into sending their army to our lands. Not to conquer us. Or as retribution for the death of one of their High Commanders. No. We would get them to send their own people here to kill Anron for us.

Winds whipped through my hair. The straps along my legs would keep me in place no matter what I did, so I eased up my death grip on the front of the saddle. Golden afternoon sunlight fell across my face and warmed my cheeks. I looked down at the water below.

The beach was growing smaller.

Ahead, a vast ocean glittered in the light of the sun.

Giddiness sparkled inside me and mixed with nervous anticipation. Spreading my arms wide, I drew in a shuddering breath and let the winds rush around me as I gazed towards the pale blue horizon.

We were going to Valdanar.

BONUS SCENE

Do you want to know what happened when Mordren followed Hadeon and Idra to that pond during the birthday celebration? Scan the QR code to download the **exclusive bonus scene** and learn exactly how Mordren ended up in the pond as well.

ACKNOWLEDGMENTS

As usual, I put my poor main character through hell in yet another book. Man, if any of my characters ever came alive, I would be so dead. But at least I let Kenna celebrate her birthday in this book, and gave her a few cute moments with Mordren, and allowed her to laugh and drink some wine with the endlessly spinning spatula that is Valerie. So there is that. And now they're all going to Valdanar for another exciting adventure. And some blackmailing. Yes. Because it wouldn't truly be a Marion Blackwood book without a little blackmail, now would it?

As always, I would like to start by saying a huge thank you to my family and loved ones. Mom, Dad, Mark, thank you for the enthusiasm, love, and encouragement. I truly don't know what I would do without you. Lasse, Ann, Karolina, Axel, Martina, thank you for continuing to take such an interest in my books. It really means a lot.

Another group of people I would like to once again express my gratitude to is my wonderful team of beta readers: Alethea Graham, Deshaun Hershel, Luna Lucia Lawson, and Orsika Péter. Thank you for the time and effort you put into reading the book and providing helpful feedback. Your suggestions and encouragement truly make the book better.

To my amazing copy editor and proofreader Julia Gibbs, thank you for all the hard work you always put into making my books shine. Your language expertise and attention to detail is fantastic and makes me feel confident that I'm publishing the very best version of my books.

I am also very fortunate to have friends both close by and from all around the world. My friends, thank you for everything you've shared with me. Thank you for the laughs, the tears, the deep discussions, and the unforgettable memories. My life is a lot richer with you in it.

Before I go back to writing the next book, I would like to say thank you to you, the reader. Thank you for joining me and Kenna on this mission. If you have any questions or comments about the book, I would love to hear from you. You can find all the different ways of contacting me on my website, www.marionblackwood.com. There you can also sign up for my newsletter to receive updates about coming books. Lastly, if you liked this book and want to help me out so that I can continue writing, please consider leaving a review. It really does help tremendously. I hope you enjoyed the adventure!

Printed in Dunstable, United Kingdom